Indestructible

V Plague Book Seven

DIRK PATTON

Dirk Patton

Published by Voodoo Dog Publishing, LLC

2824 N Power Road

Suite #113-256

Mesa, AZ 85215

Printed in the United States of America

First Printing, 2015

ISBN-13: 978-1508565079

ISBN-10: 1508565074

Indestructible

Table of Contents

Author's Note

Thank you for purchasing Indestructible, Book 7 in the V Plague series. If you haven't read the first six books you need to stop reading now and pick them up, otherwise you will be lost as this book is intended to continue the story in a serialized format. I intentionally did nothing to explain comments and events that reference book 1 through 6. Regardless, you have my heartfelt thanks for reading my work and I hope you're enjoying the adventure as much as I am. As always, a good review on Amazon is greatly appreciated and the best way to ensure more books are published.

Determination that is incorruptible

From the other side, a terror to behold

Annihilation will be unavoidable

Every broken enemy will know

That their opponent had to be invincible

Take a last look around while you're alive

I'm an indestructible

Master of war

Indestructible – Disturbed

1

Pain. Pain and darkness. And pressure. I didn't know where the hell I was or how I'd gotten there. Or what was on top of me. Crushing me. It was hard to breathe. Impossible to take more than a very shallow breath of stale air.

And the smell. The raw stink of urine and feces. The coppery odor of blood. But whose blood? For that matter, whose bladder and bowels? Then it came flooding back in a rush of vivid, brightly colored memories, almost like watching a movie where the director is trying too hard to be artistic and as a result fails to tell a cohesive story.

The fight in the casino. Finally finding Katie. Both her and Martinez on the floor, bleeding. Killing Roach. Piling into an Osprey that was taking us to Tinker where the two women could get proper medical attention for their wounds. The aircraft's engines shutting down. Cradling Katie in my arms as we quickly lost altitude. Meeting Rachel's eyes and seeing her acceptance of our fate a moment before we struck the ground.

That's where the movie ended. No closing credits. No little flashes of action to help wrap up the story. Just a memory of an incredible impact accompanied with the horrible sounds of the Osprey disintegrating on impact, then nothing. OK, more like a poorly ended movie or TV series that leaves the fate of some poor bastard to whatever the audience imagines by just cutting to black.

I'm not sure how long I lay there, conscious, but feeling like I was in a bad daydream. I might have lain there until thirst or hunger spurred me to action, however long that would have taken, but I remembered that Katie had been shot and needed my help. That snapped me fully alert and I tried to move my legs, banging against something with my boot.

A hard tug on my foot. Then a second tug, harder than the first, and the snarl of an infected. That got me going as about a gallon of adrenaline dumped into my bloodstream. I should have already been analyzing my situation, trying to figure out what was lying on top of me and how I'd extricate myself, but instead I'd been too caught up with worrying about how I got there in the first place.

I was on my left side, something that I was reasonably sure was my rifle trapped between the hard deck and me. A large piece of the Osprey was on top of me, crushing me. Trying to turn my body to get my hands up and push, I grunted when the infected pulled and twisted on my foot hard enough to send a jolt of pain all the way into my hip.

Pushing down rising panic, I managed to wrench my upper body around, turning at the waist. My hips and upper legs were pinned tightly and I couldn't move them at all. Shoulders flat to the floor I placed my palms on the piece of debris and pushed. Nothing moved, other than the infected's hand working its way to the top of my boot.

Whatever was on top of me was large and smooth. I suspected it was part of the Osprey's fuselage, and if it was a large enough chunk, I was screwed. Just because the damn things can fly, there's really no part of an aircraft that is light when it's lying on top of you. Taking a deep breath I grunted and pushed with everything I had.

Nothing. With a curse I blew out the breath I had held while pushing and grimaced as I felt a hand clamp down on my leg just above the top edge of my boot. I needed to do something before the infected managed to squirm his way any farther up. Twisting my head around, I was able to see down the length of my body.

It was hard to tell, but looked like my feet were sticking out into open space. The sun was shining brightly and I could clearly see the male that was trying to make a mid-day snack out of me. He was dressed in a uniform and it took me a minute to remember that while we were in the casino the Osprey had extracted a small Army unit that was surrounded by infected. They must have been out in the field and never received the vaccine that was distributed at Tinker Air Force Base.

My fear for Katie and the rest of my friends ratcheted up and I tried to kick as he resumed his attack, but my legs were pinned too tightly and all I succeeded in doing was to bump the side of his head with my boot. He turned and bit down on the thick leather, fortunately unable to tear through to my flesh.

My arms had a fair degree of freedom and I reached for the object that had been digging into my side when I'd first awakened. As I suspected, it was the Sig Sauer rifle, still held securely to my body by its sling. I began working it around, trying to get it into a position that would let me shoot.

It was slow going. The sling hampered my ability to bring the weapon to bear, and while I was working on it the male had shifted his efforts at a snack to my boot's upper. Fear rising, I fumbled for the quick release button on the sling, desperate to kill the damn thing before he moved up to where there was only fabric to protect me from his teeth.

Fingers finally finding the button, I pressed it and ripped the rifle free of the sling. Twisting, I ignored the pain in my back and hips as I forced my body into a position it wasn't intended to achieve. Maybe I should have accepted Katie's offers to attend Yoga classes with her.

The rifle came onto target, but I was forced to hold it with one hand and guess whether or not the muzzle was aimed at the infected. My arm was bent at ninety degrees and I couldn't use the scope. If I was off, even a little, I would blast a hole through my foot.

With a deep breath I lined up as best I could and pulled the trigger. And missed both the male and my foot. The rifle was very quiet when it fired, but it was still loud enough to draw the attention of my attacker. He stopped biting on my boot and swiveled his head towards the source of the sound.

By now my arm was growing tired from maintaining such an awkward pose and I couldn't hold the weapon steady. The infected hissed at me and dragged himself higher until his head came up against the debris that was pinning me down. Turning my ankle as far away from him as I could, hoping to keep my foot out of the line of fire, I pulled the trigger again.

The bullet took off most of the male's ear, powder burns stippling the skin of his face. How the hell did I miss? It was a four foot shot at the most! Silencing my frantically racing mind, I struggled to get the weapon pointed where I wanted it, sweat pouring off of me as I forced my body to still itself.

Pulling the trigger again, I exhaled and let my arm flop to the deck when a neat hole appeared in the infected's forehead. I only rested for a moment before looking back up to take a better survey of my situation. My head pounded, my lower back and hips were on fire and I was sick to my stomach. Blood from head wounds was pouring down my forehead and blocking most of the vision from my right eye. But none of that would matter if I kept lying here until more infected showed up.

Forcing myself to not get distracted by worry over Katie or Rachel or any of the others, I reached down and ran my hands over my body where I was pinned. The same piece of metal that was over my chest and head also pressed tightly on my hips and thighs. Feeling around, I stopped when my fingers banged up against my holstered pistol.

The pistol was in a thigh holster, and the whole rig had been pushed up my leg during the crash. Whatever the piece of debris was, it was resting directly onto the holster, wedging my body in place. This was the first good news. Yes, I was pinned tightly, but if I could remove the pistol and holster I'd gain enough space to wriggle my hips around and start working to get out of the trap. Of course that assumed that as soon as I got the pistol off, the debris didn't shift farther down and pin me again.

It took some doing, but I succeeded in getting a hand far enough down my body to touch the upper buckle that held the holster rig. Several minutes later I suppressed a victory shout when it clicked open. Reminding myself 'that was the easy one', I rested for a moment, using my collar to wipe sweat and blood out of my eyes.

Heart rate almost back to normal, I reached for the second buckle, farther down my leg. I couldn't touch it. No matter how I stretched or twisted or contorted my body, I just couldn't get my hand in place to release the buckle. This time I had to suppress a scream of frustration.

2

I don't know how much time passed. I wanted to shout for Katie or Rachel or Martinez or Zemeck or anyone. But concern over alerting more infected to my presence kept me quiet. I struggled with the metal that had me trapped, but it was immovable, at least from the position I was in. I must have tried to reach the second holster buckle a hundred times, but I don't think I ever came close.

The blood had crusted on my head and face, and I could feel several small cuts and one large gash on my skull. The smaller ones had clotted and stopped bleeding, but the multi-inch laceration that started on the top of my head and continued down through my right eyebrow was open and raw, still weeping. I made the mistake of touching it once, the pain enough to prevent me from trying it a second time.

The blow that had caused the wound had also given me another concussion. It had only been a couple of days since I was knocked goofy when a bullet fired through the head of an infected by Irina had grazed my temple. While I had been feeling normal, I've had enough concussions in my day to know they don't completely heal that quickly, and it's not good to get another one while still recovering from the first.

A headache and nausea were the most telling symptoms of the damage. I suspected I'd also have double vision if I were ever able to get out and see anything in the daylight. Not worrying about something I was unable to do anything about at the moment, I looked over my situation again. Nothing was different or new since the last time, or the several dozen times before that. I was stuck and it wasn't looking like I'd be able to get myself free.

Then, I wasn't sure I wanted to get free. Free to do what? Find Katie dead? Rachel and Dog, too, as well as the rest of my group? They had to be dead. They wouldn't have left me behind. What the hell did it matter if I got free if everyone in the world I cared about was dead? Get free to spend the rest of my days fighting the infected? To what end?

Maybe I was better off to just stay right here and relax. Lack of water would finish me off in two or three days at the most. With a sigh of resignation I laid my head back and closed my eyes.

Dying of dehydration wouldn't be pleasant. Maybe I'd just stick the muzzle of the rifle in my mouth and end it all before the pain and thirst got too bad. "That's what I'll do", I thought to myself a moment before I lost consciousness.

I don't know how long I was out, but it was dark when I woke. Not that I could tell the difference in my little metal cave, but if I craned my head around just right I could see past my feet and into the open. Terrain that had been clearly visible in bright sunshine earlier was now hidden by the night. Dark night that hid predators.

Not wolves or mountain lions, or anything like that. It was the two legged variety that was so dangerous, especially the females. And they were quiet. Maybe it was because the virus had enhanced their senses, and with improved hearing came more awareness of the sounds they made. Perhaps this helped them to adjust and be stealthy. Maybe not. Either way, I didn't hear the female approaching until she was within a few feet of me.

The first indication she was there was when I heard her sniffing the air. Cautiously, I twisted around and could just faintly make out a pair of feet standing close to mine. Afraid if I moved again it would make a noise and alert her to my presence, I stayed in the uncomfortable position and barely breathed. I might be ready to put a gun in my mouth, but I sure as hell wasn't ready to be torn apart and eaten by an infected.

She stood there for a long time, frequently sniffing. Did she smell me? Maybe she did, but there were apparently enough smells of death in the crashed aircraft to confuse her. Finally, my screaming muscles and ligaments couldn't remain contorted any longer and I slowly straightened my back and neck. Not that I was able to move into a comfortable position, but it was better than a constant fire in every fiber between my head and waist.

I didn't think I made a sound as I slowly moved my upper body, but something caught the infected's attention. She inhaled sharply and held her breath, waiting for whatever she'd detected to repeat. I was frozen in place, hand gripping the rifle tightly even though I had serious doubts about being able to use it effectively if she attacked.

There was a thump, then even more pressure on my pinned body. She had climbed onto the debris that trapped me. The sniffing started again, her new location causing the sound to echo off the hard surfaces inside the downed Osprey. That sound sent chills up and down my spine.

She moved again, a footstep sounding right over my head. Pausing, she sniffed then stopped and held her breath. Had she found me? Did she know I was right under her feet and all she had to do was raise the debris to find a hidden prize? I thought about revealing myself and hoping the infected would be able to lift the metal off of me.

They're strong as hell. Pound for pound, at least twice as strong as an uninfected human. Maybe she could lift the weight, but as I thought about it I dismissed the idea. All it would take would be for her to search around the edges until she found my feet sticking out, then she could attack. Sure, I'd been able to kill the male, but he was moving slow, and in reality I had shot a stationary target. It wouldn't be nearly as easy with a fast and agile female.

I stayed absolutely still and silent. Breathed shallowly through my mouth and willed her to grow bored and move on. That was unlikely, as I've seen the infected demonstrate an amazing degree of patience when they believe there is prey to be had. That was the question. Was she sure enough something was here that she would wait it out, or was I hidden well enough?

Time stretched out, and more than twenty minutes must have passed before she finally moved again. Unfortunately not back out, but a few steps in the direction I'd come to think of as farther into the aircraft. She took two steps on the metal object covering me, then stepped off and slipped as lose debris shifted under her weight.

Numerous metallic objects fell to the deck, making a hell of a racket. Something that I couldn't identify in the dark struck me in the face, opening another small cut, and remained pressing tightly against me. I could tell it was a smooth metal rod of some sort, but nothing else.

When the debris shifted the female must have leapt backwards to stable footing because there was a thump I could feel in my legs and the object pinning me down shifted slightly. My heart leapt and I was hardly able to contain my excitement. It shifted! If it shifted, it could be moved! Had she dislodged something that was holding it in place? Didn't know and didn't care. Just wanted her to get the hell out of there so I could try to get free again. I'd decided I wanted to live after all.

3

The female finally moved back outside the Osprey, but not before she had prowled around most of the interior. There was apparently a lot of wreckage strewn about as she took to jumping from spot to spot in her inspection. Before her departure, she leapt onto the metal over me a final time, slipping and sending another collection of debris crashing to the deck.

I cringed at the noise, afraid it would attract other infected, but also excited when I felt another small shift. Once she departed I waited half an hour, calmly counting off the time in my head before I dared to move. I had no idea if she had just stepped out into the night and was standing there waiting to see what happened, or if she had headed out in search of a meal.

When I felt it was safe to move, I reached up and grasped the metal rod that had hit me in the face. It was curved with hard edges and I realized it was a rib, or strut, or whatever the proper aviation term is for the internal structure that supports the smooth skin of an aircraft.

Pulling, I worked it under the metal plate and down alongside my body.

The curve was sharp and I had to rotate the strut to get it to fit, stopping when I felt the end move past my hips. Turning my upper body, I wrapped my hands around the metal, took a deep breath and pushed. It moved a couple of inches, raising the metal that had me trapped, then the curved edge slipped and I banged my fists onto something hard enough to skin all my knuckles and draw blood.

Exhaling slowly, fighting the pain, I took another breath as I turned the strut to a new angle. Pushing again, I felt it start to slip before catching an irregularity on the surface of the plate that was trapping me. With renewed effort I pushed, barely able to stifle the scream of effort that wanted to erupt from my throat.

With excruciating slowness, the pressure on my hips and legs lessened. Arms shaking from exertion I turned my lower body until I was straight, ass flat against the floor. Strength waning, I slowly lowered the makeshift lever. I expected the pressure to come back on my legs, but it didn't. The strut let the plate down, no longer supporting its considerable weight, and I could wiggle my hips freely.

Pushing the lever out of my way, I breathed a relieved sigh and started squirming my way free. It took several minutes, and I had to move numerous large pieces of wreckage that were tumbled near my head, but I eventually stood up. Immediately I bent to rub my throbbing legs, taking the opportunity to look around.

From my new perspective I realized that the Osprey had come to rest on its roof. I had been pinned beneath a section of the floor decking that had torn lose when we crashed. A large hole was ripped in the side of the fuselage to my right, the rear door completely missing. The daylight I'd been able to see earlier had been through the opening where the rear ramp had once been.

Night vision goggles had been on my head when I'd boarded at the casino, but they were nowhere to be found. I didn't waste much time looking for them, deciding to throw caution to the wind and show a light. I was more concerned with knowing what had happened to Katie and everyone else than I was with being spotted by an infected. I was free and able to fight if the female came back.

The short Sig rifle had a small, high-intensity flashlight clipped on the right side rail. Clicking it on, I got a good look at the interior of the Osprey. What had been a Spartan space that was free of clutter was now hardly recognizable. Wreckage was everywhere. The seats that had been pulled free to make room for Katie and Martinez had almost certainly become large missiles from the force of the crash.

Ignoring the damage, I started looking for bodies, finding several. The first was the infected soldier I'd killed as he tried to snack on my leg. The two Marines who had accompanied Zemeck were tumbled within a pile of seats, both appearing to have died during the crash. Another Army uniform caught my eye, white bone poking through the heavy fabric in a couple of places. The soldier's neck was at an unnatural angle and almost certainly broken.

There weren't any other bodies inside the aircraft other than the two pilots. They were still strapped into their seats, hanging upside down, both quite dead. Looking at the large holes in the side and rear of the Osprey, I turned off the light and stepped out into the night. I expected to find bodies strewn in the wake of our crash, and I wasn't wrong.

Immediately outside, I encountered the remains of what had to be the small boy. There was nothing left other than shredded clothing, bones and a lot of blood that had soaked into the soil. Not bothering to scan the area for infected, or other threats, I ran to the closest body. A female, most likely infected and her throat most certainly torn out by Dog. I found four more dead females, then spotted a male form.

I bypassed it when I saw the Army uniform, my breath catching when I saw a crumpled form with lots of exposed skin gleaming in the moonlight. Katie had been forced to wear a thong and a small, frilly bra by her captors, and was still barely dressed when we got on the aircraft.

Relief flooded through me when I got close enough to the body to see the blonde hair. I didn't need to check anything else. Katie had tried blonde, once, many years ago. It hadn't worked and she had stayed with her natural red ever since.

Moving on, I found two more soldiers and another dead infected female. Looking ahead, back down the raw score carved in the ground by our crash, I didn't see any more bodies. Scanning to the sides I spotted more to my left. Two more of the scantily clad women. One of them had long, dark hair and a very similar build to Katie. I only had to check her hip. The absence of the small, unique tattoo was all the confirmation I needed to be certain this wasn't my wife. Then I found my friend.

Master Gunnery Sergeant Matt Zemeck was on his back, head turned up as if he were looking at the stars. A large piece of jagged metal protruded from his chest and his right leg was bent back at an impossible angle. I stood looking down at him, trying to process his death.

There's always someone you encounter in life, especially in the military, who seems larger than life. Indestructible. Like they could walk into hell itself, rip Satan's heart out and be back in time for a cold beer with their friends. That had been Matt. Now he was gone, trying to help me.

I knelt and opened his vest, removing his dog tags. I dipped my head to slip the chain around my neck and paused when something that didn't belong caught my eye. A thin, silver oval was nestled between the two, rubber encased tags.

Holding it up to the moonlight I recognized Chris, his wife, who had died during the attacks in New York. Saying goodbye to my friend, I put the dog tags in place and stood to continue my search.

After five minutes of sweeping the area I didn't find any other bodies. One soldier missing. Two of the women rescued from the casino missing. Stephanie and the other kid were nowhere to be found. No Katie, Rachel, Martinez or Dog. What the hell?

Climbing back into the Osprey I used the light to conduct a more thorough search of the debris. I didn't think I could have missed them, and the dead females indicated Dog had survived the crash, but where the hell were they? Ten minutes later I had checked everywhere large enough to conceal a body and went back outside.

Light off, I started walking a circle around the crash site, expanding the radius from the aircraft on each lap. I kept this up until I had circled beyond the initial impact point. There weren't any more bodies to be found.

With a start I realized I hadn't been looking for everything I should have. I was so focused on finding bodies that I hadn't been looking for tracks.

We had come down in a large field that was growing something green and low to the ground that I couldn't identify. The soil was soft and loose, and I cursed my own stupidity for stumbling around and mucking up any tracks that had to be present.

It didn't take me long to find what I was looking for. A large group had approached the crash sight from the east. I was able to identify more than ten different sets of tracks, some of them barefoot. Squatting over them I reached down and lightly touched the ground.

Where the toes and balls of their feet had come down, they had struck the ground with a lot of force, pushing deeply into the rich soil. The people who had left these marks were running at a sprint. Female infected.

I tried to get a better count, but couldn't find an area where they hadn't run on top of each other's footprints. There were several of them was the best I could come up with. Standing, I turned to go get a count of dead females and examine them more closely. Looking at the ground as I turned I moved right into the grasp of an infected male. It was the missing soldier.

He wrapped me up instantly, pulling against me like he was trying to give a bear hug. His head lunged forward, teeth snapping and I nearly lost a chunk of my face before I got my right hand up and on his throat. My left arm was pinned between our bodies and if I released the grip on him to reach for a weapon his teeth would be tearing me open in a heartbeat.

Struggling, I tried to break away, pushing hard and moving his head back, but was unable to loosen the arms circling my body. Squeezing with my right hand I hoped to cut off his air, or the blood supply to his brain, but he seemed impervious to my efforts.

My left arm was straight down between our bodies, and as I grunted with the exertion of keeping his teeth away I realized exactly where my hand was. Turning my wrist I grabbed between his legs, adjusting until his testicles were firmly in my hand. With a solid grip I pulled and squeezed with all my strength.

He didn't react in the slightest. His arms didn't relax an ounce of pressure and he never wavered in his attempts to bite. Continuing to apply pressure I felt one of his balls rupture, then twisted and applied force to the second one until it gave with another sickening pop. He never flinched and showed no awareness of an injury that would normally put the meanest, toughest man in the world on the ground.

4

Struggling with the male, I tried to twist in his embrace but couldn't rotate my body. He was nearly as large as me, and in his infected state was stronger. My advantage was speed and agility, and maybe intelligence, but wrapped in his arms as I was, most of my strengths were negated. Feeling desperation creeping in, I pushed harder against his throat and moved my feet to dance with him.

He was trying to move me off balance and take me to the ground. Losing my footing and ending up rolling around in the dirt would benefit him and put me in an even more compromised position. Still trying to twist my body and pull my left arm free to reach a weapon, something crashed into us and sent us sprawling.

When we hit, he landed on his back with all of my weight coming down on his chest. Whatever had struck us was attacking me, tearing at my right shoulder and arm, but the bear hug had loosened and with a herculean effort I broke free and rolled. I left the male behind, but my attacker came with me, screaming right next to my face. A female had joined the party.

Still rolling, I reached for the new arrival, hands finding long hair, which I grasped and pulled hard to control her head. I was caught off guard when I was able to pull the body completely off of me and send it tumbling away towards the male. Scrambling to my feet I grasped the hilt of my Kukri and whipped it up as the little girl we had rescued with Stephanie leapt at me.

A month ago the sight of a child would have caused hesitation, but I'd learned they are just as dangerous and determined as an infected adult. Turning the blade I met her charge and buried the weapon to the hilt in her small throat. Yanking the Kukri free, I killed the male who was just rising to his knees.

Weapon still in hand, I stayed in a partial crouch, knees flexed, scanning all around me for any more attackers. Not seeing any within range of my vision, I quickly cleaned the steel on the dead male's uniform, sheathed it and pulled my rifle up. With the night vision scope I repeated my scan of the surroundings, standing up straight and relaxing slightly when I didn't spot anything else moving.

With a deep breath I turned a full circle again, still finding the area clear. Moving quickly I checked each body I could find. Nine dead females that I didn't recognize. Four of them appeared to have been killed by Dog, their throats torn out and deep, defensive wounds on their arms where they had tried to stop him.

Five more had large wounds in their torsos and heads. Large, ragged holes. I stood staring down at one of them, finally turning my flashlight back on after checking the area again for threats. It came on, then quickly dimmed. Squatting down for a better look before it completely died, I was at a loss. These were definitely not bullet holes, or wounds from any type of firearm I was familiar with. Neither were they knife or dagger wounds. What the hell had killed them

Putting it aside for the moment, I started looking for tracks again. I had to move well away from the crash sight and all of the disturbed ground before I found where they had walked away to the east. A mix of shoe prints and bare feet. And right in the middle, every track clear and crisp, Dog's paw prints. Moving to the side of their path so I didn't disturb them I followed the tracks for close to a hundred yards.

For long stretches, Dog's trail was pristine as he'd obviously been following. Then it would swing out to the side and make a large half circle that would intersect with the trail and all but disappear in the jumble of marks in the soft soil. This told me he was shadowing the group.

Sometimes at the back, which is when he would leave clear tracks, others ranging ahead which is why some of his prints were lost in the passage of human feet. There was also one time where a set of three tracks left by unshod horses had come in from the south and intersected Dog's circle around the group, but they had peeled away to the southeast and didn't seem to be following the infected.

But had they taken my group? I didn't see any other explanation. I couldn't imagine Rachel, Katie or Martinez willingly leaving me behind. For that matter, the last time I saw them, Katie and Martinez weren't in any condition to set off on a hike across Oklahoma. Fear sent a thrill through me. Had they turned? Maybe they weren't taken. Maybe they had joined.

I was only sure of one thing. Rachel, uninfected, must have been with the group or Dog would not have followed. But I was still at a loss as to why I was left behind, alive. I forced myself to not think the worst. Katie was fine, not turned, and I wasn't going to stop until I got her and everyone else back.

Scanning around me again, I trotted back to the crash to find my pack. It took some searching and digging through the debris, but I eventually found it buried under a jumbled pile of seats. Opening it up I quickly checked the contents and discarded as many items as I felt I could do without. I was going to follow the group and needed to lighten my load as much as possible so I could move faster.

While searching for the pack I'd come across the M4 rifle that I had left with Stephanie when I went into the casino. I liked the little Sig that Zemeck had given me, but it fired low powered, nine-millimeter pistol rounds, which were perfectly suitable for CQB. But I was back outside, moving across open country and might need something with a little more oomph behind it.

Pushing the Sig onto my back, I slung the M4 and scavenged full magazines from the dead Marines and Soldiers. Taking a few minutes to prepare an MRE, I stood thinking about my situation as I wolfed it down.

We had taken off from the casino, heading south to reach Tinker Air Force Base. It was about ten minutes, I thought, into the flight when the engines shut down. Why the hell had that happened? I had no clue, and it didn't matter. It had, and we had crashed.

Ten minutes in the air before going down meant I was somewhere between twenty and thirty miles south of the casino. I remembered driving through that area the previous night and not seeing anything other than an occasional farmhouse. It had been dark, but there had been enough moonlight to see fields under cultivation stretching away to the horizon.

The crash had been shortly before sunrise of the day that had already passed. And now it was dark again and I had no idea what time it was. Had the sun only gone down an hour ago, or...? It didn't matter. I could run at night just as easily as in the day. There was enough light from the moon for me to see, and I'd probably cover more ground without the heat of the sun beating down on me.

Finishing the last of the meal I tossed the packaging onto a pile of debris and drank deeply from my water. Working the pack onto my shoulders, I adjusted the straps and took another look around the area with the rifle's night vision scope. Satisfied all was clear, I set off at a run, following the tracks that went east.

5

Running across the fields was just as difficult as I expected. My direction of travel was perpendicular to the rows of cultivated produce, so rather than a normal stride I had to lift each foot and pay close attention to where I brought it down. Miscalculating a step could result in a sprained ankle at best, a broken leg at worst. The former would be a serious problem, the latter most likely a death sentence.

After covering close to a mile, and several fields, I had to slow to a walk. The extra effort required to move on the difficult footing coupled with the weight of my pack was quickly draining my energy reserves. I was panting and sweating heavily, fighting dizziness that I was sure came from the concussion I'd suffered during the plane crash.

Striding along, spanning a furrow with each step, I finally succumbed to my injuries and leaned to the side to throw up. Most of the MRE and water I'd consumed before heading out came gushing, my stomach continuing to spasm long after it was empty. Straightening up, the world around me spun for a moment and I almost pitched over. I must have looked like a drunk, standing their swaying as I fought the waves of nausea.

Closing my eyes I breathed deeply through my nose, willing my body to settle down and let me push on. Eventually the worst of the disorientation passed and I was able to open my eyes without getting sick. My head pounded and my vision was blurry, but at least I was able to stay on my feet. I took a mouthful of water, swished it around and spat it out, then took a few small sips. Thankfully my system didn't rebel.

With another deep breath I began walking again, stepping over the next row and onto a clear paw print. I was moving slow, wiping blood from the gash on my head out of my eye, and I'm not sure if I was walking a straight line or not. But I was able to follow the tracks of the group I was pursuing.

Pressing on for what felt like hours, I glanced down to check on their trail and came to a stop. Nothing but undisturbed dirt and a row of low, dark green plants in front of me. I looked to either side, but failed to find the tracks. What the hell? How long had I been walking in a daze?

Reversing course, I began following my own tracks, alarmed to see the weaving path I had taken. Pausing, I wiped sweat off my face and more blood out of my eye, then took a few more sips of water as I looked around. My vision was blurry, my head pounding like a jackhammer, but I did feel more stable.

With a start I realized I hadn't scanned for threats in I didn't know how long. Lifting my rifle I looked through the night vision scope and began to turn. I had only completed a quarter of the circle when I stumbled sideways as the world around me started whirling in the opposite direction. Lowering my rifle, I closed my eyes and waited as a wave of heat rolled across my face and a fresh bout of nausea struck.

When the flushing passed, I swallowed twice, trying to keep myself from throwing up again. Stomach settling, I breathed deeply, slowly feeling better. Ready to try looking at the world again, I opened my eyes and was startled to see an Indian standing a few feet in front of me.

He was taller than me, broad across the chest and shoulders and narrow in the hips. He wore jeans and boots and a leather vest that exposed powerful, dark bronze arms. His hair was black as midnight and pulled into a long ponytail. He had deep-set eyes and a face that was all planes and angles. His skin was difficult to differentiate in the dark from the leather he wore.

He stared back, an assault rifle held loosely in his hands. Was I that out of it that he had managed to walk right up without me even knowing he was there? I've worked with Indians in the military and not for a second did I buy into any of the mystical warrior bullshit. A man is quiet in the field because he has learned how to be quiet, not because of any magical powers granted by the earth mother.

"What do you want here?" He finally spoke in flat, American tones. No Hollywood stereotype accent here. Just a voice that sounded like any other male born and raised in the United States.

"Just passing through," I said, assessing him.

He may have been holding his rifle loosely, but that didn't mean he didn't know how to handle it. It was being held almost exactly the same way I hold mine. The man had had some training.

His face remained unreadable and he didn't move a muscle. "Army?" He finally broke his silence.

I nodded, instantly regretting the movement that caused my dizziness to flare up. He tilted his head as he watched me sway slightly.

"You're hurt," he said. "And on Osage land. You have no right to be here and no authority. Or is the white man going to take our homes and move us again?"

"Fuck you, Tonto." I said. "Whatever was done happened long before you or I were born, and there's not enough people left alive in the world to give a shit."

That pissed him off, his eyes narrowing as he made a small adjustment to his grip on the rifle. My right hand was hovering a few inches from my pistol and I was confident I could draw it and put a round through his forehead before he could raise and fire his rifle. Well, maybe I could if I was able to figure out which one of him I was seeing was the real one. Dizziness and double vision without tequila is a real bitch.

"Fuck you!" He snapped back. "You come onto my land and insult me? You need to go back the way you came before I stop being friendly."

"Friendly?" I snorted. "That was being friendly? Well, hell. Where *are* my manners? Thank you for being so welcoming to travelers."

The tension ratcheted up a few notches when I finished speaking. Even in the darkness I could see his eyes flash in anger, the muscles in his arms twitching as he squeezed the rifle. Things were about to go south in a hurry.

"Look, I'm sorry." I said, genuinely apologizing for having been a dick. "It's been a bad day and I was tracking a group that took my friends and got a little lost. I was in a plane crash a few hours ago and took a good blow to the head. I just want to get back on their trail."

He stared at me for a long time. Long enough that the silence was growing uncomfortable, but I wasn't going to break it. I've played the game before and knew the rules. The next one to speak would be compromising some of his position.

"The only group to come through in the past two days was a bunch of infected women." He finally said.

"When? Going east or west?" I asked.

"West, around midnight yesterday, then back east an hour after sunrise this morning." He answered after a very long pause. "They were carrying two on their way east."

"Did you see a German Shepherd?" I asked, feeling the stirrings of hope.

What I didn't voice was a question of why he hadn't tried to stop them. The Osage were fierce warriors, one of the most feared Indian nations at one time, and he didn't look that far removed from his heritage. Then the answer hit me. He was alone out here and was either out of ammo or was so low that he couldn't engage the group.

He looked at me, maybe finally believing my story. "Yes, I did. But he wasn't really with them. More like he was trailing them, then he'd race ahead for a bit before circling back to trail them again. Kind of strange."

“That’s them,” I said. “The ones being carried and the dog belong with me. We got separated after the crash.”

“You don’t want to be messing with them,” he said.

“Yes, I do. And I am. They have my friends, and my wife.”

6

He stood looking at me, either trying to figure out if I was seriously deranged or tilting at windmills. The inscrutable act was wearing thin and the longer I stood here wasting time with him, the farther away the group moved.

"Look," I said in a calm voice. "I'm not turning around. I'm going after them. If that means crossing your land and we've got a problem because of that, well… we'd better settle it now because you're wasting my time."

I moved my right hand and placed it on the butt of my pistol. Yes, I was still dizzy, but my vision was improving and instead of seeing two of him I was only seeing one and a half. Kind of like he had an identical twin that was standing partially in front of him. If I had to shoot, I'd go for center mass, but I didn't think I'd have to shoot. Hoped I didn't have to shoot.

"That way," he finally said, carefully taking a hand off his rifle and pointing in a direction slightly north of due east.

I nodded, very gently, and began to move around him. I wasn't thrilled with the thought of turning my back on his rifle and sidestepped a few yards down the row I was standing in. Still angled so I could see him, I started striding across the rows, stopping after the third one. I turned back to see him watching me, rifle now hanging down his side on a sling.

"Here," I said, pulling two loaded magazines out of my vest. "You're probably going to need these."

I held the mags up and the surprise on his face was evident. I'd finally gotten something out of him other than a blank stare.

"Take them," I said, extending my arm and shaking them in the air. "I know you're either out or very low on ammo."

He had recovered from his surprise and pasted the blank look on his face again. With a sigh of frustration I dropped them on the ground.

"Suit yourself. I'm out of here." I said, turning my back on him and resuming my direction of travel.

I can say that for the first couple of hundred yards there was a spot in the middle of my back that itched and twitched, waiting for a bullet. But the farther I walked, the more confident I was that I hadn't misread the man. If he'd really wanted to kill me he could have done so when he first walked up while I was standing there with my eyes closed. He hadn't then, and other than a few insults I hadn't given him a reason to do so now.

Not bothering to look back and see if he picked up the magazines, I pushed on. Several hundred yards later I found the group's trail. I had wandered way off course in my dazed state. The good news was I felt better. My vision had mostly returned to normal. I was no longer seeing double or partial-double. Now there was just some fuzziness around things, but at least there was only one object when I looked at something.

My head still pounded, but I was stronger and no longer sick to my stomach. Sipping more water, I adjusted the straps on my pack and broke into a jog. I can't say I was moving appreciably faster than I was when just walking, but I needed every fraction of a mile per hour I could get. With no idea how fast the infected that had my friends were moving, all I could do was push as hard as possible to close the distance between us.

After half an hour of jogging I reached the edge of the agricultural area. The soft soil of the field ended at a narrow, hard-packed dirt road. I slowed when I reached the road, noting the scuffing of the surface made by passing feet. Moving to the far side there was a slope down to grass-covered prairie and the path to follow was clear. All of the feet had trampled the vegetation down, changing its color and texture.

With relatively smooth ground to traverse I was able to push my speed up to a run. Not having to step over every row as I jogged eliminated the worst of the jarring impact from every step. The new terrain was a physical relief and for the first time I began to feel that I was actually making progress.

The trail followed the geography, sticking to the easier route. It wound through low areas, seemingly avoiding climbing small rises. It took a while for the significance of this to dawn on me. Humans, at least modern humans who grew up in towns and cities and did all their walking on smooth concrete and asphalt will normally follow a straight path when walking through nature.

Maybe it's because we've been conditioned since birth to get from point A to point B in as straight a line as possible. Maybe not. I just know it's the way people behave. Animals, on the other hand, will almost always follow the terrain. The path of least resistance. Use as little energy as possible because they can't count on a grocery store or fast food restaurant being just around every corner.

The infected were moving like animals. Like humans travelled throughout history until we began building and living in cities. I didn't know how this helped me, but it did give me some insight into the infected's minds. A lifetime of conditioning to move in straight lines had been stripped away by the effects of the virus, the infected operating on a more instinctual level.

These thoughts and half a dozen others went through my head as I ran. Running is boring, and my mind found things to occupy itself while only devoting enough attention to what I was doing to keep me from stepping off a cliff or smashing into a tree. So I let it wander. And not surprisingly, all I could think about was Katie and Rachel. Rachel and Katie.

I was thinking about how this would all shake out when I got them back. Katie was the love of my life, there was no question of that, but Rachel had a piece of my hard, black heart and the thought of hurting her broke that little piece. I would be dead half a dozen times over if not for Rachel, and I owed her more than I could ever repay for helping me find and rescue Katie.

Tabling the internal discussion, I slowed then came to a stop when I reached a wide river. I cast around, checking the tracks that transitioned from the prairie grass to the dirt banks, but their direction of travel didn't deviate. Straight into the water. A few yards downstream I found a clear set of prints where Dog also went into the river.

This was really odd. I looked across the water, estimating it to be nearly a hundred yards to the far bank. I couldn't tell how deep it was, the water moving so slowly that if I didn't pay close attention I couldn't even detect a current. I had not seen infected willingly enter any body of water unless they were in hot pursuit of prey. They couldn't swim, or at least I'd yet to see one that was capable.

The river had to be shallow. If they weren't crossing it there was no reason for them to wade out into it. Starting to step into the water, I froze when my little early warning system sent a wave of prickles up my back. Frozen in place, I cut my eyes back and forth in search of any threat while I calmed my breathing so I could hear anyone or anything approaching.

Seeing and hearing nothing after a few moments, I slowly turned my head first to the right, then left. My rifle was up to my shoulder by now and I gently clicked it from semi to burst mode. Still detecting nothing, I suddenly dashed to my left to take cover behind a large willow tree. The tree's roots were exposed due to the erosion of the river, thick and rough where they were above the surface.

Standing in water to my knees, I looked through the night vision scope. Thoroughly scanning my back-trail I didn't see anything, so I began checking each side. What the hell had got my spidey-sense all excited? OK, I know it's not really super powers. I heard, smelled, saw or felt something that was so subtle my conscious mind wasn't aware of it, but my subconscious picked up on it and sounded an alarm.

Staying still, I kept watching. Several minutes later I detected movement as a figure broke cover from behind a stunted tree and dashed to conceal itself behind a low mound of dirt. I didn't recognize the features through the scope, but his build and long ponytail told me who it was. Maybe he'd had second thoughts about letting me cross his land. The fucking Indian was following me.

7

Climbing out of the river, I crawled up the low bank. Working my way over the top, I silently moved at an angle to the mound the Indian was behind. Pausing, I checked the area and spotted a clump of bushes that I was willing to bet was his next destination. They provided the best concealment and were a forty-yard dash from the mound. I intended to get there first and be waiting for him.

I didn't know what his game was. Was he stalking me with bad intentions, or was he just following along to make sure I didn't do something disrespectful while I was on Osage land? Frustrated, I slipped into place ten yards to the side of the bushes. I was prone on the ground, mostly hidden behind a couple of rocks. In the dark I knew I was invisible to anyone that didn't have night vision or thermal imaging.

My rifle had just settled in against my cheek, aimed at where I expected him to stop when he suddenly appeared right where I'd predicted. Damn he was quiet. I'm good in the field. I'm not bragging, just stating what I know from years of having survived because I was taught how to move stealthily. But this guy was a fucking ghost. Watching him suddenly appear in my sights was like watching something on TV with the audio muted. It happened with zero detectable noise.

"You're not faster than a bullet," I said, just loud enough for him to hear me.

He remained frozen in a crouch, head lifted to see over the bushes to the river. After a few long heart beats he turned to look in my direction, not moving any other part of his body. His rifle was in his right hand, on the far side of his body and he knew there wasn't a chance in hell he could bring it around before I pulled the trigger.

"Why are you following me?" I asked.

He just stared back, not saying anything.

"I don't have time for this shit," I finally said in frustration. "I think it's time to put a bullet in your head so I can go about my business without worrying about you. Now, if you don't like that idea I'd suggest you knock off this silent routine and speak up. I'm out of patience."

"I know where the females are going," he said without his usual hesitation. "Where they're headed is sacred ground. I tracked a large group of them there a few days ago."

"So... what? You were going to sneak up behind me and kill me to protect your sacred ground?" I growled, getting really tired of this.

"No," was all he said.

"Then what? Seriously, I'm getting pissed off and don't have time to be jerking around with you." I said, clicking my rifle's fire selector from burst to semi. I didn't need to expend three bullets if I decided to put him down.

"Relax. OK?" The sound of the rifle had gotten his attention. "I might have killed you before, but leaving me some ammo was pretty stand-up. You were right. I was out. Been fighting these bitches for a long time. I was just going to tie you up and drag your white ass back to where you came from."

"I'm supposed to believe that bullshit?" I asked.

"Honest Injun." He said, showing the first glimmer of a human being behind the intractable warrior façade.

I lay there looking at him through my scope, finally snorting a laugh but not relaxing. Just because he had cracked a joke at his own expense didn't mean he wasn't still a deadly threat.

"Well, I'm not going to let that happen. So I see two ways out of this. First is, I put a bullet through you and go on my merry way. Second, you get it through your head that all I care about is getting my wife and friends back.

"I don't give a flying fuck about your sacred ground. If that's where they are I'll spill a lot of blood to satisfy whatever spirits you're worried about. Either way, you're not going to stop me, so make up your mind how you want this to go."

I had been watching him closely as I spoke. Looking for the subtle tells that reveal the moment a man decides to fight or not. I saw it as I finished talking. A slight lowering of his eyes and his rifle. It was only two tiny movements, and I doubt he was even aware he had made them, but they told me all I needed to know. He wasn't going to fight. Why didn't matter.

"There's a third choice," he said after a couple of moments. "I go with you. I know this land and I know where they're going. And I know how to fight. My father was in Vietnam and when he got back he made sure his boys knew how to fight. He always thought there would be a day the Osage would rise up again."

I was surprised by his offer of help, unsure if it was sincere or a tactic to get me to relax.

"What about your sacred ground?" I asked. "How do we get around that?"

"That's all bullshit," he answered. "Well, not to most of my tribe, but I don't believe in that shit. It's just something the old men and women use to try and hold on to the past and control the younger generations."

"Then why the hell were you giving me such a hard time?" I asked.

"Look at me and what do you see?" He asked, the anger clear in his voice.

"An asshole," I answered, drawing a snort from him.

"No, you see a redskin savage. A lazy, out of work drunk with nothing that hasn't been handed to him by the white man." His voice was getting louder as he talked. Apparently there was some pretty deep-seated resentment there.

"You're wasting my time," I said. "I don't give a fuck if your red, black or purple. And I sure don't give a shit what you think the white man has done to you. When you're ancestors were being herded onto reservations, mine were literally starving to death in Ireland and selling their souls to get on ships to America so their children would have a chance at survival. None of our people had it easy."

I expected more arguing. More accusations of prejudice. Anything other than a genuine, deep laugh as he slowly stood up, rifle held out to his side in one hand to make sure I didn't open fire.

"Let's go find your wife, white man. I'll tell you a story to pass the time while we run." He said.

After a moment I got to my feet, finally lowering my rifle but keeping both hands on it. This guy was either certifiable or playing some really weird game. I didn't know which, maybe a little of both, but I wasn't ready to start trusting him.

"After you," I said, gesturing at the river. I wasn't about to let him behind me again.

He grinned, turned and led the way into the water.

8

The current in the river was slow. No more than a mile an hour at best. And the water was warm; unlike the frigid dunking I'd taken in the Mississippi when I jumped in after Rachel and Dog. The footing was easy, feeling like packed sand with an occasional rock. As we approached the middle, the water rose above my waist and stayed there until I was within ten feet of the far side. It was an easy crossing and neither of us had any trouble keeping our rifles high and dry.

On the opposite bank I called a halt long enough to draw my pistol and make sure no water was trapped anywhere inside. Weapon ready, I motioned to my new traveling companion and he set off at a fast trot. I fell in slightly behind and to his side.

The tracks out of the water were clear in the damp earth, then we moved back onto the prairie grass and were easily following the trail their passage had created. The Indian's legs were longer than mine and he settled into a steady, ground eating lope that I had to concentrate to keep up with. I reminded myself of our different heritages; his one of running to hunt and survive, mine one of hard physical labor on small plots of land. I still kept up with him.

Half an hour after we left the river he started talking. He asked my name, which I told him. He asked what my story was, which I didn't. My silence didn't deter him, and now that I'd broken through he couldn't seem to shut up.

His name was Joseph Revard. It wasn't an Osage name, which he assured me would be unpronounceable to my tongue. Revard was French, a legacy of the trading alliance that was formed in the 1600s between the Osage nation and French traders. He talked for miles about the history of his people, not sugar coating any of the injustices perpetrated by the US Government, both real and perceived. Many of them I'd heard before, growing up, some of them I hadn't. None of them were something that should ever have happened, but there's no changing the past.

Then he began talking about himself and I was so surprised I began to fall behind and had to run hard to close the distance that opened up between us. Joe had left the reservation when he was 19 to go live amongst the white man. He had encountered open and hostile prejudice, and the subtle kind where people were overly polite and solicitous. He said he preferred the ones that were open with their racism because at least he knew exactly where he stood with them.

When he was 20 he was washing dishes in a greasy spoon truck stop, ready to give up on dreams of making it in the white mans' world. That was when he met Mary. She was young, pretty and as white and blonde as a tourism poster for Oklahoma. Mary was a waitress in the truck stop and the moment they met he could feel something different about her. When she looked at him, she looked into his eyes and saw the man he was. He wasn't even sure she realized he was an Indian.

Mary was a student at Oklahoma State, and when she wasn't waiting tables at the truck stop she was in class or the library. Totally enamored with the beautiful girl, Joseph began hanging around the campus to steal a moment with her between classes or when she would take a break from studying. She was always happy to see him and he quickly fell completely and hopelessly in love.

There was a small contingent of Osage students at OSU and it didn't take them long to discover and befriend Joe. With their support, and Mary's encouragement, he enrolled in the University. He had no goal, no idea what he would do with an education, but knew if he was going to be part of Mary's life he couldn't continue to be an uneducated dish washer.

Federal programs paid for Joe's tuition and books, and by the end of his first semester he and Mary were sharing a small apartment within walking distance of the campus. They studied hard, worked hard and made time for each other whenever they could. By the end of his freshman year, Joe had discovered that he had an interest in and an affinity for the biological sciences.

Three years later he graduated with an honors degree in bio-chemistry, walking across the stage hand in hand with Mary, his new bride. After graduation came graduate school for both. Mary studied literature, but Joseph began working on a degree in virology. He had completed his Masters and was awaiting word on whether or not he had been accepted into the Doctoral program when the attacks happened.

Life had remained relatively normal in Oklahoma for the first few weeks, then secondary outbreaks began occurring. Joe was spending twenty hours a day in the lab, working with senior researchers who were looking for any way to battle the Chinese engineered virus. Then the Air Force had shown up with a data stick and vials of a liquid that they claimed were a vaccine.

The team had worked around the clock to verify that they did in fact have a viable vaccine in hand. Exhausted, yet excited, Joe had rushed home to share the wonderful news with Mary and had almost been killed when he walked in the front door. Mary had been in the back of the apartment when he opened the door, screaming and charging. Joe had barely gotten the door closed before she slammed into it in her efforts to rip his throat out.

While he had been working, she had turned. The screaming devil that had attacked when he opened the door wasn't his wife any more. But he couldn't bring himself to leave her. For a whole day he sat on the porch as Mary prowled their small home, occasionally screaming her frustration and anger.

Joe was still sitting there when his friend, Robert, found him. Robert was also an Osage and a fellow graduate student at OSU. He was on his way to the reservation, fleeing the city, and had stopped to check on Joe and Mary. He had sat down and held his friend, crying with him for his loss. Wrung out, Joe had stood and asked Robert if he could borrow the old Colt pistol he was wearing.

Weapon in hand, Joe had slowly approached the door. With a deep breath he had turned the knob and shoved the door open, pistol raised and pointed into his home. Mary charged. Joe hesitated, unable or unwilling to defend himself. Only Robert's warning shout saved him, snapping him out of whatever reverie he was in and making him pull the trigger and kill his wife.

Handing the gun back to Robert, he'd walked past his friend and climbed into his pickup. Robert had gotten in a moment later and started driving them out of the city, but Joe redirected him to the University's Health Science Center where he'd been working. Going in by himself, he'd taken an empty backpack. By this time production of the vaccine had begun and he filled the pack with as many vials as it would hold.

Bringing the pack, he and Robert had returned to the reservation and immediately begun administering the vaccine. Joe had been gone a long time and had forgotten the mistrust of white man medicine that was prevalent amongst the tribe. Less than a third of the Osage were willing to be vaccinated. He did what he could, then begged the tribal elders to help him convince those that had refused to be inoculated. They turned him down, and he'd gone to his family home in despair.

Over the next several days the Osage that hadn't received the vaccine began to turn, and kill anyone around them. Soon the infected outnumbered the living and Joe and Robert barely escaped with their lives. They ran to the open plains, battling females that had tracked them until they were almost out of ammo. The day before I encountered Joe, Robert had been killed by a female. Joe had shot her with his last bullet, then buried his friend.

"Where are we going? How far?" I asked when Joe finally finished his story.

"It's a little over a day's run from here," he answered. "Canyon country. The Potawatomi tribe slaughtered hundreds of Osage women and children hiding there in the 1800s. There was a treaty in place and the American government was supposed to provide protection. They didn't."

I didn't feel like debating two hundred year old events with him. I had little doubt that the problems of any of the Indian tribes were at the bottom of the priority list for the Army at the time. Not that I wasn't sympathetic, but I had more pressing problems to worry about. Besides, I was feeling dizzy again and was having a hard time focusing on Joe's running form.

9

Colonel Crawford leaned back in the base commander's office chair and rubbed his eyes. He was tired. Bone weary tired. But the ranks of infected at Tinker Air Force Base's perimeter fence were growing by the hour as more and more of the civilian population succumbed to the infection, and he didn't have time to rest. The high altitude EMP intended to disable the satellite the Russians were using to control the herds had knocked out the electrical grid on the base and he was now working in an office lit by the pale green glow of several chemical sticks.

While this was inconvenient for him, it was downright dangerous for the Rangers, Marines and Airmen defending the fence. They had no light. Few of their night vision goggles and scopes were still working as they'd had most of them turned on when the pulse happened. Any electronic device that had been in operation at the time of the nuclear detonation had been permanently destroyed.

The only good news was that there had been very few vehicles and aircraft in operation at the time, so they were still able to use trucks and Humvees as well as put helicopters in the air to support the battle that was raging.

"They're landing at Fort Hood, sir." Captain Blanchard said from the shadows on the far side of the office where he had been softly speaking on one of a handful of radios that had survived.

"What does it look like down there?" Crawford asked without bothering to open his eyes.

"All quiet at the moment. Runways are clear and they're not seeing anything moving on post. But there's some bad news."

"Do tell, Captain." The Colonel said with a note of sarcasm.

"They passed over a herd north of Dallas that they estimate to be at least eight miles long and over two wide. If they're bunched up as tightly as we've seen elsewhere, that's estimated to be close to twenty-five million infected. Still headed straight for us." Blanchard said.

Crawford opened his eyes and stared at him, rubbing his temples in a vain attempt to ward off the headache that was threatening to explode into a migraine. He'd sent two squads of Marines and three C-130s to Fort Hood in Texas to raid the armory. They needed ammunition. Desperately. Recon flights throughout the day after the EMP had found other herds still bearing down on Oklahoma City, but none of them were as large as the one that had just been reported.

"What's the word from the Navy? Did the EMP do the job, or not?" Crawford asked.

"They're still trying to figure that out, sir. We lost everything that was over North America except for two NSA birds. The Navy never had access to them in the first place, and since the NSA doesn't exist anymore they're having to try and hack their way in."

"If they can't get in, how do they know they're functioning?" The Colonel asked, shoving papers around the desktop until he found a pack of cigarettes.

"They're showing as active nodes on the Echelon network which they wouldn't if the EMP had disabled them. But being NSA assets, they're encrypted very heavily and it's not a simple job to break in and take control. We don't even know what they're for or what their capabilities are. Hopefully once the Navy cracks them we'll have eyes over CONUS as well as orbital intel again." Blanchard raised the radio to his ear as he finished speaking.

Watching his aide listen to the muted voice, Crawford lit a cigarette and leaned his forearms on the heavy, walnut desk. The desk belonged to Air Force General Triplett, but the man was currently under house arrest in the base commander's quarters with his wife. A full platoon of Rangers were making sure that he didn't leave, didn't have any visitors and wasn't able to communicate with anyone.

Their arrest of the General for siding with the traitorous US President had started out benign enough the previous evening, but had turned ugly in a hurry. Twenty Air Force Security Forces had been guarding the General. Colonel Crawford had personally led a platoon of Rangers to arrest him and seize control of the strategically vital Air Force base.

The Rangers had moved into position, undetected. Two snipers had set up to cover each end of the large home, both of them also having a clear view of most of the Security Forces. Crawford's plan had been to move his men forward and capture the Air Force personnel, the advantage of speed and stealth on his side. Once the guards were neutralized it would be a simple matter to affect the General's arrest.

But things rarely go according to plan. As the Rangers were moving into position, close to the residence of the base's Deputy Commander, gunfire erupted from one of the second story windows. Unable to sleep, the Air Force Colonel had seen the Army moving into position and rather than sounding an alarm he had grabbed a rifle and started shooting at the two Rangers that were visible from his bedroom window.

"Weapons free for defense!" Crawford had reluctantly shouted into his radio.

He had wanted to do this without shedding any American blood. His heart sank when he heard the suppressed return fire of his men, which quickly silenced the Air Force Colonel. He was sick to his stomach when the Security Forces opened up with their Humvee mounted machine gun. Three Rangers died before the snipers took out the gunner, and they had to kill five more of the

General's guards before the rest of the men put their weapons on the ground and surrendered.

Crawford had rushed forward, a squad on his heels, intending to kick in the General's front door. Murder and mayhem were in his eyes as he approached the front porch, the squad snapping their weapons up as the heavy wooden door swung open. It was the General's wife, wearing a thick robe over her nightgown. She moved to block the opening with her body and stood facing Crawford.

The Colonel stood on the first step, the General's wife staring him down. They remained that way for a few moments, neither moving nor speaking. Finally the woman had stepped back into her home and waved Crawford inside. Leaving the Rangers on the porch he had stepped cautiously through the door, which she left standing open and pointed down a hall. Crawford had removed his beret and walked quietly in the indicated direction.

At the end of the hall had been a heavy oak door, stained dark and highly polished to match the décor of the home. Pistol in hand, Crawford had opened the door and stepped into General Triplett's den. The General was seated in one of a pair of high backed, leather wing chairs. He was wearing pajamas and a dressing gown, smoking a cigar and swirling a tumbler of amber liquid. Another glass and a cut crystal decanter of the same drink sat on a silver tray that rested on a table that separated the two chairs.

"Good evening, Colonel. Drink?" He held up the glass, his tone belying the gravity of the moment.

Colonel Crawford holstered his weapon and moved slowly into the room, taking a seat. Triplett held up the decanter and when Crawford nodded he poured a healthy slug into the waiting glass. The Colonel picked it up, his eyes never leaving the superior officer.

"To the United States of America," The General leaned forward and held his glass out towards the Colonel. Crawford picked up his drink, clinked it against the other man's glass and they drank together.

"You know why I'm here, sir." Crawford said, placing his glass back on the silver tray with most of the bourbon still in it.

"How many dead outside?" Triplett asked as if Crawford hadn't spoken.

"I'm not sure. Several of mine and several of yours. One is too many. This didn't need to happen this way."

"I'm not the one in the room committing treason, Colonel." The General's eyes flashed.

"No, sir. You're not, and neither am I. The only person guilty of that is President Clark. I admire and respect your conviction to your oath, but the office that you swore to defend has been corrupted. That only leaves our oath to defend the Constitution, and I'm truly sorry you don't see it that way." Crawford's words were respectful, but his voice was like cold iron.

The General sat quietly, puffing on a cigar that he finally placed in a gleaming crystal ashtray. Downing the remainder of his drink he gently set it next to Crawford's glass.

"Are you here to kill me, Colonel?" He met Crawford's eyes, his gaze steady.

"No, sir. I'm not. You and your wife are restricted to your quarters. My men will search the house and remove any weapons and means of communication, then you will not be troubled further unless you try to leave. You will not be allowed any visitors and my men will be outside and not intrude on your privacy. If you need anything, just ask, and if we can accommodate you we will." Crawford said, noting the shadow at the door as the General's wife listened in from the hallway.

Crawford had left, placing a Lieutenant in charge of guarding the General. The next several hours had been tense as word spread across the large Air Force base of the arrest and detention of their commanding officer by the Army. The Colonel had spent the remainder of the night speaking personally with every Air Force officer over the rank of Lieutenant, explaining the situation and even playing the recording of President Clark talking to the Russian President.

Three officers who were loyal to General Triplett refused to accept the circumstances and follow Colonel Crawford's orders. They were also placed under house arrest. The rest were aghast when they heard their President negotiating for her new home in Russia in exchange for ordering the US Military to stand down, and pledged their support. A couple of them were too quick to agree to take orders from Crawford and the Colonel singled them out for Captain Blanchard to keep an eye on.

“Don’t suppose there’s any word from our wayward Major,” Crawford asked.

“No, sir.” Blanchard responded. “I had the satellite feed streaming to storage and am waiting for the techs to get me a working computer. The servers are heavily EMP shielded, so I should be able to access the files and see where he was when the pulse burned out our birds.”

“When will the drones be on target?” Crawford was referring to four Predator drones that had been launched to check on the movement of the massive herds that had been approaching Tinker. Without satellite coverage they were scrambling to get surveillance flights in the air to find out if the EMP had shut down the Russian transmission.

“Within the hour, sir. I’ll update you as soon as I have eyes on target. If you’d like to get some sleep I’ll wake you as soon as I know something.” Blanchard said.

Nodding, Crawford stubbed out his cigarette and headed for an adjoining office where a cot had been set up for him. He was asleep almost before his head hit the pillow.

10

My dizziness came and went as we ran. For a while I felt perfectly fine, then for no discernible reason the dark horizon would start to tilt and I'd have to slow down so I didn't stumble and fall on my face. After this happened a few times, Joe pulled up to a stop and turned to look at me.

"How bad are you hurt?" He asked, not even breathing hard. I was slightly winded, nauseous and once again sweat was running off me in buckets.

"I'm fine," I said, fumbling for some water. He stood watching me drink, saying nothing.

"You're a stupid, fucking white man," he said. "I don't know why I'm helping you, but if you want my help you need to tell me what's wrong with you. I might be able to do something about it."

"I said I'm fine!" I snapped, starting to move past him.

He reached out, grabbing my arm as I passed him. I spun; fist coming up as I tried to jerk my arm from his grip, but when my body stopped spinning the world kept going. And accelerated. I wobbled and his restraining hand became all that was keeping me from falling to the ground. Taking my other arm he helped me to a seated position on the grass.

"Deep breaths and put your head between your knees," he said, moving out of range in case I decided I still wanted to hit him. "The gash on your head. It's bleeding worse."

I reached up with a trembling hand and touched my face. It came away wet with blood that was running out of the wound. Wiping higher, I realized blood was still flowing, running into my right eye and blocking nearly all its vision. I took a few moments and used some water to rinse my eye out and felt a little better when I could see clearly, but a giant bass drum was going off inside my skull and the world around me was tilted at a forty-five degree angle.

"Stay here," Joe said, standing up. "I'll be back."

"What are you doing?" I asked.

"Getting something to help your big, dumb ass." He said, turned and trotted off.

The headache and vertigo got worse for a few minutes, then improved. I sat on my ass with my knees pulled up and my head down, taking slow deep breaths and occasional sips of water. Eventually I started feeling better, the dizziness passing and the headache retreating, but not leaving. Lifting my head I looked around, but didn't see my companion. I carefully used the night vision scope to check in the direction he'd gone, but didn't see anything.

Fuck him. Whatever he was doing, I didn't have time. Katie was shot, so was Martinez. Rachel could have been hurt in the crash. They needed me and I wasn't helping anyone sitting on my ass in the middle of a giant goddamn prairie. Taking another drink of water I got to my knees, still feeling better. Standing, I swayed like a sapling in a windstorm, but managed to keep my feet under me until the horizon slowed down.

Raising my rifle, I peered through the night vision scope and started to turn to scan the area. First, the horizon began to warp. The stars were whirling, phosphorescent trails tracking their path through the night sky. Then the soil under my feet rippled in giant waves and I was falling. I don't remember hitting the ground.

When I opened my eyes I didn't understand what the hell was happening. The last thing I remembered was a dark, night sky with spinning stars. Now there was bright sunshine. I peered through slit lids and noted the sun was just above the horizon, but I had no idea if that meant it had just come up or was about to go down.

"He lives," Joe said from somewhere off to my left. "Here, drink this."

He thrust a small gourd into my hand. Half of it had been cut away; leaving a crude cup, which held a liquid that was reddish-brown and stank worse than any slit trench I've had the displeasure of using.

"What's this?" I croaked, levering myself up to a sitting position. It took me a moment to realize I was able to do this without my head splitting open or the world turning upside down.

"Ancient Indian remedy, with a little help from modern science," he said. "I've been pouring it down your throat for the past few hours. Feel better?"

"A little," I grudgingly acknowledged. "What's in it?"

"The right roots, berries and bark," he said, motioning for me to drink. "And some Tylenol I had in my pocket."

It took a bit to get past the smell, but I raised the gourd and sipped some of the thick liquid. It tasted worse than I expected, and the small pieces of whatever was floating in it nearly sent me over the edge.

"Oh, and I pissed in it." He said with a grin after I had swallowed.

"I don't know whether to thank you or beat you to death," I said, grimacing as I drank the rest.

My stomach flopped a couple of times, but the concoction stayed down. Unfortunately the incredibly foul taste had coated the inside of my mouth and didn't seem to want to go away. But I did feel better. The headache was mostly gone and the dizziness had stopped.

Joe stood up and extended a hand. After a moment I reached up and took it and he pulled me to my feet. I was prepared for the headache and vertigo to come roaring back, but they didn't. I turned my head to look around us, noting that the sun was climbing higher in the sky, happy that other than tired and weak I felt relatively ok.

"Thank you," I finally said, looking at him.

"Let me get something to write on!" He cried. "For the first time in history a white man has thanked an Indian!"

"Oh, fuck off." I said, unable to suppress a small grin. "How long was I out?"

"About four hours," he said.

Remembering the wound on my head I started to reach up but his hand darted out and grabbed mine, stopping me from touching it. "It's been cleaned and sealed with a bark paste. Don't disturb it. You were already starting to show signs of an infection."

I wanted to touch it, wanted a mirror to be able to inspect my injuries, but decided to trust him and let it go.

"Drink some water and let's go," he said. "We lost a lot of time and there's a long way to go."

"How much farther?" I asked between gulps of water.

"At least twelve hours, probably more like fourteen or fifteen. And that's if we run the whole way." He said after thinking about it for a moment.

Putting my water away I nodded and scooped up my pack and rifle, which he had neatly stacked next to me. Getting everything on my body and adjusted, we set off. I let him set the pace with his fast loping run, content to stay on his shoulder.

"So why are you?" I asked after we'd covered the first mile.

"Why am I what?"

"Helping me. You said you didn't know why you are, and neither do I. You seem to have a pretty deep seated dislike of white men." I said.

"Grow up on the Res and you're taught from birth to hate the white man." He finally answered after most of another mile went past. "The older generation still blames you for everything, and doesn't want to take any responsibility or do anything to make life better. It just gets passed on from generation to generation. Things are changing, but very slowly. Truth is, I don't really know how I feel, just know how I was conditioned to feel every day of my life until I left."

I didn't have a good answer to that. He was describing human nature. I'd grown up around people whose generations old hatred of anyone with skin a different color than theirs had been preached to them since they could walk. And it wasn't isolated to a small west Texas town. It's just the way people are unless something happens to open their eyes.

Personally, I've never understood disliking someone simply because of skin pigmentation. There's a whole lot more compelling reasons. For example, the world's full of assholes. If there's one human trait that transcends racial and cultural divides, it's being an asshole. Doesn't matter what color your skin is, which god you worship, where you fall in the political spectrum, who you like to get naked with or how educated you are or aren't. Becoming an asshole is an equal opportunity for everyone. But... I digress.

"You didn't answer the question," I said, looking around at the sun-bleached prairie and wishing for a pair of sunglasses.

"Your wife," he said after a couple more minutes of running. "They have your wife. I couldn't save mine, but maybe I can help save yours."

I'm not sure what I expected him to say, but that wasn't it. I'd been prepared for a tirade about how bad the white man was, but that I wasn't as bad as the infected. Something along those lines. I certainly wasn't prepared for such a raw, basic human emotion, or the pain that was obvious in his voice when he said he couldn't save his wife.

"Thank you," I finally said. "Sorry I've been such a dick."

"Wow. I bet that hurt to say." He quipped.

"You have no idea," I said and kept running.

11

The sun climbed as the morning wore on, the heat and humidity of the day intensifying. By mid-morning the grass in front of us shimmered under the baking sun and my pack felt like it weighed five hundred pounds. But, we maintained the pace. Joe had two canteens strapped to his belt, but one was empty and the other he finished quickly.

"We should have filled up at the river we crossed," I said, sharing my dwindling supply with him.

"We probably should have done a lot of things we didn't do," he said, wiping his mouth with the back of his hand. "There's another smaller river a few miles ahead. If it's not dry this time of year we'll be able to fill up."

"And if it is dry? Where's the next water?" I asked.

"About an hour's run to the north," he said after thinking for a moment. "Couple of windmills that keep a stock tank filled."

"Let's hope the river is running," I said, not wanting to even think about having to detour for water.

Part of me wanted to just ignore it and focus on staying on the trail. But I knew better. As hot as it was, it was hardly 10 in the morning. Both of us were sweating freely in the humidity and if we tried to run through the heat of the afternoon without water we'd be in serious trouble. It wouldn't do Katie and the rest any good if I showed up to rescue them so dehydrated that I wasn't able to fight.

We pushed on, rationing the small amount of water we had. I didn't have a hat and my head was burning under the relentless sun. The downside to shaving one's head. I envied Joe his heavily pigmented hide.

I guessed it was around 1100 when we crested a small rise, and started down into a shallow valley that was noticeably greener than the surrounding terrain. A ten yard wide channel of sand and rock wound along the floor of the valley, but so far I hadn't seen any water flowing in it. Slowing as we approached, we stopped on a grassy bank, looking at several small puddles of muddy water. They were all that remained of the river.

"We can filter the water," Joe said, starting to jump down into the dry riverbed.

I reached out and placed a hand on his arm to stop him, pointing a few yards upstream. "I don't think we want to drink this."

"Shit!"

Joe was looking at a corpse lying partially submerged in the largest puddle. There were six distinct puddles and they were all connected with thin tendrils of water. Whatever bacteria were leaking out of the body would have contaminated the entire supply.

"Is that way upstream?" I asked, pointing to our left.

Joe nodded, turning and following the bank to the north. We walked for five minutes, but all we saw was dry riverbed. Backtracking, we moved downstream, hoping to find some isolated puddles that would be free of contamination, but there was only more dry soil. Pausing in the shade of a small tree I drank half our remaining water then handed the drinking tube to Joe.

"How sure are you that stock tank will have water?" I asked as he sucked the bladder dry.

"I haven't been there in several years, but before I left the Res it always had water. It would freeze in the winter and someone would have to ride out and break up the ice so the cattle could drink, but I've never known it to be dry." He said, shading his eyes as he scanned the horizon. "We go there, or we go back to the river we waded across."

Mimicking him, I raised a hand to my brow and turned a slow circle. Nothing but miles and miles of dry grass with an occasional stunted tree to break things up. He'd said an hour's run. That meant roughly six miles. Twelve mile round trip, and we'd already run at least that far. We'd be approaching marathon distance by the time we made it back to where we stood and still had another ten to twelve hours of running ahead of us.

I cursed myself for not having had the foresight to refill at the river. Sure, I'd been hurting and dizzy and worrying about my new companion, but that's still no excuse. My failure might very well cost my wife and friends their lives.

There was nothing I could do about it other than keep running.

"Lead off," I said. "And pray there's water there or we're in a world of shit."

Joe didn't respond, just jumped down off the bank, crossed the dry river and climbed up the other side. Back on grass he broke into a run and angled slightly to the east of due north. I fell in beside him, shutting my mind down. It didn't help to be chastising myself over my mistakes, and could very well distract me to the point that I made another, even more serious, error.

"You may be in a world of shit if we run into the a-ki-da."

"The what?" To my ears he had just spoken gibberish, though I suspected it was a word or words in his native tongue.

"A-ki-da," he repeated, slowly. "Each Osage chief hand picks ten warriors. Not so much now, but a few hundred years ago they weren't all that different from the Japanese Samurai. They were the best fighters from different clans and families and it was a great honor to be chosen.

"The tradition has continued. It's mostly ceremonial now, but there are some that take it very seriously. My father was an a-ki-da and my older brother was chosen too."

Well, that explained a lot about Joe. He didn't exactly come from a slacker family. I didn't need to know the details to understand what he was telling me. Kings, chiefs and warlords have been doing the same thing since the dawn of history. Select the smartest and strongest fighters to surround you. Hell, we're still doing it today, only now we call it Special Forces.

"So, if we run into one of these... ah, ah, ah... however you say it, I've got a fight on my hands?" I asked.

"A-ki-da, dumbass. Maybe. Probably. If we do, do what I say and keep your mouth shut." He said, sidestepping a snake that our approach had flushed out of the shade of a bush.

I didn't have a good feeling that if it came to a fight he would be on my side, so I settled for keeping my mouth shut and maintaining my pace. The heat continued to build, the sun approaching its zenith. Each of us was continually scanning the horizon to our front as well as frequently checking behind us. When we had covered what I estimated to be half the distance to our destination I was looking to my right and pulled to a stop with my hand on Joe's arm when I detected movement.

Bringing my rifle up, I could just make out a form worming its way through the grass. It would move for a few moments, then go still before starting all over again. Joe didn't have the benefit of a scope, having only iron sights on his rifle, and settled for peering under the shade of his hand. Motioning him to follow, I began moving slowly to my right.

As I walked I kept up a constant scan, looking for any other signs of life. But all I saw was dry grass waving in the breeze. I flashed back to my encounter with the razorbacks in Arkansas and asked Joe if there were any of the animals in this part of the country.

"Nothing big enough for us to worry about," he said. "Used to be mountain lions, but they're long gone."

I nodded and kept walking, trying to get a better view of what was moving. A few yards later I was able to see enough to tell it was human. But infected or not? Pushing on, I got a better look and identified it as a male. Then I could see something sticking up from the body. A couple of minutes later I was close enough to recognize an arrow sticking straight up from the man's back.

"Got to be an infected," I said after I told Joe what I could see with the scope.

Keeping a very close eye on our surroundings, we continued on until we were within a few feet of the male. It was infected. An arrow was lodged dead center in its lower back, and had presumably severed the spinal cord. It was pulling itself along with its arms, dead legs dragging behind it.

The wind shifted and it must have smelled us. Its head raised and turned in our direction as it emitted a low hiss and began trying to pull itself towards us. The male was dressed in what I presumed was traditional Osage garb. I glanced at Joe who was staring mesmerized at the poor soul on the ground.

"Know him?" I asked.

"He's a-ki-da," he nodded. "One of the ten for the Sky Chief. Never been off the Res, and didn't even speak English as far as I know."

"What about the arrow?" I pointed at the long shaft protruding straight into the air from the male's back. The shaft was obviously made from a straight tree branch and had what looked like real bird feathers. It was stained a bright red, a color so brilliant and deep it had to have come from a berry.

"Traditional warrior arrow," he said. "May I borrow your rifle? Mine makes too much noise."

I looked at him for a moment, then worked the sling over my head and handed over the weapon. He clicked the selector to semi, stepped forward and fired a single round into the infected's head. The skull deformed before rupturing, then the male lay still.

Returning my rifle, Joe leaned down and grasped the arrow's shaft, wrenching it from the body. When it came out the resulting wound looked just like the wounds I hadn't been able to identify on the female infected back at the crash sight. Snapping the shaft in half with his hands, he mumbled something in Osage and tossed a piece of the arrow on either side of the corpse. I didn't bother to ask what he was doing. He'd tell me if he wanted me to know.

"Let's go," he said, turned and resumed our run to water.

12

Half an hour later Joe slowed to a walk. We were approaching the edge of a cut in the terrain and before we could silhouette ourselves on the high ground he dropped to his belly and began crawling forward. Not needing to be told, I followed suit and together we moved to a sharp edge and looked into a large bowl shaped depression, about eighty yards across.

If I had to guess, I'd say the dent in the earth was made by an ancient meteor strike. The terrain for the past several miles had been perfectly flat, then for the past few hundred yards we had made a gentle climb to reach the lip. Spread out below us was a perfect circle, pressed fifty feet into the ground as if a giant had come along and stuck his finger into the dirt.

In the middle were two tall windmills, their towers raising the blades high enough to catch the wind that seemed to be constantly blowing across the prairie. Between them sat a large, circular tank full of water. It reminded me of an above ground swimming pool, no more than four feet deep. Both windmills were turning in the stiff breeze and I could see a disturbance on the surface of the tank as more water was pumped in.

In several places around the perimeter of the depression there were well-defined trails leading down from the prairie. These had to have been worn into the ground by the heavy hooves of the cattle that came to drink. There weren't any cows in sight, but there were three horses tied to a leg of one of the windmills. Two men stood in the shade of a willow tree that grew close to the far edge of the tank. The tree was massive with lush, green branches, almost certainly well watered by overflow from the stock tank and well fertilized by the animals that frequented the location.

"More warriors?" I mumbled to Joe, looking at them through my scope.

"Yes. For the same chief as the man we found. The extra horse must be his." He answered.

I was still watching them through the scope and neither had moved. Something didn't seem right, and I took a moment to scan the open ground to our rear. Nothing was moving other than wind tossed grass. Turning back to the front I focused again on the two Osage warriors. They still hadn't moved or even shifted a foot.

"You said there were a lot of Osage that refused the vaccine. Right?" I said.

"Well over half. Why?" Joe asked.

"I'm guessing your tradition bound warriors all refused." I said, still watching the two men stand perfectly still.

"Shit," Joe muttered, understanding where I was going with my questions. "Infected?"

"Can't tell from here, but neither of them has moved a muscle since I started watching. Not definitive, but that's kind of odd." I said.

We stayed where we were for a few minutes, watching and waiting, but the men never moved. The horses were calm, which threw me off, but then I didn't have any idea how a horse would react to an infected. People think horses are smart, and in some ways I guess they are, but in my experience they are one of the dumber animals. Don't get me wrong. I love horses. I'm just not sure they're terribly smarter than a stick.

Standing up to get a better view I scanned the area, but couldn't see over the far lip of the bowl to my front and sides. Behind me, the prairie stretched away, seemingly to infinity. There wasn't anything concerning in any direction that I could see. I got back on my belly and settled into my rifle, zeroing in on the man to the left.

"Joe," I said, making sure I was solidly on target. "Would these guys have a problem with you if you went down there by yourself?"

"No. I might not be friends with them, but we're the same clan. Why?"

"Because we either need their help, or we need their horses. And we definitely need water. Go talk to them and see what you can do." I said.

I was fairly well convinced these two had turned. Humans don't just stand rock still like a statue for no reason, and they certainly had no reason to behave this way. Not out in the open like this. We'd been watching them for several minutes, and not once had either of them turned to check the area around them.

"You think they're infected, don't you." He said.

"I do, but I don't want to start shooting until I know for sure. You're the bait. If they are, I'll drop them before they ever get close to you. If they're not, I'll stay right here with the rifle in case you have a problem." I answered.

After a few moments he got to his feet and stepped over the edge, slowly working his way down the slope. He had covered half the distance to the tank and neither of the men had moved. Joe paused and after waiting a short time he called out something in Osage. His voice was clear and strong in the hot mid-day air.

Both men jerked, immediately starting to turn around in a stumbling and uncoordinated fashion. That removed all doubt. They were infected. Adjusting my aim slightly, I pulled the trigger and one of them spun to the ground and lay still. Shifting slightly to the right I fired as soon as the red dot settled on target.

The second man fell and I quickly stood and made another scan of the area. Still clear, but it bothered me that I couldn't see a large swath of the horizon because of the upper edge of the depression. Standing, I started down, catching up with Joe where he waited for me.

“I was hoping you were wrong,” he said when I walked up.

“Me too.” I walked past him, heading for the tank and a long drink.

The water was cool and it felt wonderful to bend over and submerge my sunburned head. We both drank our fill and replenished our supply. I took a few moments to dig through my pack , finally remembering that I had a shemagh stuffed in the bottom. Soaking it in the water, I wrapped it around my head and face. Re-energized, I walked over with Joe to check out the horses.

There was an appaloosa and two roans, contentedly munching the thick grass growing in the damp soil at the base of the windmill. The appy raised its head and watched us with big, brown eyes as we approached, the roans continuing to graze.

“You know how to ride?” Joe asked.

I looked at the horses, none of which had saddles. True to tradition, the Osage warriors had been riding bareback. I hadn’t been on a horse in probably twenty years and had never been on one without the benefit of a saddle.

“Fucking white man,” Joe said when I just stood there looking at the big animals, not saying anything. “Just don’t fall off and break your stupid neck.”

“Really funny, asshole,” I shot back. “How the hell do I get on his back?”

“Her, dumb ass. Jesus, you really are thick, aren’t you?” Joe laughed at me. “OK, first, you’d better get to know the horse. The appy’s the biggest, so you’re on her. I’ll take one of the roans. Come up in front of her, no sudden moves, and get to know her. Talk to her in a calming voice, then rub her head once she relaxes.”

Following his instructions I got to know the animal. There were a couple of false starts when I thought she and I were going to have a problem, but soon we were getting along famously as I rubbed her head.

“OK, so what now?” I asked, keeping my hand going.

“Get on.” He demonstrated.

Watching him, it looked so damn easy. One second he was standing next to the horse, grasping its mane at the animal’s withers with his left hand, then the next second he made a little skipping-leaping motion and was seated on its back. He looked at me and shook his head, dismounting with the same fluidity.

"Stand like this," he said, positioning himself next to the horse's left front leg, facing rear. "Grab a fistful of mane right here, take a little skip and leap up as you throw your right leg over her back. While you're jumping, reach up and grab her withers with your right hand to pull yourself over. Like this."

He did it again, and it looked just as magical the second time, but the hell with it. I'll try almost anything once. Making sure my rifle was slung securely down my back I moved down the side of the horse and grabbed her mane where Joe had showed me. Taking a breath I took a small skip and leapt, reaching for her far shoulder with my right hand.

I slammed face first into the side of the horse and crashed to the ground. Fuck that hurt! Joe began laughing in a deep, loud voice and I briefly thought about shooting him just to shut him up. Standing, I refused to dust myself off and repositioned to try again. And achieved the same results. Joe laughed harder and I was about ready to drag his ass off his horse and beat on him when he finally shut up and hopped down.

The horse had taken me crashing into her side without so much as a twitch, merely bending her long neck around to stare at the crazy human lying in the dirt. I kept waiting for her to start laughing, but all she did was lift her tail and spray a stream of urine onto the ground.

"Try it without your pack and rifles," Joe said, walking over and extending a hand to help me to my feet.

I dropped the pack on the ground and worked the rifle slings over my head. Probably fifty or sixty pounds lighter I took a moment to rub the horse's neck before attempting another mount. This time I jumped too hard, my momentum carrying me onto her back and nearly dumping me to the ground on the far side. Only a fistful of mane kept me from going all the way over.

"Say one word. I fucking dare you!" I said to Joe as he held my pack up.

He shook his head, a smirk on his face as I took the pack and slipped my arms through the straps. He handed me the rifles, walked to his horse and sprang onto its back with little apparent effort. Asshole.

13

We spent several minutes walking the horses around the bottom of the depression. Joe obviously knew what he was doing, but I was struggling just to stay balanced. Fortunately the big appy was calm and steady, forgiving all my errors as I got the hang of how to let her know what I wanted her to do. Eventually I was able to get her to walk, stop and turn as she responded to my body. I thought I was going to wind up on my back the first time I pushed her into a trot, but held on for all I was worth.

"I'll learn the rest as we go," I said after completing two circles around the area at a slow run.

Joe nodded and turned his mount to head up the closest game trail. He had released the second roan and it stuck to the tail of the horse he was riding. Shifting pressure and pressing with my legs as I leaned slightly forward, my horse fell in behind them and we were off. I still had a death grip on her mane, thankful she wasn't objecting to me using the only handle I could find.

"Would it have been too much to ask for your warriors to use saddles?" I called out. Whatever Joe said in return was lost in the sound of the horses' hooves on the rocky soil of the slope. Probably just as well. I doubted it was anything flattering about either my heritage or me.

We crested on the far side of the bowl from where we had arrived. More endless prairie stretched away to the north. Joe had pulled to a stop and I maneuvered until I was sitting next to him. The view from the horse's back was dramatically better, being nearly twice as high as when I had been standing on the ground. Far to the northeast a massive dust cloud spread across the horizon, appearing as a heavy, brown smudge against the blue sky above.

"What the hell is that?" Joe asked.

"I was hoping you were going to tell me that's a storm," I said, but he shook his head. "That's a big herd of something, then. Unless the buffalo have made a miraculous recovery, it has to be infected."

I had raised my rifle and was looking through the scope as I spoke, but whatever was churning up the ground was too far away. It was at a point over the horizon from where I sat, only the dust rising in the air letting me know something was happening. Joe turned to me, a look of horror and revulsion on his face.

"How many does it take to do that?" He asked, pointing at the billowing dust cloud.

"A lot," I said. "I saw a herd in Texas a couple of days ago that was miles long. Probably three million or so."

He turned back to the front, staring ahead with his mouth open in awe.

"But how the hell are they surviving? There's no water up there and they're still human. They have to drink." He said in a frightened voice.

"Beats the hell out of me," I said. "They can do things and endure injuries that would kill you and me. You studied the virus that came with the nerve gas. You should know more about it than I do."

"Studied the virus, yes, but only to find a way to combat it. Not what its long term impacts on the human body are. Jesus Christ! How the hell do we stop them?"

"We kill every single one of them. That's all that's worked so far. Like you said, they're still human. They will die. It's just a lot harder to kill them than it is a normal person." I answered.

"We need to get moving," I finally said when Joe just sat there, staring at the horizon.

Urging my horse forward, I got her turned and circling the bowl so we could head south to pick up the trail we'd had to abandon in pursuit of water. Soon Joe was riding beside me, the third horse following along behind. Once we had reached the southern edge of the depression I was able to see the path we had left in the grass as we came north. After a little coaxing I got the appy moving at a trot.

What had been an hour's run for us was covered in less than fifteen minutes on the horses, then we reached the dry river. Two vultures were intently tearing flesh off the corpse that had fouled the water, both of them turning their ugly heads to look at us when we rode up. I got the horse stopped, watching them just standing there, unmoving, staring at us.

Vultures were one thing I was accustomed to seeing in Arizona. I spent a lot of time out in the desert, and they were always present, cleaning up the remains of any animal that had died. They are loud, raucous and always in motion. If they're not eating, they're spreading their large wings to scare away any competing scavengers, especially when approached as we had done.

But these two were just sitting there watching us. No ear grating cries. No wings extended in an attempt to appear large and intimidating. Just still as statues. With mounting concern I raised my rifle and looked at them through the scope. Red eyes. They were infected. Then it struck me that these were the first scavengers I'd seen since this all started.

Sure, I'd seen a bear in the Tennessee woods feeding on a corpse, but bears don't fall into the scavenger category even if they will help themselves to an easy meal. I remembered the truck stop in Arkansas where I'd gotten the Lexus, and all the corpses lying around without a single scavenger in sight other than insects.

The larger of the two birds suddenly spread its wings, extended its neck and hissed at us. Before it could take flight I pulled the trigger and put three rounds into it. There was an explosion of feathers and blood as it was punched back by the impact of the bullets. The second one continued to stare at us, not reacting in the slightest to the death of its companion. I put three rounds into it, following up with a single shot when it didn't die right away.

"OK, just what the fuck was that?" There was a note of hysteria in Joe's voice. "They were infected?"

I nodded, taking a moment to scan the horizon, then the sky to make sure I didn't see any circling buzzards that were about to swoop down on us.

"Seriously?" He sounded like he was about to lose it, and if I hadn't seen everything I'd seen up to that point I'd probably have been right there with him.

"Let's go and I'll tell you while we ride." I said, getting my horse moving in the right direction.

14

Joe rode beside me and I talked as we worked our way east. I told him about the razorbacks, and the bats I'd seen in Texas. As we moved he calmed and began thinking about what I was saying. He asked a lot of questions I couldn't answer, then began making some of the same assumptions that Rachel had when we had first encountered infected wildlife.

"We didn't know it was communicable to other species," he said after I was finished with my horror stories. "We didn't even test for that. I guess from a purely scientific standpoint it doesn't matter. Wouldn't have changed any of the approaches we were trying."

I didn't know what to say to that. The concept of studying and understanding viruses and how they work was something I knew nothing about. It was something that every time I read or heard about, sounded like science fiction. Very scary science fiction. How the hell do you fight when something as simple as taking a breath or a drink of water could be the last thing you do?

"Maybe we should have been working on a Terminator virus." He mused.

"What's that?" I asked, shifting my aching ass enough to get a little relief without sending the horse in a direction I didn't want to go.

"Something one of the senior researchers at the lab was talking about. It's like... well, how much do you know about how a virus works?"

"They make you sick. Not much more than that." I said, wondering where he was going with this, but curious nonetheless.

"OK, I'll dumb this down as much as I can. A virus isn't alive. It's not an organism like say bacteria. It's just a tiny little bundle of genetic material, DNA or RNA, surrounded by a protective coat, called a capsid, which is made up of proteins. When viruses come into contact with host cells, they trigger the cells to engulf them, or fuse themselves to the cell membrane, so they can release their genetic code into the cell. Basically they hijack the host.

"Once inside a host cell, viruses take over its machinery to reproduce. Viruses override the host cell's normal functioning with their own set of instructions that shut down production of host proteins and direct the cell to produce viral proteins to make new virus particles. That's why we feel sick. The virus is making our body's cells do something different than what they're supposed to be doing.

"Some viruses insert their genetic material into the host cell's DNA, where they begin directing the copying of their genes, or simply lie dormant for days, years or a lifetime. Either way, the host cell does all the actual work: the virus simply provides the instructions.

"Viruses are able to infect and reproduce in more than one kind of animal, but the same virus can cause different reactions in different hosts. Flu viruses infect birds, pigs, and humans. While some types of flu viruses don't harm birds, they can overwhelm and kill humans.

"What we do know about this particular virus is that it's elegantly simple. It only has two instructions for the host cells. First, brain cells where it rewrites the host's DNA and causes both rage and triggers an exponential increase in output from the adrenal, thyroid and pituitary glands. That's why the infected are so strong and tough.

"Second, and we were just starting to look at this, it invades the nervous system. It... ok, the best way I can describe it if you don't have a bio-engineering degree is that it amps up the nervous system. Hearing, smell, taste, touch, and vision. And it drastically improves your reaction times. It's like a super charger for your senses."

I had been listening closely and understood most of what he was telling me. I'd seen infected behave in nearly superhuman fashion.

"But why the difference between males and females?" I asked. "And why are the males blind?"

"Human physiology," he answered, sighing when he saw the blank look on my face.

"OK, I'll try. Male and female bodies are different, not just in appearance, but there are also basic physiological differences. Different organs, different chemistry and they use their brains differently. I could spend hours detailing the subtle differences, so you're going to have to trust me that they're there." He said.

"That male and female brains are different? You don't have to convince me of that." I said and he smirked at me before continuing.

"So are the nervous systems. Not so different that it matters, normally, but different enough that once the virus corrupts the host's cells, there's a different end result. What is a glaring difference between an infected male and female to us is a tiny fraction of a percent difference at the genetic level. Personally, I believe that the virus was developed and tested by researchers who only used female test subjects. They probably didn't know it would be different in males, or they would have tweaked it a little."

"OK, but why are the females getting smarter?" I asked.

"They aren't getting smarter, the virus is mutating and having less of a detrimental effect on their higher brain functions. Think of it this way. Have you ever used a copy machine to make a copy of something?"

I nodded, wondering where the hell he was going with this.

"Good. The copy you made wasn't quite as perfect as the original, right? Now, what happens if you make a copy of the copy? And then a copy of the copy of the copy, and so on. Each copy will be progressively different from the original until eventually you could place a thirtieth generation copy next to the original and couldn't tell they were the same document.

"This is really over-simplifying it, but the concept with viruses is the same. Every time a strand, or any fraction of a strand, of DNA is copied there's a possibility for something to go wrong. And it does. All the time. That's why there's a different strain of the flu virus every year. It's not technically a new flu virus; it's just a mutated version that came about because nature isn't perfect.

"So, with the virus lose in the world it has been replicating in host organisms and has obviously started mutating. That's what you're seeing. Something in the DNA code didn't copy correctly and the effect of the virus has changed. Does that make sense?"

I thought about what he said and it did make sense. Sick, twisted sense, but from what I knew about China it didn't surprise me at all to consider that they had used females as test subjects. Maybe I was being unfair, but they didn't exactly have a good track record when it came to how they treat women.

Or unwanted female children, I thought with revulsion at the mental image of a lab full of little girls being continually exposed to different versions of the virus until the scientists were satisfied with the result.

“So what’s this Terminator thing you mentioned,” I asked, shaking my head to clear the horrible images our conversation was fostering.

“You map the DNA of an invading virus, which we have. Using that map, you engineer a new virus with DNA that will target it and shut it down.”

“You mean you can kill it? You can make a cure? But what about the mutated version?” I asked, excitement causing me to bring the horse to a stop. Joe stopped his and turned it to face me.

“Kill it, yes. Cure? No. There is no cure. When the Terminator virus targets the original virus and rewrites its DNA, the host cells die. And the mutation is so insignificant that if we have the original base code to target, the Terminator will also target the mutations. That’s why it’s always so important to find the source of an infection, or a patient zero.” He said.

“If there’s a way to kill the virus...”

"When the host cells die, the organism dies." He said. "That's why it's called a Terminator virus. It kills everything without discretion when it's activated."

"So you're telling me there's a way to kill the infected with another virus? What about people who aren't infected?"

"Yes, I think we could kill it. In theory, the Terminator virus would lie dormant in any person that wasn't infected. It would only be triggered if it encountered DNA specific to the original virus. It shouldn't do anything to you or I. The beauty of it would be if, say, ten years from now you suddenly turned. The Terminator virus would still be present in your body and would attack. You'd die, or the infection in you would die." He said.

"Then why the hell didn't you guys do this?" I asked.

"We ran out of time. We were just starting to discuss it when the vaccine samples arrived, then things kind of went to hell pretty soon after that. I don't know if there's anyone left other than me that even understands this shit."

15

We continued our ride across the grassy plain. My horse, I'd decided to name her Horse, was strong and apparently accustomed to the weather and terrain. After a few miles at a trot we slowed the animals. They weren't showing signs of tiring, but it was approaching mid-afternoon and it was hot. We didn't want to wear them down too much, never knowing when we might need them to be able to call on some energy reserves.

Two hours from the dry river where I'd shot the vultures we dropped into a small valley with a narrow stream running through it. Large trees grew at the water's edge and when we rode into their shade it was a physical relief to be out of the sun. I planned to let the horses take some water for a few moments then keep pressing on, but Joe jumped down and stepped in front of Horse to stop her from dipping her head for a drink.

"They need to cool down in the shade for a few minutes first," he said. "If they're too hot, which they will be in this weather, the water can make them sick and then they're no good to us."

I nodded and shrugged out of my pack, tossing it to the ground. I wasn't eager to try dismounting with the extra weight on my back without benefit of a saddle and stirrup.

Clumsily, I climbed down, nearly falling as my right leg came over Horse's back. Feet on the ground I winced as the pain in my ass and lower back reminded me it had been over twenty years since I'd been on a horse and that I wasn't a kid anymore. Joe watched me hobbling around bow legged and tried to hide a smile as he bent and filled his canteens.

I walked around, enjoying the shade and drinking deeply before replenishing my supply. Removing the shemagh, I dipped it in the water and rewrapped my head. As I stood up, Joe coaxed the horses forward and they all lowered their heads and drank noisily. While I was waiting, I moved out into the sun and looked at the tracks the group we were trailing had left.

Nothing new or different to see. They had walked straight into the shallow water, not pausing. Clear paw prints told me Dog was still behind them.

"How much farther?" I called to Joe who was checking each of the horse's feet.

"Maybe twenty five miles," he said after thinking about it for a minute. "Two hours if we kept them at a fast canter, but I don't think that's a good idea in this heat. It's got to be well over a hundred degrees. Won't do us any good to push them until they drop."

I didn't like the answer, but I agreed with him. It was hot as hell, and that's saying a lot for me. I've been in most of the hottest and crappiest places in the world, and I lived in Arizona for the past several years. I'm used to dealing with not just a few days, but several consecutive months of triple digit temperatures. 110 Fahrenheit is nothing unusual for Phoenix, and 115 to 120 happens more often than the Chamber of Commerce and Tourism Bureau would admit.

We rested the animals for ten more minutes, drinking as much water as we could. It wasn't just the horses suffering from dehydration that we had to worry about. Finally we were almost ready to go and I took a few minutes to prepare myself. A six foot length of paracord tied to my pack at one end and belt at the other, I got in position and leapt onto Horse's back.

I made it on the first try this time. It wasn't pretty, and I had a bit of a scare when I thought I was going to roll right on over and land in the water, but I made it. Getting my balance, I used the cord to pull the pack up and got it settled on my back. Joe had watched my improvisation and once I was settled he magically transported himself from the ground to his mount's back. Fucking showoff.

We kept the horses at a walk, probably around five miles per hour. I wanted speed, but at the same time I had decided I'd rather reach our destination after the sun went down. My NVGs were somewhere back in the crashed Osprey, but I had the night vision scope on my rifle. The night had been my friend for many years, and I was going to count on it again to help me.

An hour from where we stopped to rest we came across a faint trail in the yellowing grass that struck out at a right angle to the tracks of the group. Turning Horse, I walked her around the area, then a few yards in the direction of the new trail. There was another track paralleling the one that had caught my attention.

Looking up, I could follow both of them with my eyes for close to a hundred yards before they disappeared over the top of a low rise. Whistling to get Joe's attention, I urged Horse forward and we started following the new tracks. Joe fell in beside me and together we crested the rise, stopping to look at a body.

This was a woman, lying face down, with no obvious signs of injury. Infected? Only one way to find out. I dropped my pack and swung down with less drama than the last time I'd dismounted. Rifle on burst mode and aimed at the woman, just in case, I cautiously approached and kicked her leg.

No matter how well a conscious person is pretending, they can't seem to mimic the boneless feel of a corpse. It's one of those things that I can't describe; you just have to have been around dead bodies. There's a quality to them that's more than simply limp or flaccid. Anyway, I could tell from the feel and movement of the female's lower half that she was truly dead.

Hooking a foot under her shoulder I lifted. The body came up, then flopped over onto its back, dead, red eyes staring at the cloudless sky. Infected. The front of her shirt was soaked with blood, ants and beetles already feasting. But the best part was her throat had been torn out. Dog!

Now the story of the tracks diverging from the group was starting to make sense. Someone had run. And they had been pursued, but not by the whole party. Looking around at the signs beaten into the grass I confirmed my suspicion that two infected had followed. But obviously, so had Dog, and he had killed one of them, protecting whoever had run. It had to be Rachel. Dog didn't know Katie, and anyway, she wasn't in any condition to run with a bullet in her chest.

Dashing back to Horse, I grabbed the end of the paracord and leapt onto her back like I'd been mounting horses without a saddle my entire life. Pack raised and in place I pushed her to a run, following the trail. Joe matched my pace and we raced south across the prairie, covering a lot of ground very quickly.

Ten minutes later my heart skipped a beat when I spotted another body in the distance. Approaching I could see the flowing brown hair and long, slender limbs. Rachel? I held my breath until I was close enough to see it was another infected. Her arms were badly chewed up where she'd fought with Dog, but he hadn't killed her. The skull was deformed where it had been caved in with a small, smooth rock. The rock was lying in the grass next to the corpse, blood and hair stuck to one side of it.

Horse danced sideways as I held her back, searching the ground with my eyes. There was a lot of trampled grass from the fight, but it only took me a few moments to spot the twin tracks that headed to the east. Rachel and Dog were going after the group!

I urged the horse to a run, leaning forward over her neck as we streaked along. I could hear the pounding of Joe's mount's hooves slightly behind me. Trusting Horse, I focused my attention on the ground, frequently looking up to the horizon before returning my gaze to the trail we were following. After a few minutes I could no longer hear the other horses and shot a glance over my shoulder.

They were still behind us, running hard, but Horse had the longer legs and was steadily pulling away. I didn't bother to slow and let them catch up. Nearly fifteen minutes later I topped a rise and spotted two forms lying in the grass a couple of hundred yards ahead. Horse covered the distance quickly, pulling up when I shifted my weight back and squeezed with my lower legs.

Rachel lay on her side, either unconscious or dead. Dog stood at our approach, but he was wobbly on his feet, nearly falling before he caught his balance. Putting himself between Rachel and us he lowered his head and I could see his teeth as he growled. I threw myself off of Horse's back before she was completely stopped, stumbling but managing to keep my feet under me.

"Dog, it's me!" I shouted as I ran forward.

Dog raised his head and tried to run to meet me, but all he could manage was a weak legged walk. Rushing up, I skidded to the grass on my knees next to Rachel, wrapping one arm around Dog's neck. He was hot to the touch and shaking and I knew he didn't have long if I didn't get some water in him. Taking a moment to check Rachel's pulse, I was alarmed to find it weak and erratic.

Ripping the shemagh off I placed it over Rachel's head, shielding her from the sun. By now Joe had arrived, leaping to the ground and running towards us. Dog started to growl but I calmed him and told him Joe was a friend.

We worked on the two of them feverishly. Both were severely dehydrated. We started with small sips of water for Dog and carefully poured tiny splashes into Rachel's mouth, cautious to not choke her. I also rubbed water on her face and neck, trying to slowly bring her body temperature down. She was as hot as Dog, feeling like she was running a blistering fever, but I knew it was from exposure to the sun.

An hour later Dog was much improved, drinking at will. His eyes had cleared and he finally lay down and closed them with a sigh that had the most contented sound to it I've ever heard. He was out of danger, as long as we didn't run out of water. Rachel was still unconscious, but the fever seemed to be under control as her skin was no longer hot to the touch. I had used more of our precious supply to soak the shemagh again, hoping to keep her cool.

"I've got to go get us more water," Joe said.

I nodded, looking up as he gave the last of our water to the three horses. While he did that I worked the water bladder out of my pack and tossed it to him, pausing when my eyes fell on the two waterproof battle packs of ammo for the M4 stuffed in the bottom. Each bag had a built in handle and held two hundred rounds. They would also probably hold half a gallon of water each.

Pulling them out I opened them, careful not to damage the heavy plastic, and dumped the ammunition into my pack. I handed these to Joe and he swung onto his horse and raced off to the northwest. I looked down when Rachel made a sound, like a cross between a whimper and a moan. Her eyes were open and she was looking up at me with a weak smile.

“I knew you would find me,” she said in a harsh, dry croak before closing her eyes and falling asleep.

I brushed some hair off her face and re-positioned myself to block as much of the scorching afternoon sun as possible and give her some shade.

16

Rachel threw her body across John and Katie a moment before the Osprey struck the ground. The impact was brutal, the aircraft immediately beginning to disintegrate as it carved a deep furrow into a dark field. All around her people were crying out in fear and pain, then the fuselage hit something hard, most likely a rock embedded in the soil well below the surface, and the tail rose and flipped over violently.

There were more sounds of the plane coming apart then it rumbled to a stop. Rachel was stunned, vaguely aware of sounds around her but unable to move or even form a coherent thought for that matter. She lay on something hard that was digging into her hip, but the thought that she should move to relieve the pain failed to translate into action. Eventually her mind shut down and she lapsed into unconsciousness.

Sometime later Rachel woke to the sounds of a fight. She could hear Dog snarling as he battled with something, then an infected female screamed. That scream was a catalyst for movement, spurring her to climb to her feet. She looked around for John, but couldn't find him. Another scream sent her pulse racing and she reached for her rifle, but it was no longer slung around her body.

She was turning to start digging through the debris at her feet when two females stepped into the opening at what she thought was the rear of the Osprey. Turning to move deeper into the wreckage, Rachel had barely taken a step when they sprang forward and tackled her to the ground. Struggling, she tried to fight, but they worked in concert and pinned her until she stopped struggling.

Abject terror at being helpless in the embrace of two infected turned to confusion as they did nothing more than hold her down. No slashing with ragged nails. No attempts to tear her open with their teeth. They just held her with inhuman strength until she ceased struggling against them.

A few moments later she was roughly hauled to her feet and dragged outside. She renewed her struggles, but the larger female on her left leaned in and bared her teeth inches from Rachel's face. She could see the blood red eyes and smell the stench of death on the woman's breath, and took the warning to stop resisting.

Rachel was stunned when they moved into the open air. The debris field from the aircraft was nothing short of awe inspiring when she considered that she'd just walked away from the crash, relatively unscathed. But what really drew her attention were the bodies on the ground and the large group of females.

From where she stood, still being held by the two infected, she could see several bodies that must have been ejected during the crash. She wasn't close enough to identify any of them, but recognized Gunny Zemeck because of his size. There was enough moonlight for her to see a large fragment of metal sticking out of his chest.

She also saw one of the women they had rescued from the casino, knowing it was her because of the skimpy outfit that left most of her skin bare. Then there were a large number of dead females. She could tell several had been killed by Dog, but there were several more scattered around the area that had long, thin objects protruding from their heads and bodies. Who or what had killed them? And where was Dog?

She turned her head, trying to find him, but couldn't see him anywhere. There was a smaller group of the females that were clustered together facing out into the night. Rachel looked in the direction their heads were pointed and was just able to make out Dog's form. He was thirty yards out, standing and watching. They had worked together to drive him away and keep him from coming back.

What the hell was going on? Along with John, she'd been observing the females growing smarter, but this was like nothing she'd ever seen or imagined. No mindless attacks. They were actually working together and using the strength of their numbers. But to what end? Or did they have a purpose?

Four of the females were moving around the area, pausing to check each of the bodies. Rachel stood in mute shock as one of them began pulling what appeared to be arrows from the dead infected. Arrows? Who had shot them and where were they? Had the females killed them or driven them off or, like Dog, were they waiting for an opportunity to attack?

When the female finished removing the arrows, several of them moved past Rachel and into the aircraft. Soon she could hear banging as they dug through the wreckage. But what were they looking for? As surreal as the whole scene had been, it became even more of a waking nightmare when two of them emerged carrying Martinez.

Rachel couldn't tell if she was dead or not, but the females brought her out and gently placed her on the ground. A few minutes later, after more searching, two more appeared with Katie, laying her in the dirt next to Martinez. More searching and Rachel was afraid she'd see John's body carried out next, but it was the young girl that had been with Stephanie.

She seemed uninjured, but was twitching and moaning when they put her down. One of the females who had remained outside squatted over the girl and leaned close, sniffing her body. Examination complete, she moved first to Martinez and then Katie, repeating the process. Finally she was approaching Rachel as the little boy was dragged out into the open.

Where the females had been gentle with the women, one of them had a grip on the boy's ankle and pulled him along, dragging his body across the debris, unconcerned for any damage that might be done. The female that was approaching Rachel turned and looked at the child, then up at the one dragging him. There was some form of silent communication between them and the boy's leg was dropped before half a dozen females rushed forward and began consuming him.

Rachel's state of confusion quickly became one of revulsion. She wanted to look away, but couldn't stop herself from watching as the small body was quickly stripped to the bone. Gore rising, Rachel snapped her head to the side when a scream from within the downed aircraft split the night. All of the females turned their heads to look as another woman charged out into the night. It was Stephanie.

She paused, looking around, then screamed and charged when she spotted Rachel. The female that seemed to be the leader stepped forward and with a vicious blow sent Stephanie sprawling in the dirt, immediately falling on her. She thrust her face into Stephanie's and screamed, lips skinned back and teeth bared less than an inch from her face. Stephanie didn't struggle against the woman, going completely still. After a long minute, the woman relaxed her posture and sniffed just as she had with the girl, Katie and Martinez.

When she stood, Stephanie slowly climbed to her feet and stood docilely as the woman turned and came up to Rachel. Thrusting her face into Rachel's she sniffed, weaving her head slightly before dipping it to smell part of the way down her body. After a brief examination she turned away and looked into the aircraft, testing the air. For a moment Rachel thought she was going to enter the wreck, but there was the sudden sound of a horse from the darkness and one of the females in the group watching Dog fell to the ground with an arrow quivering in her head.

Their leader screamed and four of them peeled away, racing into the night at a frightening speed. The woman walked over to the freshly killed female and wrenched the arrow out of her head, adding it to the bundle she carried in her left hand.

Rachel stood there in shock. She wasn't sure whether or not she was suffering hallucinations as the result of a head injury during the crash. None of this made sense. This wasn't behavior she'd thought the females were capable of. For that matter, why was she still alive? And

Katie and Martinez? The infected never hesitated to kill. That seemed to be their single minded pursuit in what remained of their lives.

A few minutes later, three of the four females that had chased the horseman returned. The leader was still moving around the wreckage, checking bodies. The young girl's condition hadn't improved and Rachel started to take a step towards her but was roughly yanked back into the spot where she'd been standing with her two guards. She caught her breath at the strength of the females' hands on her arms, then movement from the far side of the Osprey caught her attention.

It was one of the Army soldiers that had been picked up while they were in the casino. He was infected, stumbling his way around, apparently following a scent. Seeming to zero in, he turned and began walking directly towards where Katie and Martinez lay on the ground. The females ignored him, until he came within a dozen feet of them and started snarling.

One of the females who had been watching over the two unmoving women leapt at him with a snarl, smashing her fist into his face and sending him sprawling. He was unfazed and began an uncoordinated effort to get back to his feet, looking for all the world like a drunk. The female pounced on his chest and hit him several more times until he lay still, breathing raggedly through his damaged nose and mouth.

"The females are protecting us!" Rachel realized with a shock, her head swimming. But why the hell are they doing that? Different scenarios raced through her head, each of them more frightening than the last. The most terrifying thought was that they were going to be the guests of honor at a feast. Maybe main course was a better description.

After a few more minutes of milling around the area, the infected leader made several guttural sounds that Rachel tried to recognize as language, but settled on them as simply being subdued screams. The grip on her arms tightened and four females bent to lift Katie and Martinez into the air. Rachel couldn't tell if they were still alive, but couldn't imagine why the infected would be messing with them if they weren't.

She had gotten both women's bleeding under control before the crash, so barring new injuries they should be OK for a while. "For a while," she reminded herself as the group began moving to the east and she was forced to start walking. Both of them needed a hospital, but Rachel didn't think any of them would live long enough for something as mundane as gun shot wounds to kill them.

17

The females set a fast pace. Not faster than Rachel could manage without having to break into a jog, but close. Not for the first time in her life she was thankful for her long legs. If she was shorter she would have been trotting, as failing to keep up wasn't an option. The iron grip on each arm hadn't lessened at all as they moved.

After a couple of miles, Rachel had settled in to the rhythm of their movement. The horizon they were walking towards was growing lighter by the minute as sunrise approached. It had been a warm and humid night and she was sweating from the exertion of the forced march. Once the sun came up it was going to be a blistering hot day. Would the females stop and seek shelter from the heat, or would they push on?

Not happy that her prediction was accurate, Rachel squinted as the sun climbed into the sky and began baking the earth. The heat kept building but the females seemed to be impervious to its effects. When they came to a wide, shallow river the group waded directly in, stopping in the middle as each female bent and drank.

Rachel took as much as she could force her stomach to hold, not knowing when she would get water again. While they were stopped, the grip on her arms was released and she took a tentative step towards the females that were supporting Katie and Martinez. One of her guards snarled a warning, but didn't make a move to stop her. After a moment Rachel kept moving, wading through the gentle current.

Katie was conscious when Rachel reached her, and she was glad to see that one of the females was helping her drink.

"What the hell is going on?" Katie asked in a quiet voice when she saw Rachel.

"I have no idea," Rachel answered in an equally subdued voice. "I don't know if we're being kidnapped or protected, but either one is something I didn't think the infected would do. How are you feeling?"

Rachel moved closer, skin crawling as she came within a foot of the female holding Katie's upper body. Cautiously reaching out she moved a filthy bra strap aside so she could see the bullet wound. Before the Osprey had crashed she had determined that nothing vital had been damaged as the round punched through, and had successfully stopped the bleeding with a powdered blood-clotting agent pressed directly into the entry and exit holes.

"Hurts, but I've felt worse. How's... I don't even know her name." Katie said, looking to her left.

"Martinez," Rachel said. "She was hurt worse than you. Hang in there. I'm going to check on her."

"Wait," Katie reached out and grabbed Rachel's wrist. "Did you see John after the crash?"

"No. But you know as well as I do that if there's a breath in his body he'll be coming for us." Rachel placed her hand on Katie's.

"If he survived," Katie said. "He's always seemed so damned indestructible, but..."

"He is." Rachel said firmly. "And just in case we don't have another chance to talk you should know he never gave up on you."

"Thank you," Katie said looking into Rachel's eyes. "Roach told me some things about you two. Things I don't want to believe, that I'd normally never worry about, but times aren't normal."

"He's my friend and I love him," Rachel said, her honesty spilling out before she even thought. "He's had the opportunity, more than once, but you don't need to worry. He's still yours. You should have seen him when he found out your were alive and Roach had you. Nothing and no one was going to stop him."

Katie smiled and squeezed her hand, tears forming and threatening to spill down her cheeks. Rachel smiled back at her and moved to check Martinez. She didn't look good, skin pale and clammy with sweat. The bullet wound in her leg was a through and through in the meaty part of her thigh, but other than spoiling the view in a short skirt it wasn't anything to worry about.

The wound in her abdomen was a different story. The bullet was still in her, and Rachel had no idea what internal damage had been done. There was always a possibility that nothing vital had been hit, but even if that was the case there was still a contaminated foreign object inside the woman's abdomen. Infection leading to sepsis and death was nearly assured if that bullet wasn't removed.

The leader walked over and Rachel took an involuntary step back. The woman was obviously of Indian heritage, tall with broad shoulders and heavy muscle. Neither attractive nor homely, she was just intimidating as hell with her size and blood red eyes that seemed to pierce all the way to Rachel's soul when she looked at her.

She stood staring at Rachel for a long moment, then looked down at Martinez. She leaned forward, sniffing deeply as she inspected the injured woman. When her nose came close to the abdominal wound she jerked her head back and scrunched her face into an expression of disgust. She made a guttural sound and the woman holding Martinez released her and stepped aside as the sluggish current started to take her away.

"No!" Rachel cried, lunging forward to reach for Martinez.

The female that had been carrying Martinez grabbed Rachel to stop her. Rachel struggled, fighting to break free, screaming as she tried to get to Martinez before the river carried her too far away. The leader stepped in front of her and slapped her hard enough to knock her free of the other infected's grasp.

Rachel stumbled backwards, lost her footing and went under the surface of the water. She was only submerged for a second before the leader latched on to her upper arms and violently pulled her back onto her feet. She pressed her face forward, her nose an inch from Rachel's as she snarled and bared her teeth.

Tears streaming down her face, Rachel stopped struggling against the much stronger woman. She understood the warning, and part of her knew that without a hospital Martinez was doomed the instant the bullet entered her body. But that didn't make it any easier to watch the woman who she had come to think of as a friend slowly spin away on the lazy current.

Still crying, Rachel finally relaxed her body and the female released her. Looking around, Rachel met Katie's eyes. Saw the tears and also the fear that reflected her own emotions. What the hell were the infected doing? Why take them? What could they possibly want with them?

The questions tumbled around in Rachel's head as her two guards prodded her back into motion. Grief threatened to consume her, but she bottled it up and focused on her anger at the death of another person. A death that could have been prevented if the infected hadn't interfered. She convinced herself that she could have saved Martinez if she'd only had the medical kit from the Osprey.

18

The group moved for the rest of the day, only stopping twice when they crossed water sources. Rachel was almost delirious from dehydration when they reached the first, a nearly dry river with just a few muddy pools of water evaporating in the sun. She used her shirt to filter as much of the muck and debris out of the water as she could, helping Katie drink.

Katie had been walking for the past several miles, and was holding up surprisingly well. She was well tanned from living in Arizona, but this wasn't saving her from a sunburn that was spreading across all of her exposed skin. Rachel, dressed in clothes that covered most of her skin was faring much better. Except for her legs. She was still wearing the impromptu booty shorts she'd created to distract the sentries at Tinker so they could escape.

Once they had drunk their fill she helped Katie scoop handfuls of mud and smear it on her body for protection from the sun's rays. Katie spread it on the backs of Rachel's legs.

"I'm sorry about Martinez," Katie said softly as they worked, afraid to draw any attention from the infected.

"It's going to really hurt John," Rachel replied. "He kind of adopted her. Like a little sister, or something."

"He has a way of doing that," Katie said with a sad smile. "There used to be a woman that worked for him that was more a sister than an employee. And, I'm sorry I questioned you earlier."

"I'd ask questions too, if I were you." Rachel smiled as she rubbed mud across Katie's exposed back.

"How did you two meet?" Katie asked.

"The morning after the attacks," Rachel answered, reaching for more mud. "I was in trouble. Infected chasing me through a swamp. Then, there he was. Saved me, and we've been running ever since. Just a few days after the attacks we were only hours away from getting on an Air Force flight to Arizona, then the second outbreak hit and what had been bad turned into a nightmare."

"Second outbreak? What are you talking about?"

Rachel stared at Katie with her mouth open. She didn't know about the secondary outbreak? How was that even possible? The infected had been a daily part of her life since the attacks. Was it really that much better to the west? She wanted to keep talking to Katie, but the females all suddenly got to their feet as one and soon they were trudging to the east again.

Neither Rachel nor Katie was being closely guarded any longer and they fell in next to each other. Movement far to their right caught Katie's eye and she turned to look.

"Did you see that?" She asked.

"What?" Rachel turned to look in the direction Katie's head was facing.

"Looked like a dog racing along. Paralleling us." Katie was still looking in the direction but didn't see any more movement.

"Dog!" Rachel said, tamping down her excitement. After a moment she told Katie about Dog.

"Do you think that means John is out there too?" Katie asked in a hopeful voice.

"Maybe. John and I got separated for a few days in Arkansas, and Dog tracked me down. I think he thinks he's my guardian angel. Well, he is my guardian angel."

"OK, I've got to hear the story. We've got nothing but time while we're walking. Start from when you met John."

Rachel took a deep breath, collecting her thoughts as she scanned the horizon for any sign of Dog or John. She didn't see either of them, but had no doubt that help was on the way. Just like he'd come for her in Georgia when she'd been taken, then jumping off the bridge over the Mississippi River and later finding her in eastern Arkansas.

"Well, I was at work the night of the attacks." Rachel began.

"At a hospital? You're a nurse or doctor, right?" Katie asked.

"Almost a doctor," Rachel smiled. "Only had a year to go. But that night I was at the job that paid the bills..."

Rachel talked for miles as they trudged across the prairie. The sun was brutally hot, the mud they'd smeared on their bodies quickly drying and turning to a brittle shell. But it did its job and protected their skin.

Katie was a good listener, not interrupting as Rachel relayed everything she, John and Dog had been through. Rachel told the story in a near monotone, for the first time leaving nothing out. Not even the parts where she'd professed her love to John and her attempts to seduce him. She was expecting questions, or possibly scorn, and was mildly surprised when she received neither.

When she finished she took a breath, feeling more comfortable around Katie now that everything was out in the open. As she had talked she'd kept a close eye out and had spotted Dog two more times, ranging along beside them.

"Thank you for telling me," Katie said. "I'm glad he had you with him. Sounds like you two made a good team."

"We did. We do." Rachel said. "We did, I guess. When we get out of this you don't have to worry about me. You don't need me in the picture, and honestly, I don't think I could handle being around."

"Let's cross that bridge when we come to it," Katie said after a long silence. "First things first. I don't believe that whatever they have in mind for us will be a good thing. It's going to be dark soon. You should try to get away if there's a chance. Find John and Dog."

"I'm not about to leave you," Rachel protested. "We go together or we don't go."

"You're smarter than that," Katie said. "I'm hurt. It's all I can do to stay on my feet. I'm feeling better, but there's no way I can run. You've got a shot, especially with Dog out there, and John probably not far behind. At least I hope he is. Either way, when you get a chance, you go. Understand?"

Katie looked at Rachel who finally lowered her eyes under the intensity of the gaze. She wasn't surprised Katie was such a strong woman. She couldn't be married to John if she wasn't. Not that he needed to be told what to do, but there had been a few times she'd had to insist on a course of action and had been surprised he'd actually listened to her. After meeting Katie, she understood why. John had been trained well by his wife.

Just before sundown they reached a small river, well shaded by the spreading branches of several large trees. Rachel hoped the females would decide to spend the night near the water, but after a brief pause to drink, they set out again into the twilight. Within a few minutes the sun had dropped completely below the western horizon, night falling as they continued their journey.

Katie seemed stronger, but slowed as they walked, moving slightly slower than the pace of the group. One by one the females passed them until there was only one infected remaining behind her and Rachel.

"Soon," Katie said in a low voice.

"What?" Rachel asked, then realized that Katie had been slowing on purpose. She wanted as many of the females in front of them in the dark as possible so Rachel could make a break and have a head start.

"I don't want to leave you," Rachel said as the rearmost infected pulled abreast of them.

"You have to," Katie said. "If John was out there he'd have attacked by now. He wouldn't still be waiting. If you can get away, maybe you can find a way to come back and get me. But we won't make it together."

Rachel wanted to argue, but everything Katie said was right. Maybe John hadn't survived the crash, or if he did he was hurt too badly to have come for them. Either way, it was looking like it was up to her. If she could reach Dog, she might have a chance as long as the whole group wasn't in pursuit. She didn't think that would happen. The majority would stay on course. Maybe three or four of them would come after her. That many... well, that was a lot, but with Dog's help, maybe. It was a chance.

"Have you seen Dog?" Katie asked.

"As it got dark I saw him way off to our right." Rachel answered.

"Then that's the way you go. As soon as this one is a couple more feet in front of us, just come to a stop. They aren't paying attention, and maybe won't notice you're not there until you're out of sight. Either way, you'll have a head start. I'll do what I can to slow them down." Katie said.

Rachel nodded, then said "OK" when she realized Katie couldn't see her gesture in the dark.

"One more thing," Katie said. "When you find John, tell him I love him and I didn't give up on him either. Now... STOP."

Rachel automatically did as she was told, coming to a halt. The group of infected, with Katie trailing behind them, continued on, starting to fade into the night. Turning to her right, Rachel began moving through the grass, failing to see the low anthill in the darkness. Her toe caught on the loose soil and she stumbled, not making a lot of noise but enough to cause several of the females to turn their heads.

Not waiting to see what would happen, Rachel broke into a sprint. There were several screams behind her, then a shout from Katie as she tried to slow the rush to pursue the escaping prisoner.

19

Joe returned quickly with water and I carefully poured some of it into Rachel's mouth. I trickled more over her hair and onto her throat and chest, trying to bring her body temperature down some more. Watching me, he reached out and placed the back of his hand against her forehead.

"We need to get her out of the heat," he said, standing up. "It's only a few minutes to the river on horseback. If we don't get her body temperature down she's in real trouble."

I nodded, hesitating for a second. He was right about Rachel needing to cool down, but if this was the condition she was in, what was happening to Katie and Martinez who both had bullet wounds? Making my decision, I scooped Rachel up in my arms as Joe turned Horse to the side. Lifting, I draped her over the horse's back, just behind the withers. Despite being moved and put into what had to be a very uncomfortable position, she didn't wake.

Joe bent and laced his fingers together, offering me an impromptu stirrup. With his help I swung onto Horse's back without knocking Rachel off, got the big animal turned and moving. Dog was on his feet and trotting next to us, but he hadn't recovered fully, his head and tail drooping. Soon Joe was riding next to me, the third horse trotting along behind us.

As I rode I spread the shemagh across Rachel's back and poured water on it. I wanted to press the horse to a full run and get to the river as fast as I could, but I was worried about Dog. He would push himself, not wanting to be separated from us, and I was concerned he'd run flat out until he died.

Moderating Horse's speed, it took us close to 20 minutes to reach our destination. Coming to a stop in the shade I jumped down, sparing a glance at Dog who flopped onto his belly in the cool mud, panting so hard his whole body shook. Pulling Rachel down I cradled her in my arms and waded into the water.

Half an hour later her eyes fluttered open and she began struggling. I raised her head slightly and spoke to her as I rubbed water across her face. She relaxed when she heard my voice, closed her eyes for a few moments then reopened them and looked at me. The delirium that had been there earlier was gone.

"You found me," she said with a smile. "We knew you would."

"We?" I asked, unable to contain my hope.

"Katie is still with them. She's alive. She talked me into escaping."

"That sounds like her," I said with a smile. "Goddamn woman is always more concerned about everyone else than she is about herself. What about Martinez?"

Rachel's face changed, a look of sadness darkening her features. "She didn't make it," Rachel said, then told me the whole story.

"How long have you been out there?" I asked, grimacing at the pain the loss of Martinez was causing.

"I escaped last night. Maybe an hour after sunset. I was really thirsty by sunrise and was wandering around trying to find water. Once the sun came up it got worse. Much worse. Dog wouldn't leave me, either. I thought we were both dead." Rachel looked over at Dog, his tail thumping the mud when their eyes met. He had consumed a lot of water and was lying quietly, keeping an eye on us.

"Any idea what they want? Why they took you?" I asked.

"None. Don't know if they think they're protecting us or were leading us to the slaughter." Rachel said, finally moving and sitting up in the water. When she did she looked down and ran her hands over her hips.

"Why don't I have any pants or boots on?" She asked, then reached up under her shirt. "Or a bra?"

"We needed to cool you down. Fast," I said. "Feeling better?"

"Much. I'm actually cold," she said, trying to get her feet under her to stand up. "And weak."

I helped Rachel to the edge of the water where she sat down in the shade next to Dog. Joe had turned away to give her some privacy and I handed over her cut off pants, boots and bra.

"How bad is Katie?" I asked as she dressed.

"She's not great, but she's tough as nails. The work I did before the crash stopped the bleeding, but she's got to be in some pretty serious pain. She's walking, and I'm amazed she is, but we need to get her somewhere so that wound can be cleaned out and she can get started on antibiotics before an infection sets in."

I helped Rachel to her feet and steadied her as she pulled her pants up and fastened them. She didn't hesitate to pull her shirt off to put her bra on, Joe looking over just as her breasts were bared. He quickly turned away, and for a moment I swear I thought I saw him blush.

While Rachel finished dressing I stepped out from under the tree and looked to the west. The sun was heading to the horizon and I guessed we had about an hour of daylight left. Making up my mind, I turned back when Rachel touched me on the shoulder. Her hands were shaking so bad she couldn't fasten her bra, so I hooked it for her and helped her work her shirt on over her head.

"Who's you're new friend?" She asked, tilting her head in Joe's direction.

I called him over and made the introductions, surprised when he couldn't make eye contact with Rachel. She picked up on his embarrassment and smiled.

"They're just tits, Joe. No big deal." She said.

That brought his eyes up to hers and despite my worry over Katie I nearly laughed at the look of shock on his face. Grabbing my pack, I dug out two MREs and handed one to each of them.

"What's this?" Rachel asked, holding it up in an almost accusatory manner.

"You need some time to recover," I said, working the M4 over my head and handing it to her before pulling all the spare magazines out of my vest. I still had the Sig 9 mm rifle and wanted Rachel to be armed with a weapon she was familiar with. "I'm going after Katie. You stay here with Joe and get some food and more water in you. When you're ready, follow me."

"I'm good to go," she said, stepping closer to me. I recognized the look on her face.

"No. You're not. You couldn't even hook your bra two minutes ago. You need food, water and some rest. So does he," I said, pointing to Dog who rolled onto his side and grunted at me.

Rachel stared back, ready to argue, then wobbled slightly as a tremor went through her arms.

"See? Now stop arguing with me." I said as I stepped forward and wrapped her up in a hug.

Rachel's arms circled my waist and she buried her face in my chest. We stood there for a few moments, then I stepped away after kissing her on the cheek, turned and headed to where Horse stood munching on the rough prairie grass.

20

Navy Petty Officer Jessica Simmons slammed the keyboard in frustration, barely suppressing a scream. She was part of the cyber warfare group the Navy had assembled, and was deep in the sub-basement of a heavily guarded, non-descript building hidden away on Pearl Harbor Naval Base. She had been tasked with cracking the encryption that protected the NSA satellites orbiting over North America that had survived the EMP, and so far she wasn't having much luck.

The NSA had layered multiple levels of security into the software, each one unique. So far she had identified and penetrated three levels, and suspected there were at least two more. Stuck on the fourth level, she stared at the lines of code in multiple different windows spread across three large monitors and let out a heartfelt sigh.

"What's wrong, Simmons?" Lieutenant Hunt asked from across the room. He was looking up from his own terminal, the light from a monitor reflecting off the lenses of his glasses, making him appear to have computer code where his eyes should be.

"Nothing, sir. It's just that those paranoid fucks at the NSA really locked these birds down tight." She said, leaning back and rubbing tired eyes. She'd been working around the clock for nearly two days, trying to gain access to the command and control functions of the satellite.

"Go get a few hours of sleep then come back to it fresh," he said. "You're the one that got past the firewalls China set up for the Iranians last year. If you can do that, you can do this, but not if you're so tired you can't think."

After a few minutes Jessica nodded and pushed herself upright out of the chair, groaning as her back protested being forced to straighten after so many hours of sitting. Stretching, she winced slightly then leaned forward and pressed a key that locked her station down. Other than a combination of her personal password and fingerprint, only two senior officers in her division providing their fingerprints simultaneously could unlock it.

Exiting the room, Jessica passed two security checkpoints before even reaching the elevator that would take her from the sub-basement she worked in to the surface. The ride up was fast, another set of armed guards nodding at her when she exited into the main lobby of the building where she worked. A final security point that checked her out of the facility after scanning her body and personal possessions and she stepped into a beautiful Hawaiian afternoon.

The sun was bright and it would have been oppressively hot and humid if not for the trade winds blowing across the islands. The fresh air and daylight invigorated her after she got over her surprise that it wasn't the middle of the night. She'd completely lost all track of time and couldn't remember the last time she'd looked at a clock.

Changing directions from the path she'd been on that led to her quarters, Jessica walked across an immaculate grass field and took a seat on a bench shaded by several palm trees that rustled in the strong wind that was blowing the smell of the sea to her. Idly noticing the massive aircraft carrier at anchor in the harbor below, she looked up when two fighter jets roared overhead, part of the round the clock CAP – Combat Air Patrol – that the Navy and Air Force was flying throughout the island chain.

When she looked back down she was momentarily startled by the tall, ramrod straight man wearing an Admiral's stars standing at the end of the bench. He was watching the same two jets. Jessica dropped the pack of cigarettes that were in her hand and shot to her feet, her right hand snapping up in a perfect salute.

The Admiral returned the salute and smiled. "As you were, Petty Officer. Didn't mean to disturb you. Was just looking for some fresh air."

"No problem, sir." Jessica said, her eyes flicking across the uniform and noting the man's name was Packard. "I'll be on my way."

"Nonsense, young lady. Sit down and enjoy your cigarette. In fact, could I impose on you for one of them? I quit more years ago than you've been alive, but I don't think dying of lung cancer is something I need to worry about any more." He smiled again and Jessica picked the pack up, fumbled it open and held it out in his direction.

Glancing around she noticed half a dozen heavily armed Marines in full body armor spaced out in a protective bubble around the Admiral. She handed him a disposable lighter after he'd selected a cigarette and he surprised her by holding the flame out for her to light up first. Every now and then she encountered older, male officers and always appreciated their manners.

Not that her generation of male officers weren't properly courteous, but there was just something about the way the men of the older generations treated women. There was a degree of chivalry, for lack of a better word, that was missing in the younger generations. But then she supposed women had just as much to do with eroding that as men had.

"Thank you, sir." She said after her cigarette was lit. The Admiral lit his and extended a hand to offer her a seat on the bench. Once she was seated he sat next to her, making sure there was a large amount of open space between them.

"Thank you," he said, inhaling deeply. "I'd forgotten just how much I liked cigarettes. I guess that's the point, though. If you didn't like them you wouldn't keep buying them and the tobacco companies would be out of business. Well, I guess they are out of business now. Maybe it's not a good idea to start smoking again when the supply is going to run out soon." He chuckled at his own musings.

Jessica sat there, smoking, too nervous in the presence of such a senior officer to relax and enjoy herself. The man was pleasant and charming, but it was never a good idea to lower your guard around an Admiral. She had no doubt he would remember any little thing she did that he didn't like.

"Cyber warfare?" He asked after a few moments of silence.

"Sir?" She asked, surprised. There was nothing on her uniform to give away what she did for the Navy.

"Not a difficult deduction," he smiled. "I saw the building you came out of. And I recognize your name, Ms. Simmons. Just read a report from Lieutenant Hunt on your progress. He seems to think quite highly of your abilities."

Jessica didn't know what to say. She had thought this was just a random encounter, but now wasn't so sure. She took a drag on her cigarette but didn't say anything.

"Any recent progress?" Admiral Packard asked, drawing a sideways look from her.

"I'm sorry, sir. I couldn't discuss this out here, even if I was aware of what you were talking about." She replied.

The Admiral raised his eyebrows in surprise before laughing. "So right you are, Petty Officer. My apologies. I wasn't trying to place you in a compromising position."

Compromising position. The two words triggered a thought in Jessica's head that quickly headed down a path she hadn't tried.

"Sir, you're a genius!" She cried in excitement, field stripping the cigarette and shoving the butt into her pocket as she jumped to her feet. "If you'll excuse me..."

"By all means, young lady." Packard smiled as he watched Jessica race across the grass and through the doors into the cyber warfare building. Finishing his smoke he took his time stripping it of the cherry before depositing the butt in his pocket. Standing, he looked at the giant warship sitting in the blue harbor.

"The two-faced son of a bitch," he thought to himself, referring to the Commanding Officer of the Washington, Captain James. The man had decided to throw his lot in with the traitorous President and had gotten a message out that SEALs were on the way to arrest her.

That little act had resulted in the death of thirteen SEALs plus the flight crew of the plane they were on when it was shot down by order of the President. Captain James was now in the Pearl Harbor brig, waiting for Packard to decide what best to do with him. Dismissing thoughts of the traitor, the Admiral turned and followed Jessica.

He left his security detail in the lobby, passing through each checkpoint slowly. He wasn't normally a patient man, but he understood the need to thoroughly scan each person entering the building for any electronics. It wasn't only possible; it was a reality that foreign agents had successfully placed micro-electronic devices on the person of people accessing secure facilities in the past.

The people had been unaware they were carrying devices into extremely sensitive installations. US counter-intelligence had identified three such breaches in the recent past, two of them simply listening devices, but the third had been a data scavenger that was able to read and record everything that was displayed on monitors within a ten foot radius of its location. As a result, new security protocols had been enacted and the Admiral wasn't about to use his rank to hurry or bypass them.

"Right there, sir! They just changed positions between layers. All I need to do is…" Jessica was staring intently at her monitor, fingers flying across a keyboard as Lieutenant Hunt watched over her shoulder when the Admiral walked into the room.

Jessica typed another line of code, paused to read it, then hit enter hard enough to cause the keyboard to jump. The monitor went blank for a moment, then two lines of text appeared with a blinking cursor beneath them.

"We're in!" She cried, banging out commands faster than Packard could follow.

Less than a minute later a giant, high-resolution screen on the wall at the front of the room blinked to life. An incredibly crisp, wide-angle image of North America filled the screen. Jessica looked up and her face was beaming when she spotted the Admiral. Calling the room to attention she started to stand, but Packard quickly told everyone to continue what they were doing.

"I guess you answered my earlier question, Petty Officer." The Admiral said, moving to stand next to her terminal.

"You gave me the idea, sir." Jessica was grinning from ear to ear.

"Outstanding work! Can you get me a look at the Oklahoma City area?"

"Yes, sir." Jessica began typing commands, moments later the screen zooming smoothly into the middle of the continent.

"Wow!" She breathed as the image remained perfectly sharp. "Those NSA guys have some nice toys."

Soon they were looking at Oklahoma City, the scale marks superimposed on the display indicating they could also see a three hundred mile radius around the city. At multiple locations scattered around the area were massive dust plumes. Packard didn't need the orbiting camera zoomed any tighter to know what they were.

"Lieutenant," he said to Hunt without taking his eyes off the screen. "Get me through to Colonel Crawford at Tinker Air Force Base. Now."

21

The sun beat on my back as I urged Horse to a gallop. She was a strong, fast horse and we were probably moving at 25 miles an hour. The trail in the grass was easy enough to follow, but I wanted to cover as much distance as possible before the sun went down. The marks of the group's passage would still be visible at night, but would require a lot more concentration to make sure I didn't wander off course. More focus on the ground meant less speed, and slowing down was the last thing I wanted to do right now.

Dog had tried to follow when Horse and I had departed. I'd had to stop and send him back. I would have loved to have him along, but he wasn't in shape to keep up. He had nearly died in his determination to stay at Rachel's side and needed more rest and hydration. Besides, there was probably only about an hour of daylight left, and I had little doubt that Rachel would be on my trail as soon as it got dark.

We covered ground quickly, me keeping Horse in the middle of the path of trampled grass. I had briefly considered just moving in a straight line and not following all of the twists and turns the infected had made, but dismissed that thought when I realized I would have missed Rachel and Dog if I hadn't seen her tracks when she escaped.

As we kept pushing east the terrain was slowly changing. What had been nearly flat grasslands with occasional low hills was becoming rolling countryside with larger and larger hills. There were more trees as well as I moved into a part of the state that obviously received more rainfall. At sunset we came across a deeper depression in the ground that held a few inches of water.

The water was clear, rocks and sand forming the basin. I brought Horse to a stop and held her back for a few minutes before letting her drink. She stepped close to the water and began to dip her head, then shied away. What the hell?

My first thought was there was a snake in the area, but I couldn't spot anything. Curiosity piqued, I swung down off her back for a better look. First I checked the tracks we were following, frowning when I noted they veered towards the water, but cut away without reaching it. Moving to the edge I looked all around but couldn't see anything that would spook a horse, let alone a group of infected.

Kneeling at the edge of the pool I scooped up a handful of water and held it up to sniff. There was an odor I couldn't identify. At first it was sharp, almost metallic, but then it changed to something I knew I had encountered before but couldn't place. It wasn't necessarily unpleasant, especially if you're really thirsty, but after seeing Horse's reaction I didn't doubt there was something in the water that would ruin my day.

Shaking my hand, I dried it on my pants and drank from the supply I'd brought with me. I shared with my mount, watching the sun completely drop below the horizon. I had just resumed my perch on her back when a pack of coyotes began yipping. They sounded close, no more than a few hundred yards away. Horse's head came up and her ears swiveled to the same direction I was looking.

Having grown up in the American southwest, coyotes are something I'm very familiar with. They're a nuisance. A pain in the ass. Both predator and scavenger, they will eat just about anything. Singly, they're not a threat unless rabid.

In packs, they've been known to take dogs and even children. They are brazen and cunning, but not a threat to a grown man on horseback. Unless they're infected.

That thought sent a surge of adrenaline through my system and I sat quietly for a moment listening. The pack was still singing, but it didn't sound like they were moving any closer. Dismissing my fears over infected animals, I pushed Horse forward to a slow trot along the path left by the females. As we moved through the hills I kept a sharp ear out, happy to hear the coyotes continuing their serenade to our rear.

It didn't take long to move out of earshot of the pack. We had entered an area with larger hills that soared more than a hundred feet over our heads into the night sky. The trail wound around each one, sticking to the lowest ground. At times it was hard to follow as the grass had all but disappeared, replaced with hard, rocky soil.

We reached the largest hill yet, probably close to two hundred feet tall even though it was softly rounded with gentle sides. At the base of the hill the low ground forked and was so dry and rocky I couldn't see a mark in the darkness. Which way?

Swinging down, I went to one knee at the junction, head bent to look at the ground. Nothing but hard packed soil and an occasional rock. The earth was too hard to take a print or even a scuff from a passing shoe unless the person walking was trying to leave a trail. Then I saw a faint mark on the path to the right. Katie's handiwork?

Kneeling over it I looked down at the freshly made gouge in the dirt. It was no more than a quarter of an inch deep and two inches long, but it was there and it hadn't been there long. The soil that had been dug up was still loosely scattered on the path. There was enough wind in the area to erase the evidence in a relatively short period of time.

Sitting back on my haunches, I thought about the timelines. The group had left the crash sight at approximately sunrise yesterday. They had been walking at what Rachel described as a fast pace, so between four and four and half miles an hour. Say four for easier math. Thirty-six hours with a few stops for water and rest. So maybe thirty hours of travel time. That meant they would have covered 120 miles by now.

How far had I come? I tried to remember as I squatted there in the dark. I'd covered several miles before meeting Joe, then we'd run for hours before finding the horses. Our speed had increased greatly once we had mounts. In the last hour and a half I'd covered at least thirty-five miles. I had to be close. Within a few miles? Maybe. Probably, I decided, standing up and looking around.

I froze when I saw the two figures silhouetted on top of the hill to my right. This one appeared to be slightly higher than the one I stood next to, and a perfect place to get a view back to the west. I stayed quiet, hoping Horse wouldn't pick this moment to make some sound. The figures were unmoving, and only visible as outlines against the starry night sky. Had they seen me?

I was below them and it was dark where I was. Darker than where they stood, but did that help me? Were these infected with enhanced senses? Or for that matter, were they even looking in my direction? I couldn't tell, unable to see anything other than human forms blotting out the slightly lighter horizon.

After several minutes of no movement or indication they were aware of my presence, I slowly lifted the rifle to my shoulder. My movements were slow and smooth for concern over alerting them in case they weren't already watching me. Movement in darkness is what will typically give away your position to an enemy. The human eye will overlook static objects that blend with the night, but instantly pick up on motion.

Looking through the night vision scope on the rifle I had a clear view. Two females. The image wasn't good enough for me to tell if their eyes were red or not, but I didn't think there'd be two women just hanging around in the middle of nowhere unless they were infected. The good news was their attention was to the southwest, ninety degrees away from where I was standing.

I watched for a few more minutes, my suspicion confirmed when one of them twitched her shoulder up slightly and her head to the side. Definitely infected. But what were they watching? Shouldn't be Rachel, Joe and Dog. I didn't think they'd be close enough yet to be visible, plus the females were looking in the wrong direction.

Five minutes later they were still standing there, the only movement from either of them limited to the occasional tick that gave away what they really were. Muttering a curse I decided it was time to take some action. I had no way of knowing if they were about to leave, or were going to remain standing on top of the damn hill all night.

If I'd had the M4 rifle with the much more powerful cartridges, I'd have probably shot them both from my current location. But I'd given it to Rachel and all I had was a 9 mm, short-barreled rifle that was fantastic for CQB. But the same properties that made it so good for fighting in enclosed spaces worked against it out in the open.

A short barrel has a pretty significant impact on accuracy at more than fifty yards, even more so when you're firing a pistol round. There's not a lot of powder to push the bullet down the pipe. If you're fifteen feet from an enemy inside a building, the lower powered 9 mm rounds are actually preferable as a military rifle caliber will be travelling so fast it will probably just punch a tiny hole right through their body without killing them.

Yes, they'll eventually probably die from the wound, but the idea is to put your enemy down quickly, not shoot them and leave them with an opportunity to start shooting back. Not that the females were going to shoot back, but when I fired I needed to put them down instantly. No chance for a warning scream that could bring more down on my head, or even for one of them to escape and bring all of her sisters back to ruin my evening.

Grumbling in my head, I began moving forward, silently starting up the side of the hill. I moved slowly, careful with each step to ensure I had solid footing and wasn't about to send an avalanche of scree tumbling down the hill and give away my presence. It took close to ten minutes for me to approach to a point where I was comfortable with the Sig's stopping power.

Lowering to one knee, I stabilized my body and sighted on the female closest to me. Mentally practicing the motions necessary to fire, shift to the second female and fire again, I took a slow, deep breath. Letting it out I squeezed the trigger as my lungs emptied, the Sig not making much more noise than a soft pop.

I was already swinging the barrel onto my second target when the bullet impacted the female's head, her body dropping silently. The second one heard the suppressed shot and snapped her focus in my direction just in time for me to put a round through her left eye. She fell dead across the first one I'd killed without uttering a sound.

Staying on my knee, I kept the rifle trained on the females, watching through the scope. I was sure I'd made two good head shots, but I gave it a few moments to make sure neither was moving before I took my attention off of them. Swinging around I scanned the area below me.

Nothing was moving. Horse was standing quietly, appearing to be asleep. Failing to spot anything or anyone else, I worked my way to the top of the hill. The females were as dead as I'd believed and I didn't waste any more time worrying about them. First I checked the southwest, the quadrant they'd been watching so intently. Nothing. Looking to the east, the prevailing direction the infected had been travelling, I didn't like what I saw.

The hilly terrain changed again. Spread out as far as I could see was a series of small canyons. From my vantage point I could tell some of them were box canyons, while others narrowed down before opening back up and connecting with an adjacent one. It was a fucking maze and exactly where the females had taken Katie.

22

I made my way back to Horse. She wasn't asleep, but resting the way horses do when they're bored, waiting for you to return. Despite no reins to tie off, she had yet to show any indication that she would wander off if I left her alone. As I walked up she bent her neck to watch me with a large, brown eye, bobbing her head up and down when I reached out and stroked her shoulder.

OK, so I guess I needed to retract my earlier statement that horses are dumb. She was anything but, and I was starting to get pretty fond of her. After all, she'd carried my big ass for a lot of miles without complaint, didn't try to throw me or run off, and actually seemed to be happy to see me. Hope Dog doesn't get jealous.

Now I had a decision to make, and I had to make it based on very circumstantial information. I believed that the infected that had captured Katie were taking refuge in the canyons. The primary reason for this thought was the two I had just killed. They appeared to have been sentries. Standing there for no reason other than an early warning in case something or someone approached. But this was just a theory.

The group of infected could very well have passed right on through canyon country and were still moving. The two I'd killed could have been doing something that only made sense to a virus riddled brain. Why this mattered had to do with Horse.

The ground had changed from soft prairie soil carpeted with grass to hard packed dirt laced with rocks. Horse would make a lot of noise walking through the canyons, whereas I could move very quietly. But if I went on foot and found the infected were just passing through, I'd waste a lot of time backtracking to get my mount. If she was even still there when I came back.

I knew coyotes were around, and even though a pack wouldn't try to take down an animal as large and powerful as Horse, would they spook her into running? The only thing worse than the loss of time to come back for her would be to come back and find her gone.

While I thought over the situation and my options, I watered Horse and drank some myself. By the time I finished I had made my decision. I was proceeding without my trusty steed, and would hope she'd still be in the area if I needed her. Hopefully she'd still be here when Joe and Rachel arrived and they'd figure out what I was doing and why.

Rubbing her neck, she pushed her head against me and snorted, leaving a trail of snot on my vest. What is it with me and animals with sinus issues? Giving her another quick drink, I patted her neck then turned and began following the trail where I'd found the scrape mark earlier.

The path was only a few feet wide and wound between more hills. There weren't many marks to indicate recent passage by human feet, but they were there. The occasional small rock that had been disturbed or the dirt rubbed off a larger rock where someone had stepped on it. The signs were subtle, and if I hadn't had some damn good teachers earlier in my life I wouldn't have known what to look for or how to find them.

Twenty minutes later I emerged from the hills that guarded the path into the canyons. Stopping in the dark I surveyed the land in front of me. From atop the hill I'd been able to see that there were multiple canyons and was able to get a good idea of which ones connected and which were dead ends. Here at ground level, well, this was not going to be fun.

I kept moving forward, following the trail, but it was getting more difficult. The whole area looked like it flooded when it rained and I was walking on exposed rock. There was nothing to take and hold a print. I didn't think the infected were smart enough to have come here for that reason, at least I hoped they weren't, but it didn't really matter. They were somewhere I couldn't track them.

Stopping, I squatted with my back against a canyon wall and raised the rifle. Night vision let me see into all the nooks and crannies that were nothing more than dark shadows to the naked eye. I didn't see anything after a slow, patient scan, so turned my attention to the surrounding ground. I was hoping to see an area where tracks might have been left that would give me an indication of their direction of travel.

Far down the canyon was what looked like a sandy area, probably where rainwater would pool after rushing down from the surrounding hills. I didn't like the idea of having to search each canyon

I came to for ground that would show tracks, but I wasn't coming up with any better ideas.

As I moved towards the sand I thought this whole thing would go a lot faster with Horse, but her hooves would make a hell of a racket walking across the exposed rock. I could cover the same terrain in near silence in my boots. Dismissing the temptation to go back and get the horse, I moved as fast as I could while still staying quiet.

The sand, when I reached it, was pristine except for a winding track that I recognized as having been left by a snake. Raising the rifle I looked deeper into the canyon, but didn't see any other candidate areas. Reversing course I moved back to the canyon's mouth and deeper into the labyrinth.

Most of two hours later I found their tracks again. I had lost count of how many canyons I'd checked, how many times I'd been tempted to turn back and get Horse to speed up the search. But my patience was rewarded when I found a large pool of water in the shelter of a looming canyon wall. A thick band of sand surrounded the water and deep footprints were clearly visible all around its perimeter.

Looking closely in the pale moonlight I could see that the deepest part of the impressions were darker than the surface. This was due to moisture in the sand and told me these were fresh tracks. Made after the sun went down, since the heat of the day would have quickly dried them out. The damp sand compressed and held its shape, just like a sand castle, and I spent a few minutes cataloging and counting the marks.

Seven barefoot females. All of them with damage to their feet, which had probably always been protected by shoes before getting infected. Fifteen wearing some form of shoe, most of them having a tread pattern that looked like it was from some type of athletic shoe.

What had Katie been wearing when I'd seen her at the casino? Was she barefoot? I knew she'd been dressed in nothing other than a thong and push up bra, but had she been wearing shoes? I couldn't remember, and even if I could there was no way for me to identify her specific prints. Or was there?

I began re-checking each set of bare prints, smiling when I found what I was looking for. Many years ago Katie and I had lived in a small condo while she was still at the Agency and I in the Army.

One of the rare times I'd been home, we'd found ourselves naked in the downstairs living room one afternoon. Passion had overcome modesty and we had neglected to close the blinds.

A friend of mine had dropped by for a visit, ringing the doorbell and sticking his face against the glass of the window next to the door to see in. Katie had snatched a throw off the sofa to wrap around herself and sprinted for the stairs that led to our bedroom. In her haste she hadn't seen the heavy duffel bag I'd dropped on the floor when I got home.

She kicked it solidly with her right foot as she ran, breaking her second toe, the long one right next to her big toe. It was severely bent to the side and I'd popped it most of the way back into place, planning to take her to an emergency room. She refused to see a doctor and the toe healed with the final third of it bent away from her big toe at a forty-five degree angle. The print I found clearly showed her sideways toe.

The trail from the watering hole led deeper into the canyon I was facing. Before proceeding I took a minute to drink and replenish my supply. I didn't know when I'd find water again, couldn't count on coming back this way, and wanted to be as prepared for the heat of the coming day as I could.

After a careful scan with the night vision scope I started creeping along the canyon wall. I expected the infected to be close. The things I'd observed told me they were falling back on instinctual behavior, the way they moved across the terrain chief among those. Taking that into account, they were going to stay close to their water source.

Unless, of course, they had simply been passing through. I didn't think so, especially as I spent more time in the canyons. The whole area was a natural safe haven. Easily defended if necessary. And now that I'd found their water I was fairly sure they wouldn't be far away.

Moving silently, I kept my back firmly against a rock wall, the rifle's night vision scope to my eye. Five minutes later I found them. Well, I was pretty sure I found them. I could see a single female standing just inside the entrance to a cave that was well hidden in the far wall of the canyon. She was just standing there, doing nothing other than watching the approaches.

Sentry duty. Just like the two I'd killed on the hill. I barely suppressed a shudder at the thought. The concept of putting out sentries for early warning indicated a level of intelligence I had so far not seen from the infected. I'd witnessed cooperation, and even a level of communication, but this? This was a game changer.

Mindless infected didn't work together like this. They didn't post guards to keep the group safe. Was this a further mutation of the virus that Joe was talking about? Whatever it was, what the hell did they want with Katie?

23

Colonel Crawford broke the satellite phone connection with a sigh. He had been speaking with Admiral Packard in Pearl Harbor and hadn't received much good news. The only good was that the Navy's computer experts had finally succeeded in accessing the NSA satellites that were still in operation above North America, restoring both visual surveillance as well as communication links. But that had only brought more bad news.

Once they'd gotten a look, they'd seen multiple herds of infected still bearing down on the Oklahoma City area. They already had their hands full with the thousands of civilians in the area that were turning. And the number was growing daily. The arrival of any of the herds, let alone all of them, would spell disaster.

On the far side of the office, Captain Blanchard was bent in consultation with an Air Force IT specialist. The EMP had destroyed the base's power grid as well as almost all pieces of electronics that had been powered up at the time of the nuclear detonation. The two men were working on restoring a data connection so

Blanchard could access the satellite imagery and Crawford didn't have to depend on eyes that were in the middle of the Pacific.

Exhausted, Crawford stood and walked quietly out of the office so as not to disturb the work that was going on. Exiting into the evening, he stretched his back then plucked his last pack of cigarettes out of a pocket. Lighting one, he inhaled deeply and began wandering aimlessly, thinking. He absently noted the half dozen Army Rangers that arranged themselves around him, creating a protective bubble.

He had been excited when the Marines had returned from the refinery in Texas and described using crop dusters to disperse fuel oil and destroy large numbers of infected. They'd found two of the planes in the Oklahoma City area, duplicating what the Marines had done with great success. But that was the only reason they still held the base, Crawford acknowledged to himself.

The size of the herds that were bearing down on them now, well, there were just too many to fight. Tens of millions. Maybe as many as a hundred million. And now they were hampered by the damage done by the EMP, which apparently hadn't shut down the satellite the Russians were using to direct the herds.

Evacuation was the only remaining option he was able to come up with. But evacuate to where? And how? Between military personnel and civilian refugees on the base they would have to move close to thirty thousand people. They had planes, sure. Planes that were capable of reaching most places on the planet, but it would take time to move everyone a few planeloads at a time.

Frustrated, Crawford continued walking. The change of scenery from the dark paneled, base commander's office was refreshing, and he enjoyed the exercise even if he wasn't having any luck at coming up with good ideas. Lighting another cigarette he looked around at the sound of an approaching engine.

The Rangers were already focusing on the Humvee driving towards them, rifles at their shoulders but not quite aimed at the vehicle. They relaxed when it slowed and they recognized Captain Blanchard behind the wheel. He pulled up next to the Colonel and hopped out.

"I got access right after you left the office, sir." He said.

"And?" Crawford asked.

"Just like the Admiral laid out for us. Massive herds out of the Midwest and northeast. It looks like the Russians directed lots of infected to some of the bridges across the northern Mississippi that we didn't destroy, and those herds are combining and making a super-herd. More out of Texas and the Denver area, and we're also seeing them start migrating east out of all the west coast states. Texas and Denver are bad, but it's looking like nearly seventy million coming down from the northeast and the herds are growing as they progress." Blanchard reported.

"Jesus Christ," Crawford was stunned at the thought. "How long do we have?"

"The closest herd is the one coming up from Texas. We've got three days before the leading edge is at the wire, maybe a little less. That's around twenty to twenty-five million. Next comes Denver, a day later at the most with an estimated two million. Then a couple of days after that the super-herd starts arriving." Blanchard said.

"So we've got three days at the most," Crawford said, drawing on his cigarette and looking off into the distance.

The two men stood there silently as the Colonel digested what he'd just been told. Blanchard could see the wheels turning and didn't interrupt his train of thought.

"What's our airlift capability?" Crawford finally asked.

"I've been doing some modeling of that, sir." Blanchard said. "First problem was where to go that could support thirty thousand people. Second were flight times. The farther away we go, the longer it takes to deliver each load of evacuees and get back to pick up the next.

"Third, we need to find a defensible location where we don't have to move again. That also means there must be supplies or at least raw materials available at our destination. Finally, I looked for a temperate climate. Winter will come, and with it a whole new set of challenges and demands on our resources. The less we're fighting the weather, the better."

"It sounds like you're looking for a permanent home for us, Captain." Crawford met the younger man's eyes.

"Yes, sir. I am." He replied. "Or at least a fairly long term solution. Continuing to run from the infected, in my opinion, is not a prudent course of action. Attrition rates would be unacceptable. We will lose thousands of military personnel protecting the civilian population, which will be decimated once we can no longer field an effective fighting force."

"I get it, Captain, and I agree with you," Crawford said. "So tell me what you came up with."

"Nassau, Bahamas, sir."

"Nassau? Needing a little vacation?" The Colonel cut his eyes sideways at his aide and grinned.

"No, sir." Blanchard said in a firm tone. "It's an island, so we would no longer have the threat posed by the herds. It also meets the other criteria I listed. Supply and raw material availability, temperate climate, plus it is close enough to CONUS that we can send scavenging parties as needed.

"Flight time is three hours from Tinker. We currently have two Globemasters, four C5s, four B-52s and an even twenty C-130s. Combined, that's fifty-six hundred people we can move at once.

Allowing time for loading, unloading and re-fueling at each end, I estimate a round trip time of nine hours.

"That means for the evacuees we're looking at six waves, which will take a total of just over two days. We'll still need to move equipment and supplies, so add a day to that."

"We're going to have hundreds of thousands of infected breaking through the wire before we can fully evacuate the base." Crawford said after a minute of thinking about what Blanchard had just told him. "That's unacceptable. We're not leaving people behind."

"Understood, sir. But we really don't have another option. If we continue to use the crop dusters for fuel dispersal we may be able to hold off the inevitable long enough to get everyone on a plane, but that's just a delaying action." Blanchard responded.

Crawford stripped his cigarette, jammed the butt in his pocket and immediately lit another.

"What's the infected population on the island?" He asked.

"Pre-attack population was roughly a quarter of a million full time inhabitants. Post attack estimates are zero survivors and approximately seventy-five thousand infected. That's a lot, but I like our odds against that many better than close to a hundred million.

"The first two waves would be Marines and Rangers on board the C-130s with the C5s delivering Apaches and Black Hawks for air support in the first wave, then ammo resupply and the Bradley's we brought up from Fort Hood in the second wave. Beginning with the third wave we start evacuating the civilians."

"The first wave will be on their own for nine hours," Crawford mused. "That's a long fucking time to be in hostile territory with no available reinforcements or resupply. And using the C5s for equipment, that will reduce the manpower to less than 4,000 in each of the first two waves."

"Agreed, sir. But I'm not finding any other options. If we move somewhere within the continent, the Russians will just redirect the herds and we'll be in the same situation we are now." Blanchard said.

"Or they wait until we're all sitting on a tiny little island and lob an ICBM at us," Crawford groused.

"Don't you think they would have done that already if they were going to, sir?"

"Frankly, I don't understand why they haven't. What's to stop them?" Crawford drew deeply on his cigarette. "OK, get things in motion. Good thinking, Captain. How soon can you have that first wave in the air?"

Crawford headed for the passenger door of the Humvee. He needed to get back to the office and have a conversation with Admiral Packard. Maybe there were some Navy resources still active in the Atlantic or the Gulf that could assist them.

"Two hours, sir. I took the liberty of putting the units for the first wave on alert." Blanchard answered as he climbed behind the wheel and started the engine.

24

"Sir, you need to look at this." Petty Officer Simmons called out to Lieutenant Hunt.

Unfolding his lanky frame from behind his station he strode across the room and leaned over her shoulder to view the monitor. "See what, Simmons?"

"The NSA satellites, sir. I've been poking around and what we thought were two are actually six. There's two over North America, one over Western Europe, one over Russia and two more over Asia." She said, pointing at a node map laid over an image of the globe.

"And that's not all," she continued. "As I got deeper into the OS (Operating System) I started finding things I didn't understand at first, but I do now. These aren't just imaging birds. There's a full ELINT (Electronic Intelligence) suite on board and it's real Sci-Fi shit. Sir."

"Explain," Hunt said, leaning closer for a better view of the computer code displayed on two of the monitors.

"First, there's the imaging enhancers. It was obvious these birds have top tier optics on board, but the software processing the pics is light years ahead of anything I've ever seen. Here, look at this."

Jessica brought up a live image on a different monitor. Hunt looked at the screen, recognizing the Oklahoma City area they'd been looking at to monitor the herds approaching Tinker Air Force Base. With a couple of mouse clicks, Jessica zoomed the image in on a group of abandoned cars.

The picture was crisp and clear even though it was night in Oklahoma. He was easily able to discern the make and model of each vehicle and could also read the license plates that were oriented properly to the camera angle.

"Yes, it's good," he said. "But I've seen nearly the same quality for several years now, this is just a better resolution."

Jessica smiled, used her mouse to draw a rectangle on the screen and clicked a series of keys. There was a momentary delay, then the image began zooming. And kept zooming until the windshield of one of the cars filled the screen.

Drawing a smaller box with the mouse where the windshield met the vehicle's dash, Jessica hit two more keys and sat back with a barely suppressed grin as the display continued to zoom without losing any resolution.

"Holy shit!" Lieutenant Hunt said a few moments later when he could clearly read the VIN number stamped into a small metal plate attached at the front edge of the dash. He knew the letters and numbers were no more than half an inch tall.

"Yes, sir." She said. "But that's just the beginning. I've already tapped into the Russian military's C2 (Command and Control) system; just don't understand what the hell they're saying. I suppose the NSA had some super computer that would translate for them in real time. And get this!"

Jessica switched screens again and brought up the satellite's menu. She clicked through a couple of layers then pointed at the screen.

"Are you serious?" Hunt breathed. "Facial recognition via satellite?"

"Yes, sir. And not just facial recog, but facial search. Load an image and put the system on auto and it will scan every face within view of its camera until it finds a match."

"I need to brief Admiral Packard on this. No, you need to brief him. I'll get word to his aide and see if he can come over." Hunt headed for his workstation, pausing and turning back to look at Jessica. "Did you finish working the calculations on the herds for Tinker?"

"Turned it over to an Army Captain that's on the ground there in Oklahoma. He seems to know what he's doing, and he has access to the system. And just so you know, there's a whole lot more buried in here that I haven't figured out yet."

"That's fine. Keep working on it and also let's use the other North American bird to get eyes and ears on the Russians that are occupying those Air Force bases. We need to know what they're up to. Malmstrom, Ellsworth and Kirtland. Also, let's start sucking up everything that's going over their C2 as well as get focused in on the Kremlin." He said in an excited voice.

"Aye, aye sir!" Jessica said, her fingers flying over the keyboard.

25

I sat and watched the female for close to half an hour. In that entire time the only movement she made was the occasional tick that seemed to be an involuntary effect of the virus. Otherwise, she was as still as a statue just staring out into the canyon. If I hadn't come in quiet and in the darker shadow of the far wall, she'd have seen me well before I knew she was there.

It was time for me to make another decision. Did I take the female out and move inside the cave, or did I pull back and wait for Rachel, Joe and Dog to arrive. Going into a close environment I would have liked to have Dog with me, but there was a lot to be said for going in alone.

It was going to be dark inside, and fighting in close quarters with no light is not something you typically want to do with a rookie. Sure, Rachel had learned to fight and shoot, and I was pretty sure Joe was better than acceptable with a rifle on the open prairie, but there's a world of difference once you walk into a tight space.

Reaction times have to increase to compensate for the decreased range at which you find yourself facing an enemy. If you haven't trained with someone, over and over, mistakes can and will be made that could easily result in a friendly fire accident. I know I didn't want to shoot them and sure as hell didn't want to get shot.

The last thought made my decision for me. I was going in alone. I'd be able to move quieter and faster. Clearing my mind, I rested the scope's reticle on the female's head. Halfway through the exhale that would have ended with me pulling the trigger I caught my breath at the sound of a rock skittering across the ground at the entrance to the canyon. The female snapped her head to look in that direction, stepping slightly out of the cave entrance to see what had made the noise.

Traversing the rifle, I looked up the canyon and after a couple of moments spotted Rachel, Joe and Dog. To be precise I could see two human and one K9 figure. I was too far away for night vision to let me see any features, but it was them. They had frozen in place after making the noise and I only watched them for a couple of seconds before swiveling back to check on the female.

She had moved farther out into the canyon and was stalking along the base of the far wall in their direction. Out of options, I sighted on her head again and pulled the trigger. The small rifle spat out the bullet without much noise at all, a moment later the subsonic round punching through the infected's skull. She dropped to the hard ground without a sound.

I checked the cave, but no other females had appeared to investigate either the noise or the absence of the sentry, so I stood and carefully made my way towards the entrance to the canyon. Dog smelled me before Joe and Rachel were aware I was there, his tail going into motion as he trotted forward to greet me.

Reaching them I held my hand up as a signal to stay quiet and led the way to an adjacent canyon. After a careful scan with my night vision scope I was relatively satisfied that there weren't any infected in the immediate area.

"Found them," I said in a low murmur.

"Where?" Rachel asked.

"That last canyon, about half way in there's a cave. There was a female guarding the entrance that I shot when you guys kicked the rock."

"Sorry about that," Rachel said sheepishly.

"Are you sure it's just a cave?" Joe asked, moving closer so we could talk without having to raise our voices. "There's a huge system of caverns underneath us."

"Ahh, fuck me," I said. "How big?"

"Not sure," he shook his head. "They aren't well known. We're on Osage land and the tribe knows about them, but I'm not sure any outsiders do. For the most part we stay away from them, but every few years there's some kid that thinks he'll impress a girl by going in and exploring. Some of them come back, but a lot don't."

Caverns actually made more sense than just a cave. Why come all this way for a cave? But caverns, now that would make an outstanding hiding place for the infected. Their enhanced senses would help them move around in the dark, and they probably had a pretty good sense of direction.

Then I wondered how long they'd been hiding here. Because they were different I'd assumed they had recently turned, but they'd been infected long enough to find this place and come to feel it was a safe haven. Now I was really wondering what the hell was going on.

"Big or not, I'm going in." I said. "You two need to head back out into hill country. These canyons would be a bad place to get trapped by infected."

"That's not a good idea," Rachel said. "You don't know how many females are in there. There may be a whole lot more that weren't in the group that captured us. You could be walking into a whole nest of them."

"Then they're going to have a problem, because I'm not leaving Katie in there." I said.

"How do you know that's where they took her?" Joe asked. "Their trail faded out as soon as we got into the canyons. The female you saw could be part of a different group for all you know."

"What are the odds of there being another group all the way out here in the middle of nowhere?" I asked sarcastically.

"Pretty good, actually." Joe said, unphased. "There's an Osage town about ten miles to the north. Something like five thousand people, and I know for a fact none of them received the vaccine. Robert and I didn't make it this far east when we were giving inoculations.

Well if that wasn't just fucking perfect. I wanted to scream with frustration, ready to charge headlong into the caverns and lose myself in a bloody orgy of killing infected. But that wasn't the right way to go about this and rescue Katie. This wasn't about my need to vent some anger; this was about getting her back.

"OK, so if these aren't the ones, where did they go?" I asked.

"I didn't say these weren't the ones," Joe answered patiently. "I simply pointed out that they might not be."

"You're about as helpful as a case of the crabs," I growled, patience almost gone.

Rachel picked up on my mood and placed her hand on my arm. My first impulse was to shake it off, but I knew she was only trying to help. Taking a deep breath I looked away and slowly blew it out.

"Well, unless either of you have a better suggestion, I have to go in. Without any tracks or evidence to the contrary I can't just move on. Either she's in there or she's not. The only way to know for sure is for me to go in." I looked a challenge at each of them, but neither had a response.

I spent a few minutes preparing, finally succeeding in convincing them to go wait in the hills. Making sure I was well supplied with ammunition for the Sig, I shed my pack. Joe offered up his canteens so I would have water. Gratefully accepting them I checked both my Kukri and Ka-Bar as I planned that they would be my primary weapons once inside. Silence and stealth would be my friend.

"Don't suppose either of you has a very long ball of string do you?" I asked, worrying about how I would find my way out if I had to go very deep into the caverns.

Both of them shook their heads. I scratched Dog's ears and wrapped my arms around Rachel when she stepped into me. She hugged me, hard, gave me a quick kiss and stepped back. I nodded to Joe, who looked thoroughly confused about exactly what and with who my relationship status was, turned and moved back toward the canyon with the cavern entrance.

26

Moving back to the canyon I swung wide to come down the far wall in the same dark area that had kept me hidden from the female sentry. I paused to check on her body through the night vision scope, but it was still in exactly the same position in which it had come to rest when I'd shot her. Continuing my slow and careful stalk, I stopped when I was directly across from the entrance.

Taking a long look with the scope, I could tell that after only a few feet there was a solid rock face. Adjusting my location slightly I got an angled view and saw that the path turned to the left, and that's where my sight line ended. Suppressing my impulse to rush in, I took the time to scan the surrounding canyon for infected.

A slow, careful survey yielded nothing I needed to worry about. Another check of the entrance and I was ready to go. Well, mostly ready to go. Few things could have convinced me to go into underground caverns. Katie was one of those few things.

I've know guys that were tunnel rats in Vietnam, and more guys that chased Al Qaida in the caves of Afghanistan. I've heard their stories and have fought in enough different environments to understand that the odds of successfully finding my wife and getting both of us out alive were pretty damn slim. Nearly anorexic.

Pushing these thoughts aside, I let the anger bubble up in my guts and started moving towards the entrance. The rifle was slung tightly on my back and I had a blade in each hand. Even suppressed, I didn't want to use a firearm in the cave and alert everyone to my presence. Cold, sharp steel will kill just as effectively at close range, and a whole lot quieter as long as I didn't give one of them time to let out a scream.

Just inside the entrance I paused to listen before stepping around the turn. Cool, damp air flowed out of the cave, caressing my skin and bringing me the smells of human waste and an underlying muskiness that could only come from mold and fungus. Not at all unexpected for a cave.

Airflow told me there was at least one other entrance, somewhere, and these openings allowed the caverns to breathe. This entrance had to be the lowest one. Cold air sinks and will flow out as warmer air surrounding a higher opening is pulled in.

Hearing nothing, I stepped forward and looked around the turn. Nothing but the feeling of a large, open space, and darkness. I already couldn't see my hand in front of my face, and hoped that the changes the virus had caused to the female's senses didn't allow them to see in the dark. I chided myself as soon as I had the thought. That was bad, B-movie bullshit.

A virus isn't going to *change* the spectrum of light that the human eye detects. It can, however, enhance what senses are already there and I knew from experience that the infected had near-superhuman hearing. Was that how they moved around in here?

As I'd stood there, thinking about sensory enhanced females, my eyes had fully adjusted to the darkness. It had been night outside, but there had been some weak moonlight and starlight to see by. Exponentially darker in the cave, it had seemed perfectly black when I'd first entered, but now I realized I could see a very faint glow ahead.

At first I thought it might be a campfire that was deeper inside the cavern, but as I looked around I could see patches of something on the rock walls that was glowing. Maybe not glowing, exactly, more like phosphorescent. There was a bluish-white hue to the light and I could now see large patches of it on the walls.

The pale light gave me a perspective. The chamber I stood in was large, roughly circular and with a high ceiling. The fungus or lichen or mold or whatever it was that was glowing didn't extend more than a third of the way up the walls. It was heaviest near and on the perimeter of the floor, slowly fading to nothing about ten feet off the ground. It was only growing in the coolest, dampest areas.

Thankful for the light, I began silently stalking across the chamber floor. It was covered in loosely packed sand, which gave me another clue. Water ran through here when it rained, carrying and depositing soil as it flowed. I didn't think this cave would be a good place to be when it was storming and the canyons began filling up with runoff from the surrounding hills.

Ahead was a narrow opening, and the jumble of tracks on the sandy floor headed directly for it. Following them, I spotted two females. Both were lying on the ground, just to the left of the natural doorway. Asleep? Had to be. One was on her back, arms splayed out, the other about four feet away on her side, facing the wall.

I didn't break stride, continuing on, making sure I had a firm grip on both of my weapons. Creeping between the females, I dropped to a knee and simultaneously stabbed down with each hand. The one on her back received a blade through the front of her throat at the notch formed by her collarbone. I stabbed directly into the other's brain stem at the back of her exposed head. Both died in their sleep without a sound.

Wiping the blades on their ragged clothing, I stood and stepped to the opening. The air was cooler here and the light producing organism was growing in larger and thicker patches. The next chamber was almost brightly lit compared to the one I'd just crossed, and a quick peek revealed it was much smaller and empty. Just more jumbled tracks crossing to another door that looked like it would be a tight squeeze for my shoulders.

Moving through the natural doorway I could just detect a low frequency roar. Pausing, I listened intently, but it was a constant sound that I couldn't identify. Crossing the chamber, I approached the next passage at an angle, happy to see it was even better lit, but unhappy to see that it was low, narrow and snaked deeper into the ground.

Taking a breath I bent my head and continued on, shoulders brushing each wall and sending a shower of light drifting down to the soft sand I was walking on. The passage twisted and turned, and at one point I had to walk sideways and bend my knees to keep going. As I moved, I wished for a helmet. My head was bare and if I ran into a low spot in the rock ceiling, even at a slow walk, it could do some damage.

But I didn't have a helmet. Reminding myself to be cautious, I pushed on, noting the floor was beginning to slope down as I progressed. The sand was still nothing more than a jumble from passing feet and I had no idea if I was only dealing with the small group that had taken Katie, or if Rachel's concern over a "nest" was going to become a reality.

The passageway finally leveled out and opened up. I found myself in the largest chamber yet. Half a dozen females were scattered around the area, all apparently asleep. Stalking forward I hoped they were sleeping as soundly as the ones I'd already dispatched.

I moved to the closest one, pausing to make sure I could identify her in the ethereal light. It wasn't Katie, so I thrust the Ka-Bar into the back of her skull. Moving silently but swiftly from form to form, I took a second at each one to ensure I wasn't about to kill my own wife before sending them on to a permanent sleep.

When I killed the last one I had reached the far side of the chamber and the roar I'd noticed earlier was much louder. It was recognizable as water in motion. There must be an underground river, and the noise I was hearing had to be a subterranean waterfall. So, the females were deeper in the caverns to be closer to water. Their behavior was starting to make more sense.

But now I had a problem. There were multiple ways out of the chamber, and all showed heavy foot traffic. The two closest openings were several feet apart and I moved to stand between them. The roar of the water was coming from the right hand door, and there was a steady flow of cold, clammy air emanating from it.

The left door's airflow felt warm by comparison. Standing there thinking, nearly mesmerized by the steady sound of the water, I didn't hear the female that approached from behind and slammed into my back.

I landed face down in the sand, somehow managing to maintain my grip on both blades. The female was tearing at my back, trying to push her face past the protective ridge of my vest and get her teeth into my flesh. Fear that she would start screaming and give away my presence added to the adrenaline already pumping through me and with a grunt of effort I drove an elbow back into her ribs.

Several of them broke with audible snaps and I struck her again and pushed into a roll. She slid off my back as I moved, leaping to a crouch as she prepared to attack. Twisting around, I whipped the Kukri through the air, cutting into her neck as she was opening her mouth to scream. The blade sliced deeply and a gout of blood soaked my arm and splashed onto my chest and face.

Ignoring the unpleasant shower I'd just received, I looked around the chamber, happy to see that she had been alone. But where the hell had she come from? Could have been from any one of the tunnels that branched out from the chamber. OK, how many more were about to show up and surprise me?

27

Colonel Crawford and Captain Blanchard sat in a Humvee watching as the first C-130 left the ground and climbed into the night sky, black smoke trailing from each engine as it gained altitude. The C5s, an escort of eight F-18s and a KC-135 tanker were already in the air, loitering, waiting for the troop carriers to form up for the flight to Nassau.

"Only three hours to the Bahamas?" Crawford asked. "Seems like it should take longer than that."

"Straight lines, sir. They don't have to avoid any air space over major cities or worry about flight corridors." Blanchard answered.

"I suppose that makes sense," Crawford mused. "Any sign the Russians are taking an interest and might try to intercept?"

Blanchard checked his laptop for the tenth time in the past five minutes. A patchwork Wi-Fi system had finally been restored and he was connected directly to one of the NSA satellites and had an excellent view of the three Air Force bases the Russians were occupying.

The EMP had hit each hard, and so far he'd only seen a few lights restored at Kirtland in New Mexico. As he suspected, the Russians weren't in a position to launch an intercept on the aerial convoy that was traveling directly away from any of their captured bases. If they tried, it would be a tail chase across most of North America.

"No sir. Nothing. The latest intercept I had translated shows they're worse off than we are. Apparently that intelligence briefing we received a few years ago was correct and they hadn't done much to harden their equipment against an EMP.

"All of their radar sets are down as well as over half their air assets need a full overhaul of the electronics. Emergency requests for replacement parts, equipment and technical personnel have been made but they haven't gotten an answer from the Kremlin yet."

"Odd," Crawford said, stepping out of the vehicle and lighting a cigarette. "You go to the trouble and expense to send an invading force half way around the globe, then when they encounter a problem you go quiet?"

"Sir, if I may suggest, this might be a golden opportunity to strike the Russians. They won't see us coming and their capability to respond is severely degraded." Blanchard said after getting out from behind the wheel and walking around the vehicle to stand next to the Colonel.

"Or that's what they want us to think," Crawford countered. "How confident are you that they're not waving a false flag, trying to draw us in?"

"I believe the odds are good that what we're seeing and hearing is genuine, sir." Blanchard said after thinking for a moment.

"You're probably right, Captain. But I'm not sure it's a good idea to expend the munitions and risk losing any more personnel and assets." Crawford said, turning to watch another heavily loaded C-130 roar down the runway. "If we had something to gain, other than a measure of revenge... perhaps. But it wouldn't change our situation. We still have to evac before the herds overrun us and planning and executing an attack on the Russians would be a distraction and a drain on very limited resources."

"Yes, sir." Blanchard said, masterfully hiding his emotions. "Oh, and you asked for an update on Major Chase."

The Colonel swiveled his head in surprise. "You found something? I was starting to think he'd finally pushed his luck too far."

"Perhaps, sir. We identified the Marine Osprey, crashed, about twenty-five miles south of the casino where his wife was being held. Numerous bodies scattered in the debris field. We've positively identified Master Gunnery Sergeant Zemeck as one of them. The rest appear to be a mix of infected females and several unidentified Soldiers."

"No sign of the Major?"

"No, sir. He could be inside the wreckage where we just can't see him, but we're not finding Captain Martinez, Ms. Miles or the dog either. There are a lot of tracks in the area. A rather large set heading to the east. I've got someone tracing them via satellite, but it's going to take some time." Blanchard said.

"Let me go find him," a voice said from the dark behind them.

Crawford and Blanchard spun around, surprised to see a powerfully built Air Force Tech Sergeant with a cast on his arm. He came to attention but couldn't salute as his right arm was in a cast.

"Tech Sergeant Scott, isn't it?" He asked.

"Yes, sir. And I'd like permission to look for the Major and the rest of his party. I just got word of the evacuation and I don't like to leave anyone behind." Scott remained at attention, staring at a point over the Colonel's shoulder as he spoke.

"Stand at ease, Tech Sergeant," Crawford said. "I don't like it either, but you don't look like you're ready to be out in the field."

"I'm good to go, sir." Scott replied, relaxing and meeting the Colonel's eyes. "If you'll let me have our two Russian guests, a pilot and a helo, I'll go collect the Major."

"What makes you think he survived that plane crash, son?" The Colonel asked, eyes measuring the younger man.

"Begging the Colonel's pardon, but he's the goddamn toughest, hardest to kill son of a bitch I've ever met. Maybe someday a bullet or an infected will get him, but nothing as simple as a plane crash. He survived, sir." Scott sounded absolutely certain when he spoke the last sentence.

"Captain?" Crawford turned to Blanchard after looking into Scott's eyes for close to a minute.

"No helos available, sir. We've already started shipping them and the ones that are still here are having their fuel drained and rotors set for transport." Blanchard said, watching Scott's eyes fall. "However, we do have more Bradley Fighting Vehicles than we're going to be able to take with us."

Crawford looked back at Scott who was grinning. "Will a Bradley suit your needs?"

"Yes, sir! Quite well. Thank you, sir." Scott answered enthusiastically.

"Good. Captain Blanchard here will make the arrangements. Are you sure you want to take the Russians with you?"

"Yes, sir. The woman isn't a combat officer, but Igor is Spetsnaz and both owe the Major their lives. They'll be just fine." Scott didn't hesitate with his answer.

"OK, they're yours. But you need to know that there are some damn massive herds on the way here. You'll get out, but you probably won't get back in." Crawford said.

"No worries, sir. If we can't get back on the ground, Captain Martinez is a pilot. We'll be able to find something."

Crawford nodded and waved the younger man into the Humvee's back seat.

"Let's get back so you can get things in motion," he said as the last C-130 roared into the night sky.

28

Without making a conscious decision I entered the passage on the right. It was another narrow, winding tunnel, but at least it had a high ceiling and I didn't have to worry about ramming my skull into a rock. Soon I emerged into an expansive chamber, mist hanging in the air.

Water gushed out of a large crack in the wall, falling twenty feet into a broad pool. The floor of the chamber was covered in an even thicker layer of sand and there were tracks everywhere. The phosphorescent growth was the heaviest I'd encountered so far, seemingly putting off enough light that I could have read a book if I'd had one and been so inclined.

A quick scan of the area didn't reveal any infected, but to my right was a large pile of something. Moving that way to investigate I paused and wrinkled my nose when the smell hit me. I knew what it was from the odor, but still went forward for a better look.

The remains of at least thirty human bodies were tossed haphazardly against the wall. Bones had been stripped of most of their meat, the few relatively intact corpses missing the majority of their internal organs. The sand beneath was clumped and stained dark with blood and body fluids. Beetles scurried around, feasting on the rotting flesh that hadn't been stripped completely.

The clothing the poor souls had been wearing was also heaped up, but was so soiled and torn I couldn't tell if it was for men or women. I suppose eighty years ago it would have been much easier as women almost exclusively wore dresses, but in our modern age one pair of pants looks pretty much like any other. At least to my eye.

I was starting to turn away when a thought struck me. Turning back, I used the tip of the Kukri to dig through the clothing, holding various articles up for a closer inspection. No bras or panties. Maybe the lack of bras wasn't that definitive on the sex of the wearer, but I found a lot of underwear styles that I couldn't imagine any woman willingly putting on.

These were men that had been fed on by the females. Were they infected, or were they survivors that had been captured and brought here? A few days ago I would have believed they were survivors, but after seeing the female kill the male she'd mated with outside the casino, I wasn't sure what the hell was going on anymore.

Leaving the detritus behind, I took a slow walk around the remainder of the chamber to make sure I wasn't overlooking anything I needed to know about, but other than tracks in the sand I wasn't finding anything. My mind started to go down the path of wondering what the infected wanted with Rachel and Katie, but I forced myself to stay focused.

Returning to the last room, I looked and listened carefully before entering in case any more females had shown up. Satisfied all was clear, I stepped in just as five females walked out of the tunnel to the adjacent chamber. I froze in place, hoping they wouldn't see me, but the second one through the gap looked in my direction and her eyes flew wide open.

I lunged forward, burying the Kukri in her mouth and twisting it up into her skull as I stabbed the lead female in the back of the head with my knife. The three following females reacted instantly, rushing me. They hadn't screamed yet, and I wanted to put them down before they had an opportunity to alert however many more were in the caves.

Spinning, I slashed with the Kukri and took off most of the top of the next female's head, kicked the body aside as it fell and whipped the two blades into attack position. The next female was fast, ducking under my right-handed strike. She had avoided one blade, but when she lowered her body I was able to stab forward with the knife and bury it to the hilt in her chest, piercing her heart.

The blade stuck and I released it, letting the Ka-Bar fall with her body. I stumbled back when the last female rammed into me, freezing in shock when she bent and snatched my knife out of the corpse on the sand. What the hell was this?

I might have stood there musing about this new behavior, but she charged with the blade held out in front of her. It was a clumsy attack, the knife way too far out in front of her body and held all wrong, but was so fast she nearly gutted me before I twisted away. Hammering with the hilt of the Kukri I heard her wrist break and the knife fell from her nerveless fingers.

She spun, no indication of the damage I'd done other than the knife lying on the sand at her feet. I reversed my grip on the Kukri and stabbed up into her throat as she was opening her mouth to scream. Seeing the strike coming, she had raised her hands to protect herself, but the big blade wasn't slowed by her defenses, severing three fingers before piercing her body.

The corpse was still twitching as her nervous system refused to accept death, but I ignored it, grabbing my knife off the ground and wiping both blades clean on her clothing. Stepping over the body, I moved through the gap and into the tunnel they had emerged from. It was narrower than my shoulders and I had to walk with my body turned slightly to the side.

It was dryer in this passage and the floor dropped slightly as I progressed. The farther I moved, the dryer the air felt, and the glowing lichen thinned out to the point that I couldn't see anything beyond a foot in front on my face. Slowing my pace, I forced my breathing to calm and even out. I'm not a fan of caves, and even less of dark ones full of infected that would be happy to have me for dinner.

When I reached the end of the tunnel it was more the feeling of open space around me than any visual cue that alerted me to the change. There were small patches of the lichen growing in random locations on the walls and ceiling. In the darkness it seemed like I was in a planetarium or some high-tech amusement park attraction, the faint spots of phosphorescence making it seem as if I were floating in space and viewing distant galaxies.

The effect was both mesmerizing and disorienting as it was completely dark where I stood. Glancing down I couldn't see the sand beneath my feet, or anything to either side. Frozen in place I listened hard, hearing the faint sounds of breathing from somewhere to my front. But that was all I could tell. It could have been anything with a set of lungs, from a small dog to a giant dragon waiting to be roused and wreak havoc on whoever dared disturb its slumber.

Chastising myself for wasting time thinking about fantasy monsters when I should be focused on the real life ones, I silently sheathed the two blades and carefully worked the small rifle around to the front of my body. There wasn't enough light in the chamber for my eyes to be of any use, but there should be for the night vision scope.

Raising the rifle to my shoulder, I looked through the scope which amplified the available light and showed me a crisp green and black image of the area. I slowly turned my upper body, scanning across the floor. My breath caught in my throat when I got a good look at my surroundings.

At least thirty females were scattered around the large room, sleeping on the soft sand. No more than a couple of feet from my left foot lay a small woman with her arm splayed out to the side. If I'd taken another step, the odds were good that I would have stepped on her. That would have been disastrous. There was no way I wanted to face this many infected in such close quarters.

Grimacing, I made another, slower scan. As I moved the scope I counted the resting bodies and cataloged them as best I could. There was a large concentration to my left, seventeen of them bedded down in a tight group. The remaining fifteen were spread randomly around the area.

I started to wonder if there was something like a class hierarchy or clique going on with them, then shut down my thinking. It didn't matter if there was. At least not at the moment. Perhaps that was something that would be useful at some point in the future, but right now it didn't have any bearing on the situation.

Making a third scan, I spotted an irregularity in the pattern of the bodies lying on the floor. At the base of the farthest wall of the chamber, two bodies were huddled together. This caught my eye because all of the other females each had some space around them, even the ones lying in the group. Focusing on these two, my heart started racing when I realized one of them was dressed like a Victoria's Secret model.

Katie? I couldn't tell through the night vision, but the odds were in my favor this was her. After another quick survey of the area to make sure none of the females had awakened and noticed me, I focused on the ground and started making my way across the chamber. Sidestepping the female's arm to my front, I was grateful for the soft sand that was spread across the floor.

Rifle aimed down, I looked at each spot I intended to place a foot before I lifted it. A stumble in my footing or stepping on an object that could make noise, either one of those could be enough to wake the whole chamber full of females and that would be the end of my night. Sweat popping out on my brow from concentration; I pushed on, one slow step at a time.

Stopping half way across I took the time to scan again. Same count, so there weren't any up and stalking around in the dark about to attack. I was listening carefully, expecting every step to make some faint sound that would rouse a slumbering female. If that happened, I couldn't shoot.

Even suppressed, the rifle would make enough noise in the quiet chamber to give me away. I would have to hope for a silent kill with my knife, but knew the odds of being able to pull that off were stacked heavily against me. Taking a moment to ensure the Ka-Bar and Kukri were seated properly in their sheaths and would draw smoothly if needed, I resumed my painfully slow progress.

The farther I moved across the chamber, the more the skin on my back puckered. It was no longer practical to be constantly scanning behind me, and that meant there were a growing number of females that could wake up, spot me and attack before I was even aware of the threat. Hopefully

I'd hear some movement before I was tackled to the ground, but I knew I would most likely be overwhelmed and killed quickly.

I was within ten yards of Katie when I stepped on what looked like an undisturbed patch of sand and a loud crack sounded as some buried object broke under the weight of my foot. I froze, holding my breath. There were several sharp intakes of breath from the females around me and I dropped to my belly, barely avoiding a sleeping form.

If the sound woke any of them, I didn't want one to open her eyes and see me standing there. Perhaps, if I was on the ground and one of them did look around I'd appear to be just another of her sleeping sisters. Of course, I was assuming their vision was enough better than mine to be able to see in the darkness. Maybe they'd wake up, smell me, and come searching.

29

When I came down on the sand I found myself face to face with a female. It was too dark for me to see if her eyes were open, but for the moment she remained still. I lay there, my face no more than a foot from hers. Her breathing stayed slow and steady, but I was holding mine for fear of waking her.

I'd been face to face with plenty of infected, but never like this. Now, I had time to notice the smell coming from her. There was the ripe stink of an unwashed human, but there was also the sickly sweet odor of decay. I hadn't seen any sign that the infected were unhealthy.

Remembering the human remains I'd found in the other chamber I didn't have to use much imagination to figure out what I smelled. Her breath. Fetid from feasting on raw flesh. I couldn't help but think about what had to be trapped in her teeth that was generating the odor.

Dismissing the macabre images from my mind, I started to crawl, ready to give her a wide berth. I didn't think I was making any sound as I moved at sloth-like speed, but something gave me away. Maybe it was just another body being so close, or maybe she smelled me in her sleep and it woke her, but either way I knew I had trouble when I heard her breathing change.

Moving by feel, I lunged, driving my left forearm across her throat to prevent a scream. I felt her larynx crush under the pressure, pushed harder and drew my knife. She was struggling under me, hands on my arm as she tried to break free, and she was strong. I had a good angle, able to use the power in my shoulder as well as bring a lot of my body weight to bear, but she still nearly succeeded in lifting me off her throat before I rammed the Ka-Bar into her ear.

She immediately went limp, but I kept on the pressure and gave the knife a twist just to make sure she was truly finished. Satisfied, I stayed where I was, listening. I could still hear soft breathing all around me, but couldn't tell if a dozen females had heard the kill and were about to drop on top of me.

Finally, after nearly a minute of not hearing any indication the scuffle had been detected, I moved forward again. I crawled with the knife in my hand until I was clear of the body, then slowly got up onto my knee. Rifle up, I scanned the chamber, taking the time to do another count. Same number. I gave it another minute and carefully stood, keeping the rifle up and ready.

Continuing, I resumed my careful survey of the ground in front of me prior to each step. The going was slow and tedious, but losing focus could spur an attack. I had been fortunate to kill the female silently enough to not disturb any of the others. I couldn't count on being that lucky twice.

After what felt like hours, I reached the location where Katie was lying on the sand. I was now close enough to make out details in the night vision scope and felt a thrill of victory when I was able to confirm it was her. She lay on her side, knees pulled up slightly, arms under her head for a pillow, long hair tumbling across her shoulders and onto the sand.

A foot away from her another woman slept in a similar pose, back to Katie. I didn't recognize her, and couldn't tell if she was infected or not, but doubted that she was. She was wearing jeans, boots and a checked western shirt. Long, blonde hair was pulled back into a severe ponytail.

I took a few moments to check the chamber, glad to see all was still quiet. Silently dropping to a knee I leaned over Katie and placed a hand over her mouth as I wrapped my other arm around her. A second after my touch, her eyes flew open and she began to struggle.

"It's me," I mumbled directly into her ear, unable to resist kissing her cheek. Immediately she stopped resisting and started to turn her head to look at me.

"No sound," I mumbled before removing my hand. "They're all around us."

She nodded and turned onto her back and wrapped her arms around my neck, pulling me down until her face was buried against my shoulder. She was shaking, but I couldn't tell if she was crying or not. I could have stayed that way for as long as she was willing to hold me, but we had to get out of there before something woke one of the females and we were discovered.

I mumbled in her ear, telling her what we were doing. I couldn't see her nod, but felt the movement against my body.

"We have to take Glynnis," she mumbled in my ear.

I had little doubt she was referring to the blonde woman, and I sighed internally. Getting in by myself had been hard. Getting two of us out would be more than twice as hard. Three of us? The odds of being heard and all of us dying were not swinging in our favor.

Arguing with Katie would have been useless. I've been married to her too long and know better. If we had been somewhere where I could actually talk, she'd let me say my piece then tell me what we were going to do. In my heart I knew she was right. For the same reason Rachel had talked me into helping Stephanie on the way to the casino, Katie was right that we had to help Glynnis.

I nodded, Katie releasing her hold on me. Rising up I made another full survey of the chamber while Katie reached for the blonde woman. A sharp hiss caused me to snap my head down, but I couldn't see anything. Lowering the rifle I saw the woman turning towards Katie's touch, but something wasn't right. Her lips were peeled back from her teeth as she turned, her hands grasping Katie's arm.

Her teeth were inches from Katie's unprotected face when I pulled the trigger. The round punched through her temple and she lay still, but the suppressed report of the rifle sounded like a thunderclap to me after so long in the near silence of the cave. The only thing I could think to do was drop to the ground behind Katie and hope for the best.

There were several sharp exclamations from around the chamber as I hit the sand. Drawing my Ka-Bar, I pressed it into Katie's hand and scooted until my head touched rock. Slowly, I kept working my way backwards until I was sitting with my back resting against the wall. The rifle was up and I was watching as a dozen females sat up at different points around the room.

Katie wormed her way through the sand until she was sitting next to me, facing out with the knife held in front of her. I kept watching through the night vision scope as four of the females that had been woken by the shot stood and looked around. They didn't seem to be able to see any better in the dark than I could, each of them scanning through the area where I was sitting without pausing, but I still held my breath each time I saw one of their heads turn in our direction.

After several minutes, two of them made their way to the exit and left the chamber. The two that stayed behind were standing stock still, occasionally turning their heads from side to side. I didn't know if they were listening or scenting, just knew I'd have been spotted a hundred times by now if they could see me.

Time passed slowly. Katie moved her leg carefully until it was touching mine. I felt for her. Sitting in the dark, maintaining absolute silence as you watched a couple of infected through a night vision scope was nerve wracking. Sitting in the dark and unable to see the danger that you know is there would be much worse.

But, she was keeping it together, like I knew she would. You know you married well when you have a beautiful wife that puts up with all your shit and still loves you. You know you hit the jackpot when the apocalypse comes along and she manages to survive without you.

After what had to be an hour, one of the females looked around a last time before lying back down on the sand. The second one stayed where she was for another half an hour before lowering herself onto the floor. I breathed a quiet sigh of relief, but didn't dare make a move or sound.

Were they confident there wasn't an intruder in the chamber and going back to sleep, or were they setting a trap? Either way, I was in no hurry to find out. I may not have the patience of a sniper who can wait for days on end for a target, but I certainly have enough to give them time to go back to sleep before trying to escape.

I gave them half an hour, keeping my mind focused by counting off the time in my head. No, I'm not that precise, but I knew that I counted slow and if I had counted to thirty minutes it was probably closer to forty-five. Making another check of the room I finally lowered my rifle, my shoulders screaming at me for having been held in the same position for so long.

Leaning to the side I pressed my mouth to Katie's ear and mumbled what we were going to do. There weren't a lot of instructions so it didn't take long and she nodded then reached up and caressed my cheek. Old habits die hard, and she automatically rubbed the stubble on my face with one of her nails. This was the signal she'd been giving me for years that if I wanted to get close to her I'd better get close to a razor first.

Smiling, I turned my attention back to the room and slowly rose to my feet, keeping my back pressed to the rock wall. Another 'all clear' scan and I tapped Katie with my foot. A moment later she was on her feet, left hand resting on my right shoulder, Ka-Bar in her right.

Repeating the process that had gotten me across the chamber earlier, I carefully scanned the sand in front of me and took a step forward. Katie stepped behind me, transferring her hand to my left shoulder. She would follow tight against me, hopefully in my tracks and not step on anything, or anyone, and wake the females.

The progress was slow. No slower than before, but certainly no faster. Katie's hand was firm on my shoulder as we moved, and even though she was close and in my tracks I made sure to keep a buffer zone between us and any sleeping bodies. Moving like this took us fifteen minutes to cross half the chamber.

Reaching the center I looked at the ground and the sprawled bodies around us. What had been an open path on my way in was now blocked. One of the females that had stood up after the shot had lain down in a different position and her legs were in our way.

Sure, I could see them and step over them, but how did Katie manage it? I wasn't about to try telling her and risk even a low mumble waking one of the infected. Neither did I like the idea of taking the chance that Katie would misstep because she couldn't see the female's legs in our way.

Cursing to myself, I turned and scanned to either side, looking for a path we could follow. Not seeing one I turned back to my front, trying to come up with even a hair brained idea, freezing when I realized the infected's legs were no longer blocking the path. Whipping the rifle up to horizontal I started to turn to the right then saw her standing a few feet away facing directly at me.

I pulled the trigger and her head snapped back as she crumpled to the ground, falling across another sleeping female. The shot seemed louder than the last one and a heartbeat later there were bone-chilling screams from all around us.

30

Tech Sergeant Scott sat in the commander's seat of the Bradley Fighting Vehicle; eyes to the periscope that provided him a view of the gate they would pass through once the Rangers finished clearing enough infected. There weren't anywhere near enough bodies to even slow the six hundred horsepower, thirty-three ton tracked vehicle. The concern was preventing a flood of raging infected onto Tinker Air Force Base while the gate was open.

Russian GRU Captain Irina Vostov was at the controls, reclined at the driver's station. She too was watching intently through one of four periscopes that provided a 360-degree view. Scott would have preferred to be the one driving, but with an arm in a cast he had delegated the job. His initial thought had been to have Igor drive, but the big Spetsnaz soldier had settled into the gunner's seat with a huge grin.

There had been some moments of panic outside when he'd begun playing with the controls, traversing the 25 mm chain gun across a platoon of Marines that were slotted for the next flight to

Nassau. They had shouted, scrambling to get out of the weapon's line, and hadn't calmed down until Igor pushed open the hatch in the turret and stuck his head up, shouting apologies in broken English.

The Marines had let him know, in no uncertain terms, exactly what they thought of him. Even though he didn't speak English, he certainly understood enough to get the gist of their comments. Laughing, Scott had to stop him from firing up the vehicle's defensive systems and lobbing a couple of smoke grenades at the platoon.

Once everyone had calmed down, Scott had gotten them moving, issuing commands to Irina. She handled the big vehicle well and he suspected she'd spent some time training on the Russian BTR-90. The eight-wheeled monstrosity was comparable in size and maneuverability to the Bradley, but lacked the hard rubber road tracks that made the American machine look like a tank. He would have liked to know, but didn't have time at the moment for a conversation.

"Get ready," the Lieutenant in charge of the Ranger platoon clearing the area around the gate called over the radio.

"Copy. We'll clear the area fast once the gate's open." Scott replied.

For the fourth time he checked over the gauges, satisfied the idling diesel engine was healthy and operating properly. He peered through the periscope at the ten jerry cans of diesel fuel strapped to the armored sides of the vehicle. Not knowing anything about a Bradley, he'd received a crash course from an Army First Sergeant who'd commanded one for three tours in Iraq.

Scott had been surprised to learn that they only held enough fuel for a maximum range of 300 miles. He had quickly found a couple of Air Force machinists to fabricate a quick and dirty rack that would hold spare cans of fuel. He knew the Major's original destination was over a hundred miles away and had little doubt he'd wind up needing to refuel before the trip was over. The extra fifty gallons of diesel would give them close to another hundred miles of range.

Looking behind him, he returned Igor's grin and did a visual check of the ammunition. He had drawn extra ammo, loading heavier than a Bradley normally is. With 1,200 rounds for the 25 mm chain gun, 4,000 for the 7.62 mm machine gun and 10 TOW missiles they were ready for anything they encountered. An additional 5,000 rounds of rifle ammo already loaded into magazines was also piled in the back.

"Go kick some ass!" The Lieutenant shouted over the radio as two Rangers began pulling the gate open.

"Let's go, Irina." Scott said as he watched the opening in front of them widen enough to drive through.

Irina didn't bother answering, just accelerated forward. She drove aggressively, and as they pushed through infected and away from the Air Force base Scott began to question his decision to let her drive. Bradley's weren't known for their smooth rides, and she seemed intent on moving as fast as she could in the urban environment. That meant bouncing over curbs and medians at near full throttle.

They whipped around one corner, Irina following the GPS display on the panel to her right, a traffic circle with a large hump in the middle just ahead of them. Scott would have slowed and negotiated the turns, staying on the pavement, but

Irina sped up. Diesel roaring, thirty-three tons of armored vehicle went airborne momentarily, crashing back to the asphalt hard enough to make him wish for a chiropractor.

"Slow down!" Scott shouted over the intercom. "Let's not break our ride before we're out of the neighborhood."

Irina said something over the intercom that made Igor laugh, but a moment later their speed dropped. She kept their pace more sedate as they worked their way through Oklahoma City, heading north. Occasionally, Scott would see small groups of survivors dashing along the street. Some of them tried to wave the Bradley down, but Irina wasn't stopping and he wasn't inclined to tell her to pull over. They couldn't save everyone.

Driving down one particularly long stretch, Scott kept hearing frequent impacts, not unlike rocks being thrown up by a car's tires and striking the undercarriage. Igor heard it too, scanning around with his periscopes and saying something to Irina in Russian.

"Igor says we are being fired on," she said.

"What? Who's shooting at us?" Scott asked in surprise.

Irina and Igor had a brief conversation before she answered. "Look to our right. About two o'clock on the top level of the parking garage."

Scott adjusted his view, a moment later spotting the wink of a muzzle flash a second before he heard another impact on the exterior armor. Some jackass was taking pot shots at them. Really? Firing a rifle at a vehicle that can battle tanks?

"Igor wants to know if he can take them out," Irina said after another exchange in Russian.

"No. They can't hurt us. Let's not waste ammo we may need later," Scott replied after a moment's thought. "And tell Igor not to engage any targets unless he sees something that could actually cause us damage."

"He says you're taking all the fun out of the end of the world," Irina said a few moments later.

Scott swiveled in his seat and looked at Igor. The big Russian met his eyes with a broad grin and a shrug. Shaking his head, Scott turned back to watch the road as they kept moving north.

Close to three hours later they arrived at the downed Osprey. Irina brought the Bradley to a gentle stop fifty yards short of the main wreckage. Using the integrated night vision, Scott scanned the area, looking for either survivors or infected. He found neither.

After confirming that Igor wasn't finding any threats, he and the big Russian lowered the rear ramp and stepped out into the night. They left Irina in the idling vehicle, each of them with a tactical radio set so they could stay in communication.

"Son of a bitch!" Scott exclaimed when they walked around the right side of the Bradley.

The rifle fire that he hadn't been worried about had punched holes in the spare fuel cans on that side, and they were now all empty. He looked at Igor, knowing he'd hear "I told you so" if not for the language barrier. Running around to the left side he was relieved to find that half of their supply still intact. After a quick translation over the radio, Igor slung his rifle and grabbed the first can off the makeshift rack.

Cursing himself for having stayed Igor's hand when the Russian wanted to take out the sniper, Scott moved to the downed aircraft while Igor started pouring diesel into the Bradley's tank. Not seeing anything that hadn't been in the satellite image he'd been shown by Captain Blanchard, he stood staring at all the bodies.

"What do you see?" Irina asked over the radio.

"Dog survived," he answered. "There's at least three female infected with their throats ripped out."

"What about the Major?" Irina asked.

"Don't know. I'm going to take a look inside the fuselage." Scott answered, clicking on a high intensity flashlight and climbing through the debris.

He spent several minutes searching, finding more bodies, but not the Major, Rachel or Martinez. Moving back outside he paused, looking at the crash site. The Osprey was heading south when it crashed. On its way back to Tinker? Most likely. And the presence of Dog was pretty compelling evidence that either the Major, Rachel, or both, were on board when it went down.

While he was standing there looking, Igor walked up and joined him. The Russian didn't bother to look at any of the bodies, but started walking around the area peering at the ground. Scott had forgotten about the tracks Captain Blanchard had found in the satellite image. Igor kept moving, slowly working his way farther and farther from the wreckage. He paused a couple of times, then looked to the east and started walking across the field. Scott jogged over to see what he'd found.

Igor looked at him and started speaking rapid fire Russian into his radio, motioning for Scott to return to the Bradley with him. As they approached, the rear ramp dropped with a whine of hydraulics and they quickly boarded and took their seats.

"A large group headed to the east after the crash," Irina translated once Scott was back on the intercom. "They were followed by a dog and a man in US Army issue boots. I think we know which way the Major went."

31

"Stay on me!" I shouted to Katie and ran for the tunnel that led out of the chamber.

She kept her left hand on my left shoulder, firmly gripping the edge of the vest. I was moving fast, but was afraid to break into a full run, rather moved by shuffling my feet along the surface of the sand. Any females that hadn't gotten to their feet could easily trip me. I hoped that keeping my feet low would prevent that.

I had lowered the rifle and drawn the Kukri as we ran, feeling it slice into a body a moment before I crashed into it. The contact with the blade had given me enough warning time to lower my shoulder and bull the female aside. We kept going, screams continuing to sound all around us. Hands grasped at my arms as we moved and I began slashing back and forth.

More often than not I felt momentary resistance as the blade bit into flesh, but it was sharp and my swings were adrenaline fueled. The Kukri cut through everything it contacted. I was starting to think we were going to make it to the exit relatively unscathed when a body crashed into my right side and sent me sprawling.

I landed hard on my left shoulder, no longer feeling Katie's hand gripping my vest. Panic surged as the female that had tackled me lunged her face forward against my throat. I was able to thrust my shoulder up just in time to protect my flesh, hearing her teeth clack together on empty air, inches from my ear.

Twisting, I grabbed the female's neck and levered her up and away, thrusting the Kukri into her chest until my knuckles pressed against her body. Hurling the corpse away I stood, afraid to swing the blade because I had no idea where Katie was. Disoriented in the dark, rage took over and when the next female reached for me I yanked her close and snapped her neck.

Stepping back, I sheathed the Kukri and raised the rifle. Suddenly I could see and began pulling the trigger the moment I had a target. The females zeroed in on me as soon as I fired the first shot, rushing my location. They were close, but I had the advantage of sight and kept putting them down as fast as I could pull the trigger, sidestepping so as not to give them a static location to attack.

"Katie!" I shouted, no longer worried about the females knowing exactly where I was.

"Here!" She shouted in return a moment later, her voice coming from behind me.

Knowing where she was removed the last restraint and after changing magazines I switched from semi to full auto and started mowing down my attackers. I wasn't going for headshots, just putting bullets into legs to slow them. Going through two full mags, I popped in a fresh one as I moved backwards.

"Coming to you," I shouted between pulls of the trigger.

"No need," Katie said a moment later from right behind me, then I felt her hand on my shoulder again.

The females were still screaming, but as I scanned the chamber with the night vision scope I didn't find any that were still able to walk. Many were alive, crawling towards us across the sandy floor, but they weren't an immediate threat. I checked behind us, not at all surprised when I saw three dead females where Katie had been.

"OK, we're moving," I said, heading for the tunnel.

Three more females were on the ground, still alive, between the exit and us. Switching back to semi I put a single round into each of their heads, then broke into a real run. Katie held on tight and stayed right against my back.

Passing through the gap, I turned to the side so I would fit, Katie shifting her hand to my other shoulder. The light steadily increased as we approached the far end and I moved with the rifle at my shoulder, ready to fire. I didn't think for a moment that there weren't other females responding to the screams and sounds of the fight.

We quickly covered the length of the tunnel, emerging into the next chamber. Stepping over the bodies of the females I'd killed earlier, I froze when I heard screams coming from one of the other tunnels. A lot of screams.

"That's a whole shitload of pissed off females," I said.

"Is that the way out?" Katie asked, moving up next to me and pointing at a tunnel in the far wall. She still held my Ka-Bar and it was stained red, drops of blood falling from the tip onto the sand.

"In there," I said, pushing her toward the tunnel entrance that led to the chamber with the waterfall. It had been empty of infected when I'd checked it and if we were very lucky, the ones charging in would head straight to the sleeping chamber.

Katie dashed through the opening and I followed, still facing the approaching females with my rifle up. We melded back into the passage, moving around the first bend so we were hidden from the chamber we'd just left. I pressed my back against the glowing wall, poking my head out just far enough to see the room. Katie was next to me, pressed tight against my side.

A moment later, females began boiling into the chamber we'd just left. There were a lot of them, and they were moving too fast for me to get an accurate count. Racing across the floor they entered the other tunnel, moments later fresh screams echoing throughout the caverns.

Pulling my head back I checked my vest, unhappy when I only found four more full magazines. Not enough with this many females. But then I'm not sure four hundred magazines would have helped. There were so many of them, and they were so fast, I didn't think I'd be able to hold them off for more than a few seconds. Longer if we were in this tunnel and they couldn't rush me from a broad front, but even then there were more targets than I had bullets.

"What are we doing?" Katie mumbled in my ear.

"I don't know," I said. "I've got less than a hundred rounds left and I'm pretty sure there are more females than that."

Katie stayed quiet and I leaned out to check the tunnel entrance. Fifteen or twenty females were pacing around the chamber, looking at the floor, sniffing the air, but so far none of them seemed to be interested in our hiding place. Pulling back, I turned and quietly told Katie what I'd seen. Before I could turn my head away she reached up and grabbed my face and kissed me, hard and deep.

"Just in case," she breathed when our lips parted.

I kissed her again, a quick touch of the lips, then looked back down the tunnel. Two females were standing at the entrance, peering in. I froze, hoping they hadn't seen me, not about to move again and risk drawing their attention. After a long moment, one of them stepped into the tunnel.

Without moving my head or taking my eyes off the approaching threat I reached behind and gently pushed Katie a couple of feet away. Once she was clear I drew the Kukri and held it along my leg and waited. The female kept coming and now the second one followed her into the tunnel.

Keeping my attention on the infected I extended two fingers on the hand that was holding the Kukri and lightly tapped the side of the blade. I hoped Katie would see my signal and understand. I couldn't help but smile when a moment later I felt two taps on my shoulder. She'd gotten it and understood.

The first female moved even with me and paused when she realized I was standing there, but I was already in motion. Leaning out I rotated my shoulder past her body and drove my elbow into the back of her neck. She stumbled forward and I reversed my motion, thrusting the Kukri into the second female's throat.

I grabbed the front of her shirt and keeping the body upright, dragged it deeper into the tunnel, out of sight of the other females prowling around the chamber. Turning, I was happy to see Katie had finished the first one off with the knife. Pulling the corpse the rest of the way around the bend I dropped it on top of the first one.

We had hardly made a noise, putting both females down before they could sound an alarm, but something had drawn the attention of several of the infected in the chamber. They were stalking towards the tunnel entrance, and I snapped my head around when a scream sounded behind us. Whipping the rifle to my rear, I body checked Katie out of the way and fired three shots, dropping two females that were charging us.

There weren't any more behind them, at least that had shown themselves, so I turned back to the front. As I sighted in on the females that had broken into a sprint I felt Katie pull my pistol out of the holster strapped to my thigh.

Pulling the trigger, I noted the sounds as she checked the magazine and verified there was a round in the chamber, then felt her back against mine as she guarded our rear. Time for worry over the noise of firing the unsuppressed pistol was over. Every female in the caverns knew where we were, and it looked like all of them were charging directly at us.

32

I burned through a magazine in no time. Loading a fresh one I resumed a steady rate of fire, dropping a female with every pull of the trigger. They were so close I hardly needed to aim, and the narrow entrance into the tunnel restricted them to one attacker at a time. The bodies were piling up, but several of the females were pulling their dead sisters out of the way as fast as I could put them down.

Ammo was going in a hurry and I could see the chamber still filling up with females. In only a matter of minutes I was going to run out and then they'd push in and rip us apart. When the rifle ran dry I'd draw the Kukri and keep fighting. I'd be able to hold them off for a while, but eventually my arm would tire and slow, or the blade would stick in a body, then it would all be over.

I hadn't realized Katie was no longer at my back until she suddenly appeared next to me, shouting to be heard over the screaming of the females and the muted shots from the rifle.

"It's open behind us. We need to fall back!"

"This tunnel's all that's saving us," I shouted in between shots. "We fall back and they can spread out and rush us."

"How much ammo do you have left?" She asked.

"Not nearly enough. Maybe a minute, two if we're lucky." I said, pushing the release to drop an empty magazine then slapping in a fresh one.

"Trust me," Katie shouted as I felt two hard tugs on the front of my vest. Glancing down I saw fragmentation grenades in her hands just as she pulled the first pin.

"Don't fucking do..." I started to say, but it was too late.

She had already thrown the first one onto the sand at the mouth of the tunnel and was pulling the next pin. The second grenade landed farther out in the chamber amongst a tightly packed group of females. Firing two more times, I spun, pushed Katie around the bend and pressed my body against her to act as a shield.

The twin detonations were like the fist of God. I was deafened and not entirely sure my eardrums weren't blown out by the concussive wave. Dirt and dust was thrown into the air, reducing visibility to nothing as it quickly filled the entire chamber and rolled into the tunnel. I was aware of a vibration in the soles of my feet, but couldn't hear a thing.

Moving away from Katie I looked around the bend, seeing nothing other than a glowing cloud. The force of the blasts had torn much of the phosphorescent lichen free from the walls and it mixed with the dust in a nightmarish, glowing fog. I couldn't see any females, but then I couldn't see more than six inches. I couldn't hear any screams, but then I couldn't hear anything other than my own heart pounding.

The vibrations intensified and "cave in" flashed through my head. Grabbing Katie's arm I turned and ran for the far end of the tunnel. Grenades are devastating weapons against the human body, but they really don't contain that much relative explosive force. I was pretty sure that either the tunnel, the chamber, or both were about to be buried under a few tons of rock, but the blasts shouldn't cause damage all the way back to the waterfall chamber.

We moved as fast as we could in the tunnel, visibility slowly improving as we moved farther away from where the grenades had detonated. Finally we emerged from the cloud and into clear air. The glowing dust was just starting to roll out of the tunnel and disperse into the larger space, but it quickly absorbed the mist in the air created by the waterfall, making the dust heavier and causing it to fall to the sand.

The vibrations increased, turning to a deep rumble and a moment later a fresh cloud of dust pulsed out of the tunnel, then the noise stopped. I had my rifle up, focused on where an infected would emerge from the dirty air, but after a couple of minutes we were still alone. Slowly lowering my rifle I was glad to note that my hearing was starting to return.

The room was well lit, as it had been before, and I turned to check Katie over. She was dirty, sweaty, streaked with muck and blood, hair greasy and plastered to her head, but had never looked so beautiful.

"Can't you ever do anything in moderation?" I asked her, smiling my happiness to be standing there with her.

"How many years of marriage and you have to ask?" She smiled back. "Saved our asses, didn't it?"

"Maybe just prolonged the agony if we can't find a way out of here." I said. "How are you feeling? The last time I saw you, you were flat on your back with a bullet hole in your chest."

"I'm good," Katie said, reaching up and touching her injury.

Leaning down I took a closer look at where Roach's bullet had entered her body. The wound looked like it had been healing for a couple of weeks, not just a couple of days. Rachel had told me she'd used powdered blood clotter to stop the bleeding after determining nothing vital had been hit, but Katie shouldn't be up and running around two days after being shot through the chest.

"How does it look?" She asked.

"Good," I said. "You're doing good."

I was more than a little concerned. Unless they're in a movie, people don't just take a bullet then go on like nothing happened. There was definitely something odd here, and I didn't like the only possibility I was coming up with. The virus. Somehow the virus, without causing Katie to turn, had strengthened her body and was helping her heal at an accelerated pace.

"What?" She asked, looking at my face. I've never been good at concealing my thoughts from her.

"Nothing," I said, starting to turn away.

"Uh huh. Talk to me. What's wrong?" She reached up and touched the wound again.

"It's just that you're healing too fast," I said. "I'm a little worried that maybe the virus has done something to you."

Katie stood staring at me. She started to smile, thinking for a moment that I was kidding her, but as she looked at my face she realized I was serious.

"Did you receive the vaccine while you were at Tinker?" I asked her.

"They almost had to hold me down, you know how I am about things like that, but yes I got the shot. You don't really think..." She paused, a look of fear passing across her face. “You think I’m infected?”

“I don’t know, babe.” I said, wrapping my arms around her and pulling her close. “I don’t know. I just know you’re healing about ten times faster than I’ve ever seen. That’s a good thing, and you’re not running around screaming and trying to eat me. That’s even better.”

“Maybe that’s why they took me,” she said a minute later, face still pressed against my chest. “I’ve been trying to figure it out, but nothing’s made sense. Until now.”

Katie leaned back and looked up at my face. Started to say something but I shook my head. There wasn’t a point in talking about it right now. We were alive and together. That was all I cared about. Breaking our embrace, I surveyed the chamber, seeing nothing different from the first time I’d been in it.

Dust was still drifting out of the tunnel, but the density of the cloud was lessening and I walked over to peer inside. I couldn’t see anything other than glowing dust, the night vision scope completely useless as all it did was make the cloud look brighter. Lowering the rifle, I stood there for a moment listening.

There was an occasional groan of overstressed rock and frequent falls of dirt and small stones that sounded eerily like some giant subterranean spider skittering along the rock walls. The good news was there weren't any females trying to attack us. The bad news; I was fairly certain the tunnel was completely blocked and we were trapped.

I wanted to go into the tunnel and check how bad the cave in was, but decided to wait until I could see. Caves and caverns are dangerous enough when you can see where you're going and what your doing. With zero visibility I could stumble into a hole that had opened up in the floor, walk into the arms of a female who was lying in wait, bash my skull in on the ceiling, or any number of other unpleasant things.

"So what now?" Katie asked.

"You ask me that, dressed like you are?" I grinned. She was still wearing only a thong and bra, and the bra had definitely seen better days. It was torn and ragged, revealing much more than it concealed.

"You're amazing," she laughed. "Didn't Rachel take good care of you?"

"Hey! Absolutely nothing happened between us." I said, probably a little more emphatically than I should have as Katie gave me one of her looks.

"I was just teasing. She and I had a long talk and she told me everything. Or I thought she had. Anything *you* need to tell me?"

Katie stood looking at me with her arms crossed. I looked back at her, feeling the heat rise from my neck and spread across my face. This was hardly the time and place to be discussing Rachel, but I also didn't want to let the thought fester in Katie's head. At the moment, we were relatively safe.

"I have feelings for her, yes." I finally said in a low voice, looking at the sand at my feet. "We've been through a lot, then when I saw our house had burned I was sure you were dead at worst, or if you were alive I'd never see you again. I thought about being with her, a lot, but I couldn't. So, yeah, I feel guilty. But not because I did anything. Because I thought about it, and wanted to."

Katie stood there looking at me for what felt like an eternity. I couldn't meet her eyes. I felt like a complete ass, but at the same time I wasn't going to lie to her. She had the right to the truth, not just about what I did or didn't do, but also what I had thought about doing. Maybe I could have kept my mouth shut, but she's a smart and intuitive woman, always able to read me like a book, and would have figured it out anyway. Better to come clean and take my lumps.

"Should I be worried?" Katie asked after letting me squirm through several minutes of silence.

"Absolutely not!" I said, finally looking up and meeting her eyes.

Katie finally nodded, smiled and stepped into my arms. She wrapped me up and held me tight.

"Good," she said. "But remember one thing. I can cut your balls off and feed them to the infected if you don't behave. Got it?"

"Yes, ma'am. Got it!" I said, smiling from ear to ear as I held her against me.

33

"Who is she?" Petty Officer Simmons asked her Lieutenant as she tweaked the photo.

The image was of Rachel, taken from a security camera at Tinker and wasn't the best quality. Captain Blanchard had been talking with Lieutenant Hunt and had gotten excited when he'd learned the NSA satellite had a facial recognition feature. He had quickly pulled images of Major Chase and Rachel from the security archives and sent them to Pearl Harbor.

"She's a civilian that was with the Army Major when their aircraft went down." Hunt answered, pointing at another monitor that displayed a slightly better photo of John. "The Army's trying to find them before they bug out for the Bahamas."

"Leave it to the Army to pick a tropical paradise," Jessica said as she worked on the pics.

"That from a woman stationed in Hawaii," Hunt said with a grin as he watched her work.

Jessica snorted, but kept her attention on the monitors. Soon she had the two photos cleaned up and cropped. A few more clicks and she had them uploading to the satellite. While the files were transmitting, she configured the software to limit its search area by using her mouse to draw a box that encompassed the eastern half of Oklahoma, then pinpointed the Osprey crash sight as the beginning scan location.

"Any idea how long this will take?" Hunt asked, watching over her shoulder.

"None," she answered. "I've dug into the system and normally it would process all the faces the satellite can see through servers at Fort Meade, but since there is no Fort Meade any more, all of the processing will have to take place on board the satellite."

"That's going to take forever," Hunt said.

"Maybe. Maybe not. We're focused in on a small geographical area, and there's not that many people left. Plus, I'm excluding everyone that is within the perimeter of Tinker. Figure if these two are on the base and the Army doesn't know about it, well... Sometimes the grunts aren't too bright."

The computer beeped as she finished speaking, indicating the two files had successfully uploaded to the satellite. A moment later the system notified her that the facial recognition process was running, searching for two targets. The process would continue to run until either locating both faces, or until Jessica told it to stop.

"Yep, it's not going to be fast." Jessica said, watching another monitor. "The bird's CPU just shot up to eighty percent utilization. That's facial recog causing that. Now we wait."

"What's the status of the surveillance of the Russians?" Hunt asked.

"We're filling up our hard drives with data, and there's a team from Naval Intelligence going through it. I have no idea beyond that. Don't speak or read Russian."

Hunt nodded and watched the monitors for a few moments before heading back to his station to call his counterpart in Intelligence. He had to brief Admiral Packard in a couple of hours and wanted to find out if there was anything noteworthy that had been gleaned from all the conversations and data transmissions the satellites were vacuuming out of the air.

"This is just some amazing shit," Lieutenant Richardson, duty officer at the Navy's Intelligence unit said on the phone when Hunt connected with him. "Why the hell the NSA wasn't sharing is frankly pissing me off. I'm sitting here right now reading a transcript of all of their C2 traffic for the past twenty-four hours. And that's just the tip of the iceberg. One of my analysts found out what happened to the Alaska. One of their Akulas, the Magadan, sank it."

"How the hell did they pull that off?" Hunt asked. "Those Akulas are almost thirty years old. The sonar suite on the Alaska should have heard it long before it got close enough to fire a torpedo."

"That's the sixty-four thousand dollar question, isn't it?" Richardson said. "As fascinating as this is, I don't imagine you called to just shoot the shit."

"No. I was going to ask if you had anything for me to include in my briefing for Admiral Packard, but now I think it would be better if you came with me." Hunt said.

"Thanks, but no thanks. Last thing I want to do is stand up in front of the old man. I've heard the stories about him taking people's heads off for not having all the answers, and we haven't even scratched the surface of all the data that's flowing in. I'll have my Senior Chief write something up for you and send it over. How soon do you need it?"

"Briefing is in two hours, and trust me, you'll want to be there. As soon as I start trying to tell him what you're doing the first thing he's going to ask is where you are. Do you want me to tell him you were too busy?" Hunt said.

"You're an asshole, you know that? Anyone ever told you that?" Richardson said sourly.

"Hey, it's us assholes that take care of everyone else. So, I'll see you at the Admiral's office in two hours?"

"Fuck you, Hunt. I'll be there, but if he climbs up my ass you're going to owe me big time!"

"Sir, we've got a hit!" Jessica interrupted Hunt before he could respond.

"Gotta run, Tom. See you in two." He said and slammed the phone down.

"Already?" He asked, standing and moving quickly to Jessica's station. "Which one?"

"The woman," she said, pointing at a monitor.

The screen was displaying two images arranged side by side. The left one was the original photo of Rachel that had been uploaded to the satellite. The one on the right was an incredibly crisp, high definition color shot taken from the satellite less than three minutes ago.

Rachel was sitting on the ground in the middle of what looked like a prairie. A dog and a man with black hair in a ponytail sat with her, three horses a few yards away. To their east the terrain became hilly before transitioning into a large series of canyons. Even though the photo was taken at night, her features were clearly visible, leaving no doubt the software had correctly identified her.

"Is the man our other target?" Hunt asked, realizing he wasn't before Jessica could answer.

"Wow, that thing takes some amazing shots," he said. "OK, get her coordinates to that Army Captain and keep looking for the Major."

34

After half an hour the dust had settled enough for me to enter the tunnel. Ten feet in, at the first bend, the passage was completely blocked by tons of rock and dirt that had fallen from the ceiling. Maybe a team of professional miners with the right equipment could have dug their way out, but I didn't see any way we would be going down that tunnel again.

Katie had followed me in, walking gingerly. She was barefoot and was OK moving around on the soft sand, but the floor was now littered with small, sharp rocks. Going back into the larger cavern I stood looking around. The walls and ceiling were solid, the only other opening the large crack from which water poured into the pool. At least we wouldn't die of dehydration.

"Did you bring anyone with you? Anyone looking for us?" Katie asked.

"Rachel and an Indian I met are up top, but even if they could fight their way past the females, I don't see how they could help us." I said after a moment.

"You found Rachel?" Katie sounded surprised.

"Just in time," I answered. "She was in bad shape from the heat."

"I was afraid she wouldn't make it." Katie said as I walked over to the edge of the pool. She walked up next to me and stood staring at the water. "What are you thinking?"

"I'm thinking that's a whole hell of a lot of water pouring out of that crack every minute, but this pool is staying at the same level. That means there's an opening somewhere under the surface where it's draining." I said.

"That's crazy," Katie said a moment later when she realized what I was talking about. "We have no way of knowing how long it stays below ground or where it goes."

"You have a better idea?" I asked. "I've always said I want to spend the rest of my life with you, but I'd like more time than we have if we just sit here and do nothing."

Katie opened her mouth to argue, but couldn't come up with anything. After a long moment she finally nodded.

"I should be the one to go," she finally said. "I'm the better swimmer and I know I can hold my breath longer than you can."

"We both go," I said quietly. "There won't be any coming back. Not against the current. One of us going alone won't do any good. The other will just be left standing here with no way of knowing if the other made it."

I turned and looked at her. I really didn't want to go in the water, into an underground river that led to God knows where. Being rushed along in the current we could be slammed into rocks and killed, or trapped in a narrow opening and drown. The river could run for miles before it surfaced again. The odds weren't good, but they were better than staying where we were. Sitting on our asses until the chamber became our tomb. Not how I wanted to go out. At least the water gave us a chance, regardless of how slim.

"Let's at least take another look around before we decide." Katie said, heading for the side wall. I watched her walk away, appreciating the view of her in the thong.

"Quit watching my ass and try to find a way out," she shouted over her shoulder.

"Really? How the hell did you know?" I asked, shaking my head and turning to the other wall.

"I know you better than you know yourself," she said. "Besides, you've been checking out my ass since the first time we met in that damn jungle."

I grinned, knowing she was right. Reaching the wall to the left of the waterfall, I slowly made my way along the base, looking carefully at every inch of the surface. Rough rock covered with phosphorescent lichen was all I found. Reaching the tunnel entrance I decided it wouldn't hurt to take another look.

The rock fall still blocked it and in frustration I raised my head and blew out a big breath, puffing my cheeks until I must have looked like a chubby baby. When I raised my eyes I saw a darker patch on the ceiling that I'd failed to notice before. Raising the rifle I peered through the night vision scope. My heart started beating faster when I saw that it was actually an opening in the ceiling, not just darker rock.

From where I stood it sure looked like there was some sort of tunnel that had either been created or revealed by the collapse. I moved around trying to see farther in, but couldn't get a better angle. The opening was at least ten feet off the floor, going straight up for a foot before turning towards the waterfall. But I couldn't tell if it was just a big chunk of rock missing or the start of an actual tunnel.

"Katie!" I called, nearly jumping out of my skin when she answered from right next to me.

"What did you find?" She asked, giggling at me.

"Take a look." I handed her the rifle and she looked through the scope.

"Give me a boost," she said after a few seconds, handing the rifle back to me.

I got the sling over my head, bent at the waist and formed a stirrup with my hands by lacing my fingers together. Katie put her foot in my hands and stepped up, balancing herself with a hand on top of my head.

"When we get out of here you need to shave this," she said, rubbing the stubble on my head.

"Been a little busy, and I'm not the only one that needs a razor," I said, after grabbing her legs to steady her as she stepped onto my shoulders.

"Since when did a little hair on my legs slow you down?" she teased, reaching into the opening and feeling around.

"I think it's a passage. Let's see how far it goes." Katie lifted her right foot and put it on my head, gaining another foot of elevation, then her weight was gone as she worked her way into the ceiling. The pressure made the gash on my head feel like it was being torn open, but I bit my lip and stood steady.

It didn't take long for her to lower herself back onto my shoulders. She squatted and I grabbed her waist, lifting her off of me and gently setting her on the ground. I was surprised when my fingertips almost touched each other when I held her around the middle.

"You've lost some weight," I said when her feet were back on the sand.

"Nice of you to notice," she said, stepping away from me and looking at the ceiling. "I'm pretty sure it's a tunnel. There was some airflow coming at me. Not a lot, but it was definitely there. Only one problem."

"What's that?" I asked.

"The opening is tight for me. No way will your over developed shoulders make it through. You'd get stuck like a cork in a bottle before you made it more than two feet." She said. I stood there looking up at the ceiling.

"I guess we try the water," Katie said, pulling my attention back down.

"No. You try the tunnel. It's better odds than the water." I shook my head for emphasis.

"And just why do you think that?" She asked, hands on her hips. Uh oh. I know that body language. "You're always more worried about me than yourself. We go together, or we don't go. That tunnel could narrow down before it goes ten feet. Any number of things could be wrong with it. So, knock your shit off. We go together and that's that."

I opened my mouth to protest, but Katie was having none of it. Before I could speak a word she stepped forward and wrapped her arms around me. She squeezed, hard, and after a moment I heard a quiet snuffle.

"I was sure you were either dead, or at best alive but lost to me forever. Now that I've got you there's not a chance I'm going off and leaving you. You're stuck with me, buster. So let's work on getting out of here together, or go sit down and wait to die. As long as we're together, I don't much care at this point."

What the hell do you say to that?

35

The water was cool as I waded in. The sand floor of the chamber sloped gradually into the pool and I wasn't submerged much beyond my waist after walking ten feet. Everything was strapped as tightly to me as Katie and I could get it. My big concern was the rifle sling that could snag on something and cause me to drown, but it was now under my vest and pulled as tight as possible.

Katie wasn't wearing enough clothing to have to worry about getting caught up on anything. She stood next to me, water to the bottom of her breasts. Reaching out I took her hand and squeezed it. She smiled at me and squeezed back, then jackknifed into the pool. Her bare ass broke the surface, quickly disappearing, then her feet came up and started kicking as she dove.

Taking two quick breaths, I gave her a moment to gain some space, drew the deepest breath I could and followed. There wasn't much light in the pool, but whatever it was that was growing on the cavern walls and giving us illumination was also floating in the water. It was slightly disorienting, but I focused on my wife's kicking feet and followed her deeper.

In only a few strokes I was beyond the sandy shelf we'd walked out on and was suddenly in the pull of the underground river. The current was strong, grabbing me and sucking me down. Every instinct in my body wanted to fight against it, but I knew this was exactly what I needed. Let the force of the water do the work. The harder I worked the sooner I'd need to take a breath.

There was a time in my life when I could hold my breath for four minutes. I was young, in incredible shape and hadn't ended most of my days with a margarita and a couple of cigarettes. Not that I wasn't in good shape now, but I knew I had two, maybe two and half, minutes at the most before I was in real trouble.

Katie, on the other hand, was part fish. She loved the water and could swim circles around me. As we were drawn deeper into the pool, moving faster as the current approached the opening where the water drained, I knew her odds of making it out alive were significantly better than mine. And I was OK with that. If this was where it ended, well, I'd made sure she at least had a fighting chance.

The small pieces of glowing matter were being pulled down with us and I realized they weren't living in the water but were caught by the current when they fell from the walls and ceiling. Though not much, they continued to give us a little light. Just enough for me to see Katie disappear into a large hole in the side of the pool. A moment later I was swept into the same tunnel.

I accelerated once in the tunnel, shoulders continually banging into the smooth rock walls. The constant flow of the water had smoothed the rock and for this I was grateful, otherwise I'd have been ripped to shreds by rough outcroppings. The impacts still hurt, but at least I wasn't being torn open, and hopefully neither was Katie who didn't have any clothing to protect her bare skin.

We rushed along and my lungs began to burn. I didn't even have a guess how long we'd been in the water, having forgotten to start counting when I took the big breath. At this point I guess it didn't really matter. I'd hold my breath until I couldn't, then I'd just be another piece of debris flushed out of the caverns.

It was completely dark now; the water apparently having destroyed whatever biological reaction was in the lichen that made it glow. There was no discernible difference between closing my eyes and having them open. The only way I knew Katie was still in front of me was the tunnel was too narrow for me to have passed her without knowing it. It was like what I imagined being flushed through a large pipe would be like.

Without light I couldn't see the bend coming, unexpectedly slamming into a smooth wall. Half the air in my lungs was knocked out of me and it took a concentrated effort to not inhale water. I was in trouble and I knew it.

Still being rushed along by the current I couldn't see anything. I'd lost half of my air supply, and the half I still had felt like it was turning to acid as my body screamed at me to take a breath. It didn't care that there was only water to breathe; it only knew that it was time for me to exhale the stale air and draw in fresh. Fighting the urge, I registered a moment of pain when my head struck rock as I was shot through another bend, then I blacked out and my body drew in a breath exactly like it's programmed to do.

I was no longer caught in dark water, hurtling along beneath the Oklahoma countryside. Warm sand was under me as I lay on my back. The sun was bright in my eyes and Katie was leaning over me, kissing me, wet hair hanging around my face. But something wasn't right. Had I been drinking? Everything was dulled, like I was experiencing it through the fog of too much alcohol.

Then my chest spasmed and I coughed. Strong hands rolled me onto my side and I coughed again, feeling water coming up my throat and being expelled out of my mouth. The coughing intensified, my throat burning as I continued to purge my lungs. After what seemed like an eternity, the urge to choke and cough eased and I rolled onto my back, gulping huge lungfuls of air.

"Welcome back," Katie said, leaning over me and wiping sand and spittle off my chin.

I looked up at her, then over her shoulder at the moon. It was almost painfully bright after the complete darkness of the underground river, and must have been what I thought was the sun. I was glad to touch the ground beneath me and find it really was warm sand.

"What happened?" I croaked, trying to sit up and sending myself into another coughing fit.

"You drowned," Katie said when the spasms subsided. "I didn't think I was going to get you back. You were out for a while."

"How long?" I asked between gasps of air.

"Don't know for sure when you got the water in your lungs, but I dragged your big ass out of the river at least five minutes ago." She said, her hand resting on the side of my face. "How are you feeling?"

"I've felt worse, but I can't remember when." I said.

"Well, brain damage after drowning is common." Katie said, looking intently into my eyes. She must have seen the panicked reaction she was hoping for as she began laughing at me a moment later.

"Bitch," I said in a hoarse whisper.

"You say that like it's a bad thing!" Katie said, leaning down and pressing her lips to my forehead. "And don't you dare scare me like that again."

I pulled her to me and we just rested for a few moments until all my synapses started firing again.

"Where are we?" I asked, sitting up.

"No idea," she said. "But we're out of the caverns, alive, and there aren't any infected around. Well, not that I had time to look, but we haven't been attacked."

I struggled with my vest and rifle, finally getting everything over my head. Trying to scan our surroundings, I cursed when I realized the night vision scope was damaged. It had apparently impacted a rock as it was bent at a severe angle, the lens at one end completely missing. Water ran out of it when I tilted the rifle. Great. The one advantage we had was gone.

Standing, I flipped the quick release levers on the scope mount and tossed it away as I surveyed the dark landscape around us. We were next to a small, lazy river, the water gurgling softly as it flowed around the roots of a couple of large trees. We were obviously back on the rolling plains, but where? I turned a couple of circles and was unable to spot the low hills where I'd left Rachel, Dog and Joe. Then I looked down and realized I was a good ten feet from the edge of the river.

"How the hell did you get me all the way up here?" I asked Katie, gesturing at the open sand that showed two clear drag marks left by my feet.

"I just pulled until you were out of the water," she said, seemingly noticing how far she'd dragged me for the first time.

"Ten feet? You know how much I weigh. How the hell…" I started to ask, then stopped.

The virus? The same way I suspected it was helping her heal, maybe it had made her stronger, just like the infected. Was that even possible? I wished Joe and Rachel were there for me to ask.

36

"Yes, sir. Receiving them now." Tech Sergeant Zach Scott said.

He was speaking to Captain Blanchard over an encrypted comm channel. Blanchard had been concerned that the Russians would intercept any radio traffic, so before the Bradley had left Tinker he'd had it equipped with one of the FSOC – Free Space Optical Communications – units that the Air Force had at Tinker.

The system uses lasers to digitally transmit voice and data. The unit on board the Bradley had locked onto the orbiting NSA satellite with its laser, as had Blanchard from the secure communications room at the Air Force base. The system was eavesdrop proof, as the only way to intercept the data stream was to physically interrupt the laser beam. If that happened the system would detect the intrusion and shut down.

"That's definitely her," Scott said when the image of Rachel taken by the satellite appeared on his screen. He clicked a couple of icons on the display, causing a terrain map to appear, the location of the Bradley and Rachel showing up as blue and green pulsing dots. A fat yellow line traced the system's recommended route and next to it the distance to target and several other pieces of data appeared.

"Any hit on the Major?" He asked.

"Nothing so far. I just spoke with the Petty Officer at Pearl that is running the system and she said we got very lucky to find Rachel this quickly. The satellite's search pattern was only on its third circuit out from the starting point when it found her.

"What she explained to me is that it starts at a central point, in this case the crashed Osprey, and searches progressively larger concentric circles until it finds a match. If he wasn't somewhere that the camera could see his face when it scanned the area he's in, we'll have to wait until it re-scans the same area." Blanchard said.

"OK, sir. We're fifteen minutes away from Rachel." Scott said. "How are conditions at Tinker?"

"The Marines are keeping the infected back, but the numbers are growing. The herds from Texas and Colorado are moving slightly faster than predicted and we're expecting the leading edges several hours earlier than the original model forecasted." Blanchard answered.

Scott stared at the screen for a moment, thinking. "Is there anyway for me to access the real time satellite feed?"

Blanchard was quiet for a moment, "Let me see what can be done, Tech Sergeant. I'll have to call Pearl. I don't have admin control, just access into the feed."

"Thank you, sir. Anything further?"

"Negative. Just get a move on. Your window to make it back before being completely cut off by a herd is shrinking fast. Good luck." Blanchard cut the connection, the system beeping softly to let Scott know the call had ended.

Scott shut down his end of the link and spent a moment looking through the system to find the commands he wanted. Locating what he hoped was the right icon he clicked on it and selected a couple of options from the window that popped open.

“Irina, check your screen. Do you have a map with a route highlighted?” He said over the intercom.

“Yes, I’ve got it. Is that where we are going?” She said a few moments later.

“That’s where Rachel is. We get her and hope the Major is somewhere close.” He answered.

Irina didn’t answer, but almost immediately the Bradley lurched forward as she gave it full throttle. Scott was thankful he was wearing a seatbelt or he would have been thrown to the floor and most likely skidded all the way to the back of the vehicle. He’d ridden with aggressive drivers before, but the Russian woman would put all of them to shame.

“You know this thing has more than two speeds, right?” He called over the intercom.

“What do you mean? There’s another gear?” She sounded hopeful of finding a way to go faster.

“No, thank God. What I mean is we don’t have to either be stopped or at full throttle.”

Scott's voice was choppy from the heavy vehicle bouncing across the prairie.

The ground looked nice and smooth in his periscope, but Irina seemed to have a knack for finding the roughest path possible. Despite his irritation, he couldn't help but smile as she started laughing at him.

"This is how we drive in Russia," Irina said when her laughter died down. "Didn't you ever wonder why we build everything so tough?"

Scott was shaking his head, trying to think of something to say to that when Igor called out over the intercom.

"Zombie!" He sounded delighted and a moment later the motors that rotated the gunner's turret whined.

"Nyet!" Scott shouted before Igor could start firing. "Irina, remind him to not start firing unless we absolutely have to. We need to save our ammo."

Irina began speaking in Russian, going back and forth with Igor for nearly a minute.

"He says you are still taking all the fun out of this," she finally said. "But he agrees with you and will not expend ammo until he has to."

"Tell him thanks," Scott said. "And remind him they're not zombies. There's no such thing. What's he going to see next? Bigfoot? Maybe Vampires?"

Irina translated. Igor was quiet for a moment, then said something in a slightly more excited tone. He could see Irina adjust one of her periscopes before answering in Russian.

"What's going on?" Scott asked, peering through his but seeing nothing.

"To our eleven," Irina said. "Twenty degrees above the horizon."

Scott swiveled his scope to slightly left of their direction of travel and elevated the objective. At first he thought it was a dust cloud, but it was moving too fast. The night vision was already activated, blurring then clearing as he spun the zoom wheel. He cursed when he got a clear view of a huge colony of bats completely obscuring the horizon.

Looking down he checked the navigation screen, which displayed a marker to indicate the direction his periscope was pointed. It was directly in line with the pulsing green dot that indicated Rachel's location.

"Irina, can this thing go any faster?"

37

Rachel sat in the darkness talking with Joe, unhappy that she hadn't gone with John into the caverns. Not that she really wanted to go underground, and she might not have been any help, but she didn't like being left behind. She knew how to fight, having proven that time after time, but he had insisted on going in alone. Of course, there was a big part of her that was relieved. Caves didn't hold fond memories for her.

While still in college a guy she was dating had talked her into going spelunking. He was one of those who was always looking for the next extreme adventure. Rock climbing, base-jumping, snorkeling with sharks; the list went on and on. Rachel had reluctantly agreed and after their last class on a Friday afternoon they'd loaded his Jeep and driven to Kentucky. He had heard of some caves that supposedly had awe-inspiring rock formations deep inside them.

They arrived well after dark, and despite Rachel's objections he had decided they should make their first venture inside before going to sleep. She had argued that it was night, getting mad when he'd laughed at her that it didn't matter underground if the sun was shining or not. She almost hadn't gone in, frightened by the cave and more than a little pissed at his attitude, but she didn't like to be left behind.

Getting in had been simple enough. A steep cut in the ground led to the first chamber, and they slid down a rope he secured to the Jeep's front bumper. Once inside, Rachel had to admit the view was amazing. Mineral studded stalagmites and stalactites had met in the middle and created massive columns that supported a roof as high as a cathedral. The translucent calcium glowed under their lights, flecks of what looked like diamonds and gold embedded deep inside and reflecting back at them.

Half an hour after entering the cave they had moved through several chambers, and that was when Rachel's light went out. Her boyfriend had cursed, suddenly realizing that he'd forgotten to charge them before leaving Atlanta. Knowing it was only minutes before his light would die as well, he'd turned and hurried Rachel towards the entrance they'd used. They'd made it across half of one chamber when his light shut down.

They had continued on in the Stygian darkness. Their progress was painfully slow and soon they were arguing. Distracted, he had stepped without checking his footing. Instead of the expected smooth floor he stepped into a small hole. Rachel clearly heard his leg snap a moment before he started screaming in pain.

"What did you do?" Joe asked.

"I left him there," Rachel said, scratching Dog's ears and smiling at the shocked expression on Joe's face. "I made my way back to the entrance, climbed the rope and went for help. There wasn't any cell coverage out there and I had to drive thirty miles to the closest town. They finally pulled him up about noon the next day."

"Was he OK?"

"I guess he'd gotten really scared, trapped in there all night. It took me a long time to make my way out, then by the time I got back with help he'd been stuck for hours. Alone in the dark. He thought I'd deliberately taken my time to punish him and he said some pretty nasty things. So, when they took him away in the ambulance I jumped in his Jeep and drove back to Atlanta. Left it outside his apartment and never saw him again."

"And now you're mad at John for making you stay behind? I'd think you'd be grateful." He said.

They sat there for a long time, each of them constantly scanning the area behind the other. Dog lay stretched out between them, seemingly asleep but his ears remained at full attention. Rachel told him her carefully edited story, then watched the pain in his eyes as Joe talked about having to shoot his wife after she turned.

"So, this Terminator virus. You really think that could work?" Rachel asked.

"Yes, I do." He said.

"How quickly would it work?"

"You mean how fast would the infected die?" Rachel nodded her head. "That I can't tell you without some testing. It could be as fast as twenty-four hours, or it could take days or even weeks. No one knows how strong these things immune systems are, but I suspect they're significantly enhanced. Maybe it wouldn't work because of that? I can't tell you without being in a lab and having some test subjects."

"Could this be done at your lab in Oklahoma City?" Rachel asked, forcing herself to suppress the hope that was growing inside her.

"It could, sure. Why?"

"And you could do it?" Rachel asked.

"Maybe. I've done some very basic work like this, but nothing nearly as complex. You aren't thinking about heading to the city, are you?" He said.

"Not without John, no. Is there anyone still at the lab that has done something like this?"

"There's one guy, Rick Kanger. He's the one that was talking about it in the first place. He used to be with USAMRIID. Retired and working on a second pension. Most of what he did for the Army was classified, but the stuff that isn't is scary enough." Joe was referring to the US Army Medical Research Institute of Infectious Diseases.

Rachel sat in the dark and thought. She understood enough about how viruses worked to believe that what Joe was talking about could potentially destroy all of the infected and return the world to the survivors. Not that there were many of those outside of Russia, but there were some. And the last she'd heard there was no infection in Hawaii or Australia.

That gave her hope that there were even more geographically isolated locations on the globe where the virus hadn't reached. Destroying it before it could spread any more wouldn't bring back the billions that had died, but it was at least hope for those still fighting to survive.

Now she just needed John to come back. She didn't have a watch to check, but knew it had been several hours since he'd gone in. Should she be worried yet? Of course she should. He was in danger the moment he stepped inside, but should she be concerned that he wasn't going to come out?

Rachel had no doubt that he wasn't coming out without Katie. However long that took, and whatever he had to do. If she were alive, he'd get her. If she wasn't, he'd probably die in his efforts to kill every infected in the caverns. Knowing he'd do the same for her should have eased the pain of her broken heart, but it didn't help.

Dog suddenly raised his head and growled. Rachel and Joe instantly got to their feet and raised their rifles in the direction Dog was facing. There was a low hill in that direction, separating them from the first canyon, but neither of them could see any danger. Rachel had John's M4 with a night vision scope and she raised it to check the area.

She saw nothing as she slowly scanned the slope of the hill closest to them, then higher to check the horizon. Still nothing. Dog growled again, stepping closer and pressing his body against Rachel's leg. She glanced over at Joe without lowering the rifle, then turned her head to look at the horses when she saw where his attention was.

All three animals had their heads up, ears pulled stiffly to the front as they faced the same direction as Dog. One of them snorted, then whinnied quietly.

"What the hell?" Joe asked her.

"I think I know," Rachel said, raising the rifle to look above the horizon at the night sky. She could see a faint rippling that looked like distortion in the scope's optics, but knew it wasn't.

"Bats," she said.

"Bats? Sure, we've got bats around here but they don't bother... oh, shit. The virus?"

"Don't know, for sure. We saw razorbacks that were infected. Ran across about a million bats in Texas that we suspected were, but nothing definitive." Rachel said, still watching the sky through the scope.

"John mentioned that. Are they getting any closer?"

"Can't tell for sure," Rachel said, placing her hand on Dog's neck when he growled again.

"Maybe it's a good sign," Joe said, a hopeful note in his voice. "Maybe they got disturbed because John is down there in the caves kicking ass."

"Maybe," Rachel said after a long moment. "But I'm pretty sure they're coming this way, and I don't think it's a good idea to be out in the open."

Joe nodded, heading for the horses. "About a mile west of here is an old shack. Nothing but some walls and a roof, but if they are infected it will give us some shelter."

It took them less than a minute to be ready to go, Rachel swinging onto Horse's back on her first try. Joe led the way, urging them into a run.

Dog ran behind them, but he couldn't match the speed of the horses' longer legs.

A breeze had been blowing from out of the southeast all night, but had been steadily picking up until it was a strong wind. As he ran, Dog was bombarded with a thousand different scents, his brain automatically cataloging them. Most were just miscellaneous smells, but some were recognized as food, water, danger and pack.

To his canine mind, pack was family, and when the faint scent he knew as John reached his sensitive nose he slowed. The pack mate in front of him was quickly drawing away, but the scent of the pack leader was definitely to his left.

Coming to a stop, Dog watched Rachel, Joe and the horses continue to race across the prairie for a few moments. She was escaping the menace he could smell on the wind, but the alpha's scent was in the same direction as a strong odor of danger. Turning directly into the wind, Dog broke into a run, racing across the dark plains like a phantom in the night.

38

Irina kept the throttle wide open, the Bradley roaring along. The heavy rubber treads were throwing up a rooster tail of dirt and grass in their wake, leaving a trail that a blind man could follow. Occasionally she would turn slightly to adjust their heading, keeping the heavy vehicle on the computer generated route, but did so without any lessening of pressure on the accelerator.

Driving with only the periscope to see through was something that took some getting used to. As Scott suspected she had trained on a similar system used by the Russian military, but it had been a lot of years ago. Regardless, she was getting accustomed to the limited field of view, and kept their speed up. Barring driving off a cliff or into a deep river or lake, there wasn't much that could happen to them inside the armored hull.

Scott kept his eyes on the bats, trusting that Irina didn't need him to help pick out a path to follow across the terrain. Quickly glancing down at the navigation display he cursed upon seeing that the little flying beasts would be over Rachel's location before their arrival. He noted that Igor and Irina were having a discussion in Russian, but had gotten used to it and blocked it out.

“Igor says he’s picking up something on thermal. About a mile ahead, thirty degrees right.” Irina said over the intercom.

Scott took his attention off the bats, swiveling his periscope and enabling the thermal imager. Initially all he could see was a blob that was hotter than its surroundings. Zooming, the image resolved into two human forms, standing close together. Switching back to night vision he could see a small, rickety shack.

“At our three o’clock,” Irina said. “Igor says he sees horses running west.”

Scott turned and spotted the animals, streaking across the plains to the southwest. Remembering something from the satellite image he took his attention away from the scope and worked on the display. When the picture of Rachel came up he expanded the field of view, seeing three horses standing a few yards away from her.

“See the small shack, Irina?” He said on the intercom, focusing the periscope’s thermal vision back on it.

"Da," she said, uncharacteristically speaking to him in her native tongue.

"That's where they are. Go there." Scott said.

The Bradley swayed on its suspension as Irina adjusted their direction of travel. Scott took a look at the bats, relieved to see that they seemed to have changed direction. He kept watch on them for a few moments, looking at them with the thermal vision.

The swarm, or flock, or whatever the hell they were called was large, and they appeared to be shifting to a more northerly course. Back to night vision he checked the shack, noting a lone tree bending sharply in the direction the bats were adopting. The wind! It was pushing them onto a new course!

Shifting his view back to the bats he activated the Bradley's laser targeting system. Almost immediately it started displaying information about their distance, their direction of travel and several other data points that he didn't understand. What he did learn was that his visual estimation was accurate. They were turning and flying to the northwest, going with the wind.

Irina slowed as they approached the shack, coming to a stop a few yards from the rough, wooden door. She hit a switch and bright headlights came on, illuminating the rickety structure. Looking through his periscope, Scott could see the entire building swaying in the wind. It looked like it could collapse at any moment.

Releasing his seat harness, Scott moved around the tight space into the passenger area. Telling Irina to have Igor keep an eye on things with the turret mounted chain gun, he hit the button to lower the vehicle's rear ramp. With a whine it started moving down, the wind immediately finding the opening and blowing dust into his face.

Squinting, he strode down the ramp and moved into the light at the front of the vehicle. From above and behind him he heard a faint whine from the turret motors as Igor aligned the chain gun with the shack's front door. They were fairly sure Rachel was one of the forms inside that had been seen on thermal imaging, but Scott was happy to have Igor's itchy trigger finger ready in case it was someone or something else.

"Rachel? It's Tech Sergeant Scott," he shouted over the rushing noise of the wind.

A moment later the door opened and Rachel stepped out, a tall Indian hesitantly following her. She shielded her eyes against the glare of the headlights, then Irina shut them off and all of them were momentarily blinded as they waited for their eyes to adjust to the darkness.

"There's a whole swarm of bats coming," Rachel said, walking up to Scott and looking over her shoulder at the horizon.

"Saw them, but the wind is pushing them away from us. I was hoping the Major was with you." Scott said, looking pointedly at Joe.

"There are some caverns a couple of miles from here. He went in to get Katie several hours ago."

"What's Katie doing – never mind. Time for that later. Who's this?" He asked, nodding his head at Joe.

Rachel made a quick introduction and stepped closer to Scott. "Did you see Dog? He was with us when we started riding for the shack, but hasn't shown up yet."

Scott shook his head before activating the intercom he was still connected to. “Irina, ask Igor to scan for Dog.”

He heard her relay his request in Russian, then the turret began moving as Igor used the thermal targeting system to survey the area.

“You need to take Joe back to Tinker,” Rachel said. “He’s a virologist and has an idea the Colonel needs to hear.”

“No way he’s a virologist. Really?” Scott blurted.

“Fuck you, white man!” Joe bristled. “You think I can’t have an education because I’m an Indian?”

Scott barked out a laugh. "Relax, dude. I don't give a shit if you're Indian or not. I just can't believe that we find the last guy alive in the middle of nowhere at the end of the world and he happens to be a fucking virologist. What are the chances? It's like something out of a third rate zombie novel."

“Jesus Christ!” Rachel said sharply before Scott could say anything more. “Both of you shut the hell up for a minute!”

Scott stood there grinning, Joe breathing heavy, still not sure if he'd been insulted or not.

"Yes, he's a virologist, and he's a hell of a lot smarter than you or me. So, you need to get him to the Colonel." She said to Scott, glaring at him before turning her gaze on Joe. "And you. That virus doesn't give a shit if you're white or red. Park the fucking over-sensitive bullshit and see what you can do about saving those of us that are left."

"You gotta admit, dude. The ponytail and rifle in your hand don't exactly fit the image anyone is going to have when you tell them you're a scientist. Maybe gain some weight, lose your hair and get a pair of glasses." Scott still had a shit-eating grin on his face.

Joe finally relaxed a little, nodding his acceptance of Scott's comment.

"OK, can we all play nicely?" Rachel looked back and forth between them with her hands on her hips.

"Yes, ma'am," Scott said, a moment later Joe echoing him.

"Good. Now, did I hear you say Irina and Igor are in that tank? Can they see Dog?" Rachel asked.

Scott waved them to follow, walking to the ramp. He led the way inside, hitting the button to raise the ramp and cut off the dust storm that was blowing in the opening once the three of them were inside. Igor looked down from the gunner's seat, smiled and nodded at Rachel.

"No sign of Dog," Irina said, working her way back to where they stood hunched over. "There are some infected moving around half a mile to the north, but Igor doesn't see any sign of him."

"OK, where did the horses go?" Rachel asked. "I'm going to go look for Dog and wait for John. You need to get Joe back to Tinker."

"That may be a problem," Scott said. "There are herds closing in. We got out ahead of them to come find you and the Major. The base is being evacuated. Going to be something like thirty million infected arriving any time now, then a whole hell of a lot more in another day or two."

Rachel was stunned. Thirty million? She couldn't even grasp a herd of infected that large.

"But what was the plan? How were you going to get back when you found us?"

"Martinez. Figured we could find a plane or something and she'd fly us in. We've still got time to make the last flight out." Scott said.

"She didn't make it," Rachel said softly.

"What?" Scott was stunned. "What do you mean she didn't make it?"

"Roach shot her when we were getting away from the casino. After the crash we were taken by a group of infected, but she must have been dying. They left her behind in a river. Her body was floating downstream the last I saw of her." Rachel reached out and touched Scott's arm. "I'm sorry."

Scott stood mute, staring at her. He couldn't believe Martinez was gone. She'd always seemed like one of those people that nothing could stop. And what the hell were the infected doing? Taking prisoners?

"Scott!" Rachel said, snapping him out of his reverie. "Can you still get back onto Tinker? Can you get Joe to the Colonel?"

"Hold on," Scott said, moving to the vehicle commander's chair.

It took a couple of minutes for him to establish a link with the FSOC system, then several more to reach Captain Blanchard. He filled him in on their status and asked about the situation at the base. They talked for a short time then he held a headset out to Rachel.

"The Colonel wants to speak with you," he said.

"Hello?" Rachel said, adjusting the microphone in front of her mouth.

"Ms. Miles. Good to hear your voice." She recognized Crawford's baritone. "Tell me what your idea is."

Rachel started speaking, relaying her discussion with Joe to the Colonel. As she talked she saw amazement and hope flicker across both Scott and Irina's faces. Crawford listened without interrupting. When she was finished he asked a few questions, then she could hear him turn to someone, Captain Blanchard she assumed, and tell him to start looking for a scientist named Rick Kanger.

"Tech Sergeant, are you still on?" Crawford asked.

"Yes, sir."

"That virologist you have with you is now to be considered a high value asset. Do not let him out of your sight."

"Yes, sir." Scott acknowledged, looking around at Joe who glared back at him.

"Very good. Here's Captain Blanchard. He'll coordinate getting you back to Tinker."

39

Dr. Rick Kanger stood in the base commander's office at Tinker Air Force Base, listening to an abbreviated version of the conversation between Colonel Crawford and Rachel. The Colonel spoke quickly, referring to notes as he talked. He was grateful that, unlike so many science professionals, the man standing in front of him didn't feel the need to constantly correct his layman's terminology.

"The question, Doctor, is can it be done?" Crawford asked when he ran out of notes.

"Of course it can," Kanger smiled. "With the right people, the right facility, equipment and enough time and test subjects."

"That's not what I wanted to hear," the Colonel grumbled, frowning.

"You have to understand, this isn't like baking a cake. This is creating a new virus designed to target a specific DNA signature and ignore everything else. At the same time we would have to build in... well, let me put it this way. Viruses mutate. All the time. Creating a virus to kill the infected and preventing it from becoming just another plague that would wipe out the remnants of the human race, well…" he held his hands out to the side and shrugged his shoulders.

"Can you do it?" Crawford asked, irritation showing.

"Yes, I can." Kanger answered after a long pause. "But it won't be quick. And I'll need a proper facility and qualified help. You said Joe Revard is on his way?"

"He is, as well as a young woman who is a third or fourth year medical student." Blanchard answered.

Kanger frowned, but didn't complain. He was too practical to expect the Army to have a team of experienced viral researchers available after all that had happened.

"What about a facility? Can you get me back to the University?" He asked, then nodded in thought when Blanchard told him the lab building in downtown Oklahoma City had burned.

"OK then," he said, rubbing his stubbly chin. "Other than here, there's the CDC, USAMRIID,

BioGenesis in Chicago and the Allen Institute in Seattle. Any of those still standing?"

"CDC and USAMRIID are gone," Crawford said. "Captain?"

Blanchard sat down in front of his laptop and began working. It took him several minutes during which time Kanger grew uncomfortable under Colonel Crawford's gaze.

"Where in each city, Doctor?" Blanchard finally asked.

Kanger rattled off location information. He didn't have precise street addresses for either facility, but he knew enough to help Blanchard zoom in on the general area. Several clicks and minutes later he turned back to face the room.

"The whole area in Chicago has burned. Nothing but rubble. The facility in Seattle is on a lakeshore and looks to be intact. Of course I have no way of knowing what the conditions are inside, but at least the building is intact and looks to be secure." He said.

"What about infected in the city?" Crawford asked.

"There's some, but at least the general area appears clear, sir." Blanchard answered, leaning forward to peer closer at the display. "Large herds heading east, crossing mountains, The Cascades I believe, but there's still infected in the city."

Colonel Crawford stood thinking, starting to reach for a satellite phone when he was interrupted by an Air Force Security Forces Sergeant with news that one of the crop dusters being used to battle the herds had crashed and the volume of infected at the fence was growing.

"Better warn Sergeant Scott," Crawford said to Blanchard. "I'm going to call the Admiral and see what he can do to secure the facility in Seattle."

“Like hell I will!” Rachel said, anger boiling over. “I’m not going anywhere until I know what happened to Dog, John and Katie!”

Scott sighed in exasperation, looking around the cramped interior of the Bradley for support. Igor’s face was impassive, as he didn’t understand what was being said. Joe just glared back at him. Irina gave him a sympathetic look and stepped forward.

“You heard what he said,” she gestured at Joe. “He needs...”

“He sure as hell doesn’t!” Rachel shouted, tears starting to run down her cheeks. “I’m just a goddamn medical student. Not a virologist. There’s nothing I can do that half a dozen people at Tinker can’t. Now open that damn hatch and let me out!”

“She’s right,” Joe said, interjecting before emotions ran any higher. “Any of the doctors at the base can help.”

"Thank you!" Rachel said, glaring at the surrounding faces. "Now open the goddamn door!"

She started to move forward, intending to push past Scott and Igor and press the button to lower the ramp, but pulled up short when Igor held up a big hand like a stop sign. Rachel balled her hands into fists, ready to fight, but Igor stalled her by holding up a single finger for her to wait. He fired off some rapid Russian as he worked his large frame into the gunner's seat.

"He says give him a moment to check the area," Irina said.

Rachel sighed, nodding but not relaxing. Igor pressed his face to the periscope, flipped a couple of switches and started the turret rotating slowly.

"Govno," he said after a few moments of looking.

"Shit," Irina translated when everyone turned and looked at her.

Scott quickly moved to the commander's chair and peered into his scope. He scanned around the exterior of the Bradley for a moment.

"Shit is right," he finally said. "Infected all around us."

"Bullshit!" Rachel said. "Let me see!"

She pushed forward, nearly knocking Scott out of the way to get to the periscope. He had been telling the truth. Hundreds, if not thousands, of infected were all around them. Primarily females, but she could see several males in the small herd. They had zeroed in on the sound of the Bradley's idling diesel, the occupants unable to hear their fists pounding on the armor plated exterior.

"That's it. We're going to Tinker like the Colonel ordered." Scott said.

Rachel whirled on him, but she didn't know what to say. If she'd been outside like she had wanted, the herd would have run her down and killed her. Well, maybe captured like the small group had, but she wouldn't be any better off.

"Can we at least head east first? See if we can find John or Dog?" She asked, unhappy with the pleading tone that was in her voice.

"Do you think that's a good idea?" Scott asked gently. "You know the infected are going to follow us. We might drag them right to where he is."

Rachel hung her head, shaking it. A tear splashed onto the steel decking by her feet.

"Let me get you and Joe to Tinker," Scott said. "I'll fuel up and come back out. I'll keep looking until I find them."

"You'll miss the evacuation. You'll be stuck here." Rachel said, sniffing back tears.

"Not a big deal. Never did care for the tropics anyway." Scott shrugged.

"I too help," Igor said after Irina translated for him.

Rachel looked at the two men. Looked into their eyes and recognized the same driving force she'd seen in John's eyes. The same single-minded determination to succeed at all costs. Finally she nodded, dropping onto one of the troop carrier seats and staring at the floor.

"Irina, let's get moving." Scott said softly.

She looked at Rachel for a moment before turning and slipping into the driver's seat. Scott had already had the system generate a route that would take them back to Tinker, sending it to Irina's navigation screen. Glancing at the display, she raised her head and pressed her face to the periscope, took a quick look and spun the Bradley 180 degrees. Properly aligned, she goosed the throttle and the diesel engine bellowed as the thirty-three ton vehicle began crushing infected under its treads.

Scott and Igor had gotten used to Irina's driving, both men securing their harnesses just in time to keep from being thrown out of their seats. Rachel and Joe, not expecting the violence of the maneuvers, slid across several seats and barely caught themselves before they would have been thrown to the floor and pinned against a bulkhead.

As the Bradley came up to speed the ride was bone jarringly rough, but Rachel was able to muscle herself into a seat and secure a harness. She shot a look at the back of the Russian woman's head, not sure that she hadn't been looking for a little revenge for Rachel having punched her in the eye when they were in Texas.

The ride didn't get any better as they roared across the Oklahoma prairie. The terrain was slightly rolling, the vehicle lifting on its suspension every time they crested a rise. But what goes up must come down, and when something as heavy as the Bradley comes down it fully compresses its suspension as well as the spines of all the passengers.

They traveled like that for close to an hour, cutting across open plains and cultivated fields. The only thing that Irina slowed for was when they had to ford small streams. Bradleys can ford water up to four feet deep, but the way she blasted through, even after slowing, everyone on board was willing to bet all the water in each stream had been splashed well out of its banks.

The closer they came to Oklahoma City, the more small herds of infected they encountered. All of them were heading south, zeroing in on the Air Force base. When she could do so without slowing, Irina would swerve and run down groups of males, grinding their bodies into the dry soil with the heavy tracks. Females stayed out of her path, using their speed and agility to avoid the rolling monster.

Nearing the half way mark on the computer generated route, Scott struggled against the pounding motion to reach the communications panel when a red light began blinking. A coded signal had been broadcast to alert him to check in over the FSOC.

“Slow down,” he called over the intercom. “We’ve got a comm request and there’s no way we’ll stay locked on the satellite the way we’re bouncing all over the place.”

“Russian technology could,” Irina said, but slowed anyway, reducing the violent shaking and vibration to just an occasional hard bump.

Scott ignored her comment and in moments had a green light on his display indicating successful laser lock. He switched his headset from the intercom to external comms and clicked the icon to connect.

“Bad news,” Captain Blanchard said when the circuit came up. “One of the two planes the Marines were using to disperse fuel oil to fight the infected has crashed. We were barely keeping up with them with two aircraft. Now, with one, they've been able to move forward and are piling up against the fence."

"Is the evacuation in jeopardy?" Scott asked.

"We've got some concerns, but that's not why I'm calling. Unless you have a pilot with you and can find a plane or helo, you're not getting back onto the base. Infected are stacked ten deep around the entire perimeter. We can't clear enough to open a gate without being overrun." Blanchard said.

"Got no pilot, sir. What's our alternative? Can you send a helo?" Scott asked.

"Negative. We've got every air asset that's not already configured for shipping in use to hold the fence."

Scott momentarily switched to intercom, "Irina. Stop." Quickly he switched back to the comm channel.

"...found Dr. Kanger." Blanchard had continued speaking, unaware Scott had dropped off for a moment. "Getting into the virology lab at the University is a no go. Too many infected in the area and on the way, plus we flew a drone over for a look and there's been a fire."

41

"Where now?" Katie asked, looking up into my eyes.

"First things first," I said. "You need something on your feet before we go trekking anywhere."

I sat down on the ground and pulled off my vest and shirt. Drawing my knife, I cut the lower foot off the heavy fabric, handing the remainder of the shirt to her.

"Put that on. It will give you a little protection." I said, starting to work on the material I'd already cut off.

Katie held the shirt at arms length, pinched between two fingers and wrinkled her nose.

"It's covered in blood and smells like an elephant's ass." She said.

"Suck it up, buttercup. You need it." I said without looking up from my work.

Bending at the river's edge, Katie rinsed the shirt as best she could. Reaching behind her back she unhooked the tattered bra, letting it drop to the ground, then pulled the shirt over her head. It was several sizes too large, fitting like a poncho or a tent, but it covered her skin and fell below her hips. I looked up once she had it on and couldn't help but grin. I've always been a sucker for a pretty woman wearing my shirt.

"Just relax, sweetie," she smiled. "Until you find a razor and a bar of soap you're not getting any."

"Not what I was thinking," I pouted, finishing up with my knife. "Have a seat and give me your feet."

"I'm fine. Really." She protested.

"OK, all kidding aside," I said, looking up at her. "You're in my world now. I was out fighting in the field while you were sitting on your cute little ass in an air-conditioned cubicle at Langley. That means you don't argue. I'm not doing this because I love you, I'm doing it so you don't slow us down."

She stood there for a long moment, hands on her hips. Staring down at me I could tell she had several things she wanted to say, probably none of them very nice, but I know my wife. Practical almost always wins out. With an exaggerated sigh she plopped down on the sand and stuck her legs out, resting her bare feet in my lap.

I had cut the fabric into two pieces, a long strip removed from the edge of each. Doubling the material, I wrapped a piece around each foot. While Katie held them in place I used the thin strips I'd cut to bind the material tightly.

"You made me a pair of moccasins. How sweet!" She couldn't resist saying something sarcastic. Somehow I managed to keep my mouth shut. Anything I said at this point would only encourage her.

"OK," I said, resting my hands on top of her ankles. "We're going to follow this river upstream until we get back to the canyons. Once we're there we'll work our way west until we find Rachel. She's waiting with the Indian I told you about and they've got an extra horse."

"What then?" Katie asked, pulling her feet out of my lap and standing up.

"Back to Tinker," I said. "Before sundown yesterday I saw a big dust cloud to the northeast. Had to be a big herd moving this way. Last thing we want is to get caught out here on the plains with a few thousand females after us."

Climbing to my feet I turned slightly to rub a shoulder sore from impacts with the rock in the underground river. As I turned I caught a flash of movement out of the corner of my eye. There had been no warning we were being attacked, but fortunately that glimpse made me lean back as a female flew at me.

Instead of a full on body tackle she grabbed at me as I made her miss. Well, mostly miss. She grazed me hard enough to cause me to spin, but I maintained my balance even though I was staggered back a couple of feet. The knife I'd just used to fashion Katie's footwear was still in my hand, but I was turned wrong to use it effectively.

Kicking out, I caught the female solidly in the ribs, sending her tumbling across the sand and into the water. Knowing that where there's one there's usually more, I spun in time to be tackled by two more. We fell to the ground in a tangle of limbs and as one lunged for my throat I grabbed her long, dirty hair and stabbed into her neck.

Rolling, I grappled with the other one, getting a knee on her chest but unable to strike with the Ka-Bar before the first one that had missed her initial tackle slammed into my side. We rolled and I pushed her back with my knife hand and hit her hard in the face with three quick blows. With each impact I felt bone and cartilage break, but she wasn't deterred in the least.

Pushing hard, I got her off of me just in time to fend off the other one. Spinning, I slammed an elbow into her temple, sending her crashing to the ground. Changing the knife to my other hand I stepped in, batted the first female's hands aside and stabbed directly into her open mouth. Pulling the blade out, I kicked her corpse away, spun and fell on the stunned female that was still lying on the sand.

Knee in the middle of her back I slid the knife into the base of her skull. The body twitched once before going still. Leaping to my feet, I turned to face the direction the attack had come from. No other infected were in sight. Katie had snatched my rifle up and was watching for other females while I'd dealt with these three.

Grabbing my vest off the ground I slipped into it and accepted my rifle when she held it out. We didn't need to say anything to each other. We turned and started trotting north along the edge of the small river that had carried us out of the caverns. After no more than a hundred yards the dizziness and nausea hit me. Hard.

Stumbling to my knees I retched, but there was nothing to come up. Even on all fours the world around me spun and tilted and I lost what little balance I had and fell onto my side. I lay there panting, the world still twirling around me, Katie leaning over me with a concerned expression.

"What's wrong?" She asked.

I tried to focus, but I was seeing at least three of her and each of them were in motion.

"Bad concussion in the crash," I gasped between racking spasms as the vertigo continued. "Hit my head again in the water."

"Close your eyes and lie flat, face down." Katie said, pushing on my body to get me in the position she wanted.

I'm pretty sure I resisted, wanting to curl into a ball until the world decided to stop snapping back and forth, but she didn't give up until I was stretched out on my stomach. It helped a little, but even with my eyes closed I still felt like I was being spun in a sadistic amusement park ride.

Katie's hand was on the back of my neck, gently stroking my skin when I heard the scream. Female infected, and she was close. Too close. I pushed up onto my knees, immediately wobbling and falling onto my side. Another scream and I thought I could see movement in the dark, but since I couldn't focus my eyes on anything I wasn't sure.

Moments later there was the sound of bodies striking, a cry sounding that I recognized as Katie. Forcing down the rising sickness I pushed back onto my knees, then my feet, drawing the Kukri. I stood there, swaying like a drunken sailor. Katie was on the ground, fighting with a female and four more were only yards away.

Adrenaline is an amazing hormone. In small amounts it helps our bodies regulate all kinds of things, chief among them being our blood pressure. When our brain recognizes danger our adrenal glands go into overdrive, producing massive amounts, which is pumped by a pounding heart through the blood stream to our brains, muscles and organs.

When that happens, humans are able to ignore many injuries and illnesses. Not indefinitely, but the body's fight or flight mechanism is a wonder of nature. As my brain responded to the threat, my heart rate spiked, pushing freshly released adrenaline throughout my circulatory system. I don't know if the vertigo went away, or my aching brain was able to compensate for the disorientation because of the hormonal surge, but I steadied and leapt forward to meet our attackers.

I collided with the closest female with a shout of exertion, stopping her cold and slamming her body to the ground. I stomped on her head as I slashed the Kukri at the next one to arrive. I felt the skull of the one on the ground shatter and collapse under my boot's sole as the blade entered the second female's body.

With a scream I slashed up, opening her from navel to throat and continued with my momentum, spinning an elbow into the back of her head hard enough to snap her neck. I let the spin take me all the way around, building speed and aiming for the neck of the third female as she charged in from my left. If I had connected there was enough force behind the strike to have cleanly decapitated her, but at the last second she ducked under the swing and the Kukri whistled harmlessly through the air over her head.

If I had tried to stop my motion and reset for another attack I would have been vulnerable as she leapt at me. Instead I let the spin take me, twisting my body as she connected, and threw her ten feet across the ground. As she tumbled I met the last one. Kukri on the far side of my body I leaned towards her as she lunged and brought my left fist up in a wicked uppercut.

Her teeth clacked together hard enough to break. Her head snapped back and all forward momentum stopped, then her eyes rolled up in their sockets and she crumpled to the ground. Turning in time to face the one I'd sent sprawling, I let the Kukri fall to the ground as I reached out and grabbed her upper arms while she was in mid-leap. Lifting, I pressed her over my head and let myself drop back.

Falling to a seated position on the sand I drove her head first into the ground between my knees, her neck snapping loudly. The body slammed against me as it fell and I shoved it away as I snatched up the Kukri and scrambled to the female I'd knocked out. I buried the blade in the back of her skull. Spinning, I rushed to help Katie as I saw her rolling on the ground, grappling with a female.

Before I could cover the distance between us a dark shape streaked in from seemingly nowhere and slammed into the infected, ripping her off of Katie and tumbling towards the river. I dashed to Katie's side as Dog pinned the female and after a brief battle, ripped her throat out.

Katie was on her feet before I got to her, holding her hand out to me. As I reached for her I felt the dizziness return. Fight over, the adrenaline was dissipating out of my system and by the time I touched Katie's hand I had to drop to my knees to keep from falling flat on my face. She knelt beside me, wrapping an arm around my shoulders to stop me from pitching over and Dog trotted up, sticking his bloody muzzle in my face.

42

"We're going where?" Rachel asked when Scott's conversation with Captain Blanchard ended.

"Ponca City," he said, staring at the navigation display to his right.

"Northwest of here," Joe said, moving to look over Scott's shoulder. "Why are we going there?"

"Your lab at the University looks like it's damaged, plus there's about a billion infected heading for Oklahoma City." He said, scrolling the map. Finding the small town, he selected it with the mouse and the system generated a route for them to follow. "Irina, new destination on your screen."

A minute later they all held on as she whipped them through a turn and accelerated along their new route. Swiveling his seat around, Scott faced the two passengers.

"They located Dr. Kanger. He says, with both of you helping, he can engineer a Terminator virus. But he needs the right facility, and with the one at the University out of commission they didn't have many to choose from. He settled on one in Seattle called..." Scott paused to look at his notes. "The Allen Institute. Ever heard of it?"

"Yes," Joe said without hesitation. "Paul Allen started it."

"The Paul Allen that helped found Microsoft? That Paul Allen?" Rachel asked.

"That's the one." Joe nodded.

"I thought he owned sports teams." Scott said. "The Seahawks, right?"

"Yes, but he also spends millions of his own money on biological research. He's one of the good guys. The Allen Institute is actually the Allen Institute for Cell Science. Cutting edge research and approaches to understanding every different type of cell in the human body. From what I've read they're actually better equipped than the CDC was. Working there means you're at the top of your field." Joe explained.

"I still don't understand what this town we're going to has to do with Seattle." Rachel said.

"Tinker's cut off. They've had some problems and the infected are close to breaching the perimeter fence. They're probably going to fall before the evacuation is complete." Scott said, pausing long enough to check the nav display. Satisfied Irina had them on their route he turned back to Rachel and Joe, giving Irina a moment to finish translating for Igor over the intercom before he continued.

"Dr. Kanger is onboard an Air Force F-15, being flown to Washington State. There's already a SEAL team on the way to Seattle to secure the facility and be ready for his arrival. The Navy has a plane on the way to pick you two up, and the closest airport with a long enough runway that is clear of infected is at Ponca City. I'm supposed to get you two there so you can be flown to Seattle to assist Dr. Kanger." Scott watched Rachel as he finished speaking, expecting resistance from the stubborn woman.

"What about John and Katie? And Dog?" Rachel asked.

"We're not going with you," Scott answered. "Once you two are safely in the Navy's hands, we're going to find them. The satellite that spotted you is still looking. If he's out there, it'll find him."

Rachel turned and stared at the metal wall a few feet in front of her. She understood enough about how viruses worked that she believed there was a very real possibility that a weapon could be created that would destroy the infected. She also understood that her help wasn't needed for the actual engineering efforts, rather her familiarity with lab equipment.

But did they really need her? There had to be someone else equally qualified that could fill the role of lab assistant. She looked up at Scott and started to open her mouth, but he was prepared and cut her off.

"Colonel Crawford said to tell you that you don't have to like it, you just have to do it." He said. "My orders are to make sure you two get on that plane. It's not open for discussion."

"I'm not in the goddamn military! You can't order me to do something!" Rachel said, anger flashing in her eyes.

"No you're not, and before the attacks he couldn't have forced you to do anything. Now?

Everyone has a job to do if we're going to survive." Scott replied in a calm voice.

Rachel seethed, but held her tongue. She knew Scott was right, but she still didn't understand why it was so important that she went to Seattle. Then it hit her. Colonel Crawford was protecting her. Joe was important. He had to go. Rachel knew she could contribute, but also knew that anyone who had worked in a hospital lab was just as qualified as she was.

If Crawford didn't send her to Seattle, she'd be left out on the Oklahoma prairie with millions of infected bearing down on the area. With no way to get back onto Tinker and leave with the evacuees. The same fate that Scott, Irina and Igor were facing. He was doing what he could to save her life.

The anger flowed out of her, replaced by profound sorrow. She didn't see how anyone left behind could possibly survive once the herds arrived. Scott, Igor and Irina might hold out for a while inside the Bradley, but the prospects for their long-term survival were poor. And what about John, Katie and Dog?

They might be dead already, she told herself. As fucking indestructible as John was, the odds he'd faced going into the caverns after his wife were daunting. Sure, he'd proven he could survive where most would have given up, but she knew that sooner or later his number would come up.

Heart breaking as she thought about him, she hung her head and blinked tears away. Finally she lifted her head, looked at Scott and nodded.

"I'll find him," Scott said, eyes locked on hers. "And I'll make sure he knows where you are."

"Just tell him I'm OK, and that I hope he and Katie are alright. I don't want him coming after me." Rachel said, sniffing back tears and drying her cheeks.

Maybe this was exactly the break and the clean start she needed. As much as it hurt to think about never seeing him again, Rachel knew she would just be a third wheel with Katie back in John's life. If they were even still alive. If they weren't, there was nothing holding her here. If they were, then the last thing Katie would want is her hanging around.

And, Rachel had to admit to herself, it was the last thing she wanted too. Always on the outside, watching the man she was in love with as he moved on with someone else. She couldn't put herself through that. So she'd go to Seattle and work her ass off to help save what was left of the world. They'd either pull it off and she could go start a new life somewhere, or they'd fail, in which case things were just going to keep getting worse until there weren't any survivors and the infected would rule the planet.

43

They drove for close to two hours, no one talking other than an occasional comment between Scott and Irina related to their progress. Rachel sat in her own silence, in no mood to talk to anyone about anything.

"Sun's coming up," Scott's voice roused her from her thoughts. "We're approaching the southeastern edge of town."

"How does it look?" Joe asked, stretching muscles that were cramped from sitting in the tight space and being bounced around like a Ping-Pong ball by Irina's aggressive driving.

"Quiet," Scott said with his eyes pressed to the periscope. "Abandoned. At least so far. How many people lived here?"

"Maybe 25,000," Joe said after thinking for a moment.

"We've been passing infected for the past hour that are streaming south towards Tinker, but nowhere near that many. Maybe they evacuated." Scott said.

"Or maybe they all turned and they're just sitting around waiting for a bunch of idiots to show up for breakfast." Rachel said.

Igor snorted a laugh after Irina translated her comment for him. Rachel looked up at him and couldn't help but grin. John's sarcasm had rubbed off on her.

"Nice and easy, Irina. No need to go blasting through town. We're early. The Navy isn't supposed to be here for another hour." Scott said.

Irina said something in Russian that brought a big snort of laughter from Igor, but a moment later the noise and vibration reduced as she slowed the heavy vehicle. Scott chose to ignore her, splitting his attention between the periscope and the navigation display.

"Joe, do you know where the airport is? It's not showing on the map." Scott said a minute later.

"Northwest of town." He said. "Let me see where we are and I'll tell you how to get there."

Scott looked around, then nodded and vacated the vehicle commander's seat. "Just don't touch that," he said, pointing at a control station for the Bradley's weapons.

Joe slid into the seat and looked through the periscope. After a few minutes he climbed down and faced Scott.

"Stay on this road. Soon we'll cross a river and it will end. Turn left and follow that road to Waverly Street. Turn right and go about four or five miles and you'll see the airport." He said.

Scott relayed the directions to Irina as he climbed back into his seat. Soon, Rachel could hear a difference in the sound of the treads on the road surface and she assumed they were crossing a bridge over the river Joe had mentioned. Her suspicion was confirmed when less than a minute later Irina slowed then cranked the Bradley through a left turn.

They hadn't gone far when Igor said something, adjusting his periscope as he spoke. A moment later the turret whined as he traversed it to aim the chain gun to their rear.

"We're being followed," Irina translated.

Scott looked through the rear facing scope, adjusting the optics to compensate for the rising sun. “Two pickups. Loaded with armed men.”

“White or Indian?” Joe asked quickly.

“White. I think. Hard to tell with the sun filter engaged.” Scott said after a minute of watching.

“Igor wants to know what you want to do.” Irina said. “He thinks we should open fire and disable their vehicles.”

“No. Hold fire.” Scott said, thinking. “They’re just following, not doing anything aggressive.”

“Exactly what could they do against us that would be aggressive?” Rachel asked, trying hard to keep the note of sarcasm out of her voice.

“More ahead,” Irina said before Scott could answer. “They’re not blocking the road, but they’re tracking us. You sure you want them following us to the airport?”

Scott didn’t answer. He wasn’t sure what to do, having never been placed in a position where he had to make the tough decision of whether or not to be the first to engage in a fight. Once the call was made he was a fearsome warrior, but he was quickly learning that making the decisions wasn't nearly as easy as it had always appeared. How the hell did the Major make it seem so effortless?

"Stay on course," he finally said. "If they give us a reason, we'll do what we have to."

"When we were on our way to the casino to get Katie, we had to fight some local cops." Rachel said. "They were scared and sure we had some vaccine or a way to get some. That may be what's going on."

Scott thought about what she said, then shook his head. "We wait until we have to fight. They aren't doing anything other than seeing what we're up to."

Everyone stayed quiet, not arguing with him, but it was clear they didn't agree. Irina held their speed steady down the perfectly straight road. They passed two more intersections where trucks loaded with men watched them roll through. Igor kept up a steady scan, routinely adjusting the turret to send a message to the locals.

They made a right turn on Waverly, half a dozen heavily loaded pickups trailing in their wake. Two more trucks fell in behind them as they approached the airport. Everyone was tense, sweating as the armored vehicle began to heat from the sun. Scott and Igor were watching to their rear when Irina suddenly swerved and began shouting curses in Russian.

There was a hard impact followed by a grinding sound all along their right side. Scott changed his view, cursing along with Irina when he saw a civilian armored car driving next to them. It had roared out of a side street, striking the front corner of the Bradley before turning to drive next to them as its driver tried to force them off the road.

Igor didn't wait for orders, rotating the turret and firing a long burst from the chain gun. Civilian armored cars are well protected against the armaments that criminals can get their hands on. They aren't even close to being able to withstand military grade firepower.

The 25 mm slugs tore through the thick skin of their attackers' vehicle and chewed up everything and everyone inside. With a twitch of the half-moon shaped steering wheel, Irina bumped the side of the armored car and with no one left alive inside to steer, it was sent careening across the street where it crashed into the front of a small donut shop.

Igor turned the gun back to the rear but the trucks had come to a stop, watching them drive away. He activated the chain gun again, putting a short burst into the asphalt in front of the stopped pickups. The pavement was shredded, chunks breaking free and flying into the air.

"Cease fire," Scott said. "I think they got the message."

Igor had already stopped firing, nodding when Irina translated.

44

Marine Colonel James Pointere stood in a large open field adjacent to a runway, facing most of the surviving members of the Marine Expeditionary Unit. He had just come from Colonel Crawford's office where they had discussed the few options that remained available to them. Only one option, was what Pointere had quickly realized.

Pointere wasn't a speaker. He knew that. No rousing, motivational speeches from him for his men. Just a no bullshit assessment of what they were facing.

"The infected are pressing in faster than expected," he began, shouting so that everyone could hear him. His words were punctuated by distant screams and gunfire as the Air Force and several Ranger platoons held the perimeter.

"We've lost one of the crop dusters, and the rate at which the locals are turning is accelerating. There's not enough time to completely evacuate. The second wave just left a couple of hours ago, which means six hours until those aircraft are back and ready to start loading the third wave."

He paused as a pair of F-15s roared down the runway to his rear. The two fighters leapt into the air, long tongues of flame behind them as the pilots kept them at full afterburner. They were still in sight when two booms rattled every window on the base as they broke the sound barrier.

"That," Pointere pointed in the direction the planes had gone, "is a scientist on his way to a research facility. There's a plan to fight the virus and defeat the infected."

There was a murmur of excited voices and hopeful expressions appeared throughout the assembled Marines.

"But that won't happen fast or easy," Pointere said quickly. "Not fast enough to save the people trying to evacuate from this base. That's up to us."

He began pacing, looking at the faces of all the Marines staring back at him. "There's only one way these civilians are going to make it onto planes and those planes get off the ground. That's if someone stays behind and holds the infected back until the last wave is in the air."

Pointere stopped, meeting the eyes of several men sitting in the shade of a LAV. Turning, he started retracing his steps until he was centered in front of his men.

"Fox Company in Korea. Khe Sanh in Vietnam. Marines don't run. We dig in and fight. We hold the motherfucking ground that others can't!" He roared as choruses of Oorah broke out, loud enough to drown out the sounds of the battle at the fence. With a grim expression on his face Pointere held his hands up for silence.

"I'm asking for volunteers," he said when the shouts died down. "I'm staying, but I'm not ordering anyone to stay with me. Fighting men will be needed in Nassau. Anyone that wants to go, there's room on the planes in the last wave. Each of you needs to decide. I've made my decision, but I won't think less of anyone that chooses to evacuate."

As if coordinated, every single Marine in the field got to his feet and came to attention. After a moment a grizzled First Sergeant took one step forward and snapped up a salute.

"Sir!" He shouted in a booming, parade ground voice. "Request permission for the men of the 20th Marine Expeditionary Unit to join you in defense of this installation. Sir!"

Pointere stood there, looking across the ranks of his Marines, pride threatening to burst his chest. With tears forming in his eyes he snapped to attention and shouted, "Permission granted, First Sergeant!" He returned the salute and was reaching up to wipe his eyes when there was a shout from his left.

"Sir! Request permission for the men of the 5th Battalion, 75th Ranger Regiment to join you in defense of this installation. Sir!" Captain Blanchard, leading five hundred Rangers stood at attention, holding a salute.

Pointere looked at the Ranger Captain, smiled as he turned to fully face him before responding and returning the salute. Stepping forward he extended his hand, Blanchard shaking it.

"All your men know we're not getting out of here?" He asked in a low voice.

"With all due respect, sir, we just couldn't let you Jar Heads have all the fun." Blanchard answered.

Pointere laughed and clapped him on the shoulder, turning and calling over a Marine Captain to introduce the two men. Sending them on their way to coordinate the integration of the Rangers with the Marines, he looked around as NCOs began working to get the men organized and ready to protect the base until the last civilian was in the air.

Noticing a Humvee sitting fifty yards away in the field, he held up a hand to shield his eyes from the morning sun. Recognizing Colonel Crawford he walked over, the Colonel meeting him half way.

"Every single one of my Marines is staying behind," Pointere said, pride obvious in his voice.

"Not a bit surprised," Crawford replied with a wry smile. "My Captain couldn't be talked out of it. I'm still not happy I let you talk me out of it."

"Forget it, Jack." Pointere said, fishing around in a cargo pocket. Finding what he was looking for he pulled out two cigars, handing one to Crawford. "These people are going to need you to survive when they get to Nassau. Who the hell else is going to take charge?"

The conversation paused as the two men got their cigars lit. Crawford drew on his, exhaling with a satisfied sigh. “I know, I know. I don’t have to like it; I just have to do it. Right?”

“That’s what I’ve heard a certain thick headed grunt of my acquaintance say a few times.” Pointere moved so he could watch his men preparing as they talked.

“We’re leaving the Ospreys with you,” Crawford said. “Get as many men on them as you can after we get the last of the civvies out. They won’t make the Bahamas, but if you head that way I can send a C-130 to pick you up. Maybe in Alabama or Georgia somewhere.”

“Pipe dream, Jack. You know as well as I do that won’t happen. Maybe the pilots, once there’s no longer a reason for them to stay in the area, but none of us on the ground are going to make it. I accept that. Have made peace with it. You just get all these fucking people out of here. We’ll buy you as much time as we can.” Pointere said.

They stood there for a long time, not saying anything, just watching the fighting men prepare for the coming battle. Weapons were being checked. Ammunition was being distributed.

Vehicles were being gone over to make sure there wouldn't be a problem at a critical moment.

"Jim, it's been an honor." Crawford finally said, turning, coming to attention and raising a salute to the Marine Colonel.

Pointere returned the salute then the two men shook hands. After a long moment Crawford turned and started walking to the waiting Hummer, cigar smoke trailing in his wake.

45

I woke up, disoriented as hell, with a head that felt like Snoop Dog had taken up residence and turned the bass all the way to 10. The sun was shining brightly, but I was in the shade of a tree and could hear burbling water close by. An arm was draped across my chest, a shapely, bare leg thrown over mine. At first I thought it was Rachel, then my mind began creaking along when I recognized the improvised moccasin I had fashioned for Katie out of my shirt.

She was asleep, head pillowed on my shoulder. Raising my head slightly, I kissed her gently on the forehead, turning when I heard a grunt. It was Dog, sitting between a lazy river and me, keeping watch. He was looking at me, tongue hanging out of his mouth as he panted in the heat of what seemed to be the morning.

"How's your head?" Katie asked.

"I'm fine," I said, turning to look at her. "How long have I been out?"

"A few hours," she said.

Sitting up she crossed her legs and looked down at me.

"Got you down here after you went all berserker on the infected, then you passed out." She reached out and gently touched my head, examining something. "You've got one hell of a knot on the side of your head to go along with that gash."

I reached up and touched a spot that was tender enough to send a jolt of pain through my entire body. Must have been where I hit my head in the underground river.

"How bad you think?" She asked.

"Don't know, but I'm conscious and I *can* remember what happened last night, so that's probably a good sign. No more infected since the last attack?" I rose up onto my elbows, my head pounding hard enough to make my vision blur, but it passed quickly.

"Two males a couple of hours ago. Your friend there took care of them. Rachel told me about him." Katie nodded at Dog, who looked back at us, slobber dripping off his tongue.

"That's Dog," I said. "He's been with me since Atlanta and probably has as much or more to do with me making it as Rachel does."

Hearing his name, Dog got up and walked over, shoving his nose against my arm for petting.

"He doesn't seem to like me much," Katie said. She reached out to pet him, but Dog pulled away. He didn't growl, but he kept his eyes focused on her hand.

What the hell? I'd never seen him act like that with someone I was OK with. I called him, but he wouldn't approach me until Katie moved her hand back.

"I've never seen him do that," I said. "He hasn't growled at you, has he?"

"No, nothing like that. Just doesn't want me close to him. I was afraid I was going to have a problem being close to you, but he just hangs back a few feet and keeps a close eye on me. Maybe it's because I'm not Rachel."

Maybe she was right, but I wasn't convinced. Not that it was a big deal, but I made a mental note to keep a close eye on him. I remembered the conversation Rachel and I had about the virus jumping to animals and her saying that it was possible it could infect dogs.

The virus! I had suspected yesterday that Katie was healing fast because of the virus, even though she wasn't "infected". Maybe Dog could smell or sense something different and he was confirming my idea. Deciding this was best kept to myself, I sat the rest of the way up.

"So what's our plan?" Katie asked, standing and stretching. For probably the thousandth time in my life I couldn't help but admire the way the shirt stretched across her breasts.

"Would you focus on the problem at hand and not my tits," she said when she saw where I was looking.

"Sorry," I said, not the least bit sorry. I'd really missed her.

This was one of the few times in my life that I didn't know what to do. I knew where Tinker Air Force Base was. Knew we could reach it in a few days on foot, or even faster if we came across a running vehicle. But there was the approaching herd that Joe and I had seen. I had no doubt about where they were heading and didn't like the idea of being anywhere near them as they pushed into the Oklahoma City area.

I relayed the thought to Katie, watching as she stripped off the few rags of clothing she was wearing and waded into the river. Dog gave her a wide berth as she walked past him, also watching as she submerged her head in the water, vigorously rubbing her fingers through her hair. A couple of minutes later she walked out of the water and stood in the sun, naked, letting her body dry before putting the shirt and foot coverings back on.

"OK, so Oklahoma City is out. What else is around here? We've got no food and you're down to less than fifty rounds for that rifle. I checked after you passed out." She said.

I sat thinking, but I didn't have an intimate knowledge of Oklahoma. What I did know was that there was a lot of open space, just like Arizona. You could walk for days without coming across civilization. And to make matters worse, I didn't have a very good idea of exactly where we were. Somewhere northeast of Oklahoma City was the best I could come up with.

Food was going to be a real problem. I hadn't eaten in I couldn't remember when. I had no idea when the last time Katie had eaten, but knew there was no point in asking. She'd just lie to keep me from worrying about her. Not that the human body can't go for a long period without food, but food is the fuel that keeps us running and fighting. Katie didn't have any extra body fat to live on, and after the past couple of months, neither did I.

Water was a bigger concern, but I seemed to keep coming across rivers and streams. I wasn't as worried about finding water as I was food. As much of the prairie as I'd run across, I couldn't recall seeing any wildlife. Nothing that I could shoot and make a meal of. We needed a destination, relatively close, where we could find food, shelter and weapons. But exactly where the hell was that?

Standing, I swayed a little, but the dizziness retreated and I felt more or less good enough to travel. We were under a tree on the banks of the river, a gentle slope leading to a small hill to the west. Climbing up I looked out across miles and miles of nothing. Well, not nothing. Southwest of where we stood there was a massive dust cloud that obscured the horizon. At least I knew where the herd was.

Turning a slow circle I scanned in every direction, hoping to see any indication of civilization. Seeing nothing I sighed and walked back to where Katie sat in the shade of the tree.

"We're going east," I said, staring off into my proposed direction of travel.

"Why east?" She asked, not challenging, just wanting to know my reasoning.

"My parents grew up here." Katie nodded. "I remember visiting my grandparents when I was a kid. We'd drive up to somewhere close to Amarillo, then head east. Maybe I'm wrong, since that was a long time ago, but what I recall is that everything west of here is pretty much desolate grass lands until you bump up against the Rocky Mountains in Colorado and New Mexico. East of here is water, trees and a lot of towns."

Katie stood up and moved next to me, looking to the east. "I trust your memory. Let's get moving." She said, taking my hand in hers.

46

We drank as much water from the river as we could force down, not knowing how long before we'd come across another source. Setting off across the grasslands, Dog fell in on the opposite side of me from Katie. He maintained position a few feet in front, ears at full alert. I was glad to have him along, even if he was acting weird.

I guessed it was mid to late morning when we began walking. The sun was already high and it was hot. A breeze was blowing in our faces, but it seemed there was always wind moving in this area. I kept a close eye out for any movement as I walked, frequently checking our rear.

I wasn't just watching for infected, I was hoping to see something we could make a meal of. But as we kept pushing east I didn't see anything. No rabbits, which really surprised me, and no birds, which was a relief after the infected vultures I'd shot.

Several hours later we reached a stream. There wasn't much water in it, I could easily step across it without getting my feet wet, but the water was running and clear. We stopped long enough to drink our fill, Dog lapping noisily until I thought his stomach would either rupture or drag the ground when he walked.

By late afternoon we still hadn't seen a single indication that we were even close to a town or city. I still hadn't spotted any wildlife either. The prairie was completely empty, other than the three of us and the dust cloud that was still visible to our rear. As the sun began to sink towards the horizon its rays turned the dust a fantastical shade of orange. A color that I've seen artists try to recreate, but it's one of those things in nature that man just can't duplicate.

"Reminds me of home," Katie said, referring to some of the sunsets we had watched together in Arizona.

She was turning back to face east, freezing in place and reaching out to get my attention.

"Do you see that?" She asked.

"What?" I asked, looking intently in the direction she was facing. I started to raise the rifle, then remembered the scope had broken and I'd discarded it.

"I just got a glint of light. Hold on," Katie said, stepping to the side to get a slightly different angle.

"There!" She pointed. "Power lines. The big ones."

I moved to stand behind her, looking over her head. Far in the distance, just catching the rays of the setting sun I could make out what looked like strands of silver stretched across the horizon. She was right. High voltage, power transmission lines.

"They're running east and west," she said. "Will there be a town at one end?"

"Yes," I answered, already heading in that direction. "A generating station at one end and a town at the other."

"But which way?" Katie asked, rushing to catch up with me.

"Doesn't matter. Either end will have shelter, and a generating station is a big place. There might be vehicles and food there. We'll follow them east and see where they go."

We kept walking as the sun continued to drop. I was going to miss the daylight that let us see for miles in every direction, but I wasn't going to miss the heat. It had been another scorching day and we were feeling the effects. We hadn't found water since the small stream several hours earlier, and my mouth felt as dry as the Sahara.

Two hours after sunset we reached the base of a massive, steel girder tower. Eight thick power lines were suspended from a cross arm that had to be a hundred feet off the ground. A large metal plate was riveted to the tower at eye level, a series of numbers painted on it. There was just enough moonlight to read it.

"Any idea what they mean?" Katie asked me.

"Nope. Probably would tell us how far we are from the end of the line, but I've got no clue." I said.

Under the lines was a narrow dirt track carved out of the grasslands by the utility. It was hardly smooth, but it was easier walking so we moved onto it. Dog continued to stay on the far side of me from Katie, only coming up to me for attention if she wasn't close.

I'd had plenty of time to think as we'd walked, and I'd come to the conclusion that there was nothing wrong with him. Katie had to have some degree of infection from the virus. Between the rapid healing of her wound and Dog's mysterious behavior that was the only logical answer. Frankly, that scared the hell out of me.

What if Katie was going to turn, and just hadn't done so. Would I be able to shoot her? To save myself? No. I didn't even have to give that any thought. If she turned... well, then I guess it would be my time.

An hour later we moved into slightly more rolling terrain. I wouldn't exactly call them hills, but the ground we walked across was no longer billiard table flat either. The power line towers marched away from us into the distance, and we followed them, feet kicking up small clouds of dust from the dirt road.

We climbed a series of hills, each slightly higher than the last but none more than a couple of dozen feet above their surroundings. Ahead a tower occupied the crown of the tallest hill yet and when we crested we came to a stop under the skeletal structure. Below us was a broad, shallow valley and it was occupied by a small city.

Water glistened in the moonlight at several points, marking rivers and lakes scattered around the valley. There were a few lights strewn in the darkness, all of them looking like campfires. A few others, far in the distance, had the whiter look of electric lights, but it was hard to tell.

"That's not Oklahoma City, is it?" Katie asked quietly.

"No, it can't be." I said. "Wrong direction and it doesn't look right. I've got no idea what this one is, but it looks big, which means I'm betting we can find what we need."

"Right now I need water," Katie said.

I nodded and headed down the slope towards a residential neighborhood when Dog turned his head and growled. He was looking behind us and I spun, raising the rifle. On the crest of the hill where we'd just been standing was a lone figure, silhouetted by the moon. It was definitely female and I almost pulled the trigger, not really sure what stayed my hand.

Dog stopped growling and moved to stand beside me, opposite of where Katie stood. A few moments later the female walked forward, stopping twenty yards away. She was nothing more than a dark form against the lighter sky.

"Imagine meeting you here," she said.

"Martinez?" I asked, lowering the rifle in surprise.

47

Irina saw the chain link gate restricting access to the airport well before they reached it. Not bothering to slow, she wrenched the Bradley into a hard turn, blasting through the gate as if it wasn't there. Reducing speed, she drove through a maintenance lot, across a curb and between rows of hangars.

After the hangars was a long line of small, private planes that were tied down under a metal shelter resembling the roof over covered parking spaces at office buildings. Reaching the end, she slowed further and turned onto the sole runway and came to a stop.

"Drive the runway," Scott said. "Let's make sure it's clear before the Navy shows up."

Irina nodded. The Bradley accelerated to five miles an hour and held there. Driving along the edge of the long strip of pavement, she kept her attention focused on the smooth asphalt. She knew Scott was concerned about debris that could damage landing gear or be sucked into a jet engine, so she drove slow and looked carefully.

The turret whined as they moved, Igor keeping their gun trained in the direction of the shattered gate. He stayed quiet, and Rachel hoped they wouldn't have any more problems before her flight showed up.

She still wasn't happy about leaving for Seattle, but understood the necessity. She had also finally accepted that she didn't have the first idea where to start searching for John. If he had survived, she knew he'd be nowhere near the canyons. He would have gotten out of there as fast as he could.

If he were still down in the caverns, trapped by infected or still searching for Katie, she'd have no way of knowing and wouldn't be able to find him. He was lost to her and her heart ached. She'd always known this day might come, but had been so caught up in her own dreams of being with him that she'd not prepared for it.

Igor barked out something, Irina translating a beat later. "They're coming again."

Scott adjusted the direction he was looking and groaned. A massive, yellow bulldozer was trundling into view from behind the hangars they had passed. It was easily the size of the Bradley, probably more like two times. It had to be stopped before it made it onto the runway. They couldn't risk anything that would jeopardize Rachel and Joe getting on that plane.

Speaking to Irina, he issued orders for Igor. She translated rapidly, Igor nodding and grinning. He adjusted the turret slightly as he activated a laser targeting system. Satisfied with the results, he lifted a protective flap and stabbed a red button with his index finger. There was a pop then a roar as a TOW missile shot out of the launcher mounted on the left side of the turret.

TOW stands for Target-sensitive, Optically tracked, Wire-guided. When Igor had locked the laser onto the dozer, the Bradley's computer had begun feeding guidance data to the missile. Upon launch, a thin wire unspooled, connecting the missile's guidance system to the Bradley's targeting computer. The computer maintained the laser lock on the target, updating its location and distance several times per second. Igor had selected the dozer's large engine compartment, and seconds after the laser had locked on the missile arrived.

The TOW missiles fielded by a Bradley were designed to penetrate and destroy enemy armor. Tank killers, in other words. As large and heavy as it was, the cast iron, diesel engine in the dozer was sliced into like paper as the missile detonated. The driver was killed a fraction of a second after the detonation, and giant pieces of the machine were blasted into the air.

"Persistent assholes, aren't they." Scott observed, scanning for more attackers.

"They're just frightened," Rachel said. "They didn't get vaccinated and they know what's going to happen to them. A lot of them have probably already seen friends and family turn."

"So we should take it easy on them?" Scott challenged.

"No, that's not what I'm saying. I just understand their fear. But that doesn't give them an excuse to attack us." She answered.

Not having a good response, Scott grunted. He kept his eyes on the periscope, checking around the area, but for the moment the locals weren't ready to challenge the Bradley's firepower again.

"Ram two seven, this is Viper flight. Do you copy?" A strong, male voice sounded over Scott's comm panel, the high-pitched whine of jet engines audible in the background.

"Ram two seven copies," Scott answered the call from the Navy plane that was inbound.

"We're fifteen mikes from RP. What's your status?" RP was rendezvous point.

"At the RP. Runway is clear. We have hostiles in the area, but clear at the moment." Scott answered.

"Copy hostiles in area. New Jersey." The pilot spoke the challenge word.

"Giraffe," Scott replied with the correct response.

The two words were completely unrelated and meant nothing. They were simply a way for each party to verify that they were who they were supposed to be. If the pilot had failed to challenge, or Scott had responded with any other word, it would have let the legitimate person know that something was wrong.

"Confirm Giraffe," the pilot said. "We're a flight of two F-16s. How do we recognize you?"

"We're in a Bradley. The only one in the area." Scott answered, surprised there wasn't a transport coming for Rachel and Joe. "We've had to engage the locals twice so far, but they've pulled back for the moment. Contact when you're five mikes out and I'll let you know if the LZ is hot."

"Viper flight copies."

"We've got more company coming," Irina called out as the radio went silent.

Scott checked the area she was watching, sighing when he saw several hundred infected headed for them. There was a mostly even mix of males and females, the women sprinting out ahead of the group as the males shambled along behind. The sounds of the chain gun and then blowing up the dozer had almost certainly attracted them.

"What's wrong?" Rachel asked.

"Infected," Scott said. "Not more than we can handle, but still there are a lot of them."

"Don't let them get on the runway," Rachel cried out. "I watched infected get sucked up into a big cargo plane's engines in Tennessee while it was trying to take off. It didn't make it."

"Igor," Scott said. "Light 'em up."

Before Irina could translate Igor began firing the machine gun in short controlled bursts. He walked it across the ranks of the fast approaching females with devastating results. With the infected inside four hundred yards, the heavy, high velocity slugs ripped them apart. As he worked their weapons, the sound of hard impacts on the Bradley's armor caught everyone's attention.

"What the hell is that?" Joe asked, looking nervous.

Scott was searching with the periscope, finally stopping and focusing. He turned the wheel to zoom the optics and watched for a moment. There was another loud impact and he spoke without removing his attention from the view outside.

"Got some jack ass with what I'm willing to bet is a fifty." He was referring to a .50 caliber rifle. Deadly against just about anything that isn't armored. "Relax. It can't penetrate our armor. But we need to shut him down before that plane arrives. Those slugs will tear right through an aircraft."

Taking control of the turret from the vehicle commander's station, Scott activated the targeting system. He focused on the shooter's position and pressed a button that activated the laser range finder. The sniper was 447 yards away, on the roof of a two-story building with a clear line of sight to the airport.

A couple of more adjustments and the 25 mm chain gun fired a two second burst. Watching through his scope, Scott saw a large section of the front of the building disintegrate into dust and debris. There was apparently a strong breeze blowing as the air at the target cleared quickly, revealing a gaping hole in the brick façade. Neither the sniper nor his rifle was visible any longer.

"Not good," Irina said a moment later.

Scott turned his scope and uttered a curse, releasing control of the vehicle's weapons system back to Igor. A solid wall of infected was emerging from streets and alleys, approaching the large empty field to the east of the runway.

48

"I thought you were dead," I blurted out as Martinez walked down the slope towards us. Letting the rifle hang I stepped forward and wrapped her up into a hug. "What happened?"

"Beats me," she said, reaching out and squeezing Katie's hand. "I remember the crash, then being carried by the infected. The next thing I knew I woke up on the banks of a river, feeling like I'd been run through a meat grinder."

"How did you get here?" I asked.

"Been following these power lines forever. Knew they had to end somewhere, then I recognized where I was. Used to train in this area. That's Tulsa." She nodded at the city spread out below us.

"How did you survive?" Katie asked. "You were all but gone. I watched the infected leave you in the river. Last I saw, you were floating downstream."

Martinez looked at her and shrugged. "Honestly, no clue. I don't feel great, but at least I'm not dead."

"Turn around," I said, moving upslope and kneeling on the grass so I could examine Martinez' leg wound in the moonlight.

Rachel had cut off her pants leg while she was working on her in the Osprey, and her leg was fully exposed. Leaning close I looked at the wound, not surprised to see it almost completely healed.

"Do you mind?" I asked, hands poised in front of the hem of her shirt.

"In front of your wife, sir? Don't you think she'll get the wrong idea about us?" Martinez quipped.

"Shut up and show me," I said, not in the mood for banter.

Martinez lifted her shirt, exposing her abdomen. Katie leaned in next to me to see.

"It's healed. Or close enough to not matter." Katie said. "Is that what mine looks like?"

I nodded in the dark, reaching out and pressing on the skin around the puckered scar on Martinez stomach.

"Does it hurt?" I asked.

"Not so much hurts as it's tender. What's the big deal?" She asked.

"You saw Katie take the bullet, right?" I asked and she nodded. I looked at Katie and she pulled the shirt over her head. "Take a look."

"Mierda," She said when she got a good look. "What the hell's going on?"

"All I can come up with is the virus," I said.

"But we're not infected," Martinez said.

"Maybe not turned, but I'm pretty sure it's affecting you. How else do you explain both of you healing like you are? And explain this." I called Dog, but he wouldn't come to me. Stepping away from the two women I called him again and he immediately trotted over and sat down at my feet, facing Martinez and Katie.

"Now, walk towards me," I said.

Martinez took a couple of steps and Dog got to his feet and backed away. She froze in place with a look of shock and horror on her face.

"So... what, we're going to turn?" She asked, looking between Katie and me.

"I don't know," I answered. "I don't think so. I think if you were going to turn you would have already. It might not even be the virus. It might be an effect of the vaccine. I'm just guessing."

"Where's Rachel?" Martinez asked. "She might have an idea."

"Don't know," I said. "It's a long story I'll tell you when we have time. Right now we need to head down there and find some water, food and shelter."

"Food, yes. I'm starving," Martinez said. "But the hell with shelter. There's an Air National Guard base here at the civilian airport. That's where I was heading. I'm sure there's a helo there that we can borrow."

"Good to have you back, Captain." I grinned.

"I just hope you still feel that way when I find a flagpole," she said, moving past me and starting down the slope.

"Huh?" I had no clue what she was talking about.

"Remember when you carried me out of the casino? The promise you made me?" She looked over her shoulder, grinning. I shook my head. "You promised that if I survived, you'd kiss my ass at noon in front of a flagpole. It will be a red-letter day when an Army Major puckers up and plants his lips on an Air Force Captain's ass. I intend to make sure you keep your word."

I stood there for a moment as Martinez laughed. Looking over at Katie I was mildly surprised to see a smile on her face.

"You poor dumbass," she said, patting me on the chest and following Martinez towards the city.

49

The Marines and Rangers had spent the day preparing multiple defensive layers. Air Force personnel manned the fence line as they worked feverishly. About noon the transport planes had returned from delivering the second wave of evacuees. Fresh pilots took command and maintenance and fueling personnel attacked them with the same urgency as a NASCAR pit crew.

Women and children were prioritized for the third wave, but they only had so much space. Many families didn't make it on and had to wait, watching as one after another of the aircraft climbed into the afternoon sky.

With the exception of personnel actively involved in holding the fence line, every other soul on the base was put to work. Men, women and children carried supplies, weapons and ammunition. They filled sandbags. Helped the men who had volunteered to stay behind and face the infected so they could escape. There was not a single word of complaint from anyone as they toiled away in the baking sun.

Pointere's plan was simple. He knew the fence would fall, and fall soon. What he needed to do was protect the survivors that were waiting to board a plane, and he needed to make sure the runways were clear. Trying to defend the miles upon miles of fence with his small, suicide force was impossible. But he could hold a much smaller perimeter that only encompassed a few hangars and the runways.

Creating concentric layers of defense, the men worked feverishly in the hot Oklahoma afternoon. They started on the outermost ring, creating a four hundred yard buffer around the area being defended. Heavy equipment was used to carve a deep trench in the ground, a moat, completely encircling the defenders.

Buildings were knocked down and bulldozed aside. Parking lots and roadways were torn up and trees uprooted. But unlike medieval moats that were filled with water, Pointere positioned fuel trucks around its length to pump it full of jet fuel when he gave the order. Ten feet deep and twenty feet wide so the females couldn't leap across, a lot of infected would be trapped and meet their end when the fuel was ignited.

One hundred yards in from the moat, crews of Marines and Rangers had positioned mortars spaced every fifty yards. The raids of the armories at Fort Hood had yielded flight after flight loaded with all sorts of weapons and munitions, including hundreds of crates of mortar tubes and thousands of pounds of mortar bombs. Tall stacks of bombs sat ready at each firing position.

The third layer, another hundred yards in, was a double cordon of Claymore mines with a twenty foot gap between them. Thousands of Claymores had been looted and were now set up in a double ring around the flight line and hangars. Crews experienced with them were frantically reeling out thousands of feet of wire, connecting each mine's detonator to a massive, improvised master control panel.

In their haste, a mine had been accidentally detonated, killing two Marines, one Ranger and injuring half a dozen others. As NCOs screamed at the crews working on the wiring, Pointere had ordered the injured to be treated and taken to a hangar to await evacuation. Each man had accepted the medics' attention, but refused to be evacuated. They returned to work, some of them with wounds that would kill them in a few hours.

The final layer followed the edges of the pavement that defined the runways. Sandbagged emplacements were constructed. Hundreds of machine guns and hundreds of thousands of rounds of ammo were positioned. This was where the Rangers and Marines would make their last stand. All they had to do was hold out long enough for the last plane to get off the ground.

Colonel Pointere hoped there would be time for at least some of the defenders to then fall back and be picked up by the Ospreys that would be his eyes in the air once the fence collapsed. He knew it wasn't likely, that no one was leaving, but he had hope that perhaps at least a few could escape.

The day wore on, evening coming and bringing relief from the scorching sun. Most of the work completed, the civilians waiting for the next wave began circulating among the defenders, delivering food and water. Many of them thanked the tired men; confused at the almost embarrassed responses they received.

"Why are the soldiers acting funny when I say thanks?" A young girl, no more than 10, stood looking up at Pointere.

He was standing on top of a pile of sandbags as the sun touched the western horizon, surveying the monumental amount of work that had been completed. The volume of infected at the fence had grown steadily throughout the afternoon and in less than an hour he knew the Air Force personnel fighting at the perimeter would have to be recalled.

"First of all, young miss, they're Marines and Soldiers," he said, sighing when a look of confusion crossed her face. He looked up when a woman he assumed was her mother walked up. "And they're not trying to act funny. They're just... well, think about this. If you're doing something because you want to, because you believe deep inside it's the right thing to do, are you wanting to be thanked?"

"I guess not," she said, looking even more uncertain.

Pointere opened his mouth, but didn't know what else to say. Couldn't figure out how to explain why civilians thanking military men and women for doing their jobs made them feel uncomfortable. Why the thanks so often felt hollow, as if it was little more than what people had been conditioned to say to someone in uniform without even giving what they were speaking a thought.

"Thank you, Colonel," the mother said and led the little girl away by the hand.

Pointere watched them go, then returned his attention to the defenses. There were various points around the moat where large steel plates bridged the gap, creating a path for the men and women to escape across. Forklifts that were normally used for loading cargo were standing by to remove the plates as soon as the last survivor made it across and before the infected could flow through their outer defensive layer.

"Impressive work, Jim." Pointere looked down to see Colonel Crawford standing at the base of the pile, holding out a steaming mug of coffee. He jumped down, gratefully accepting it.

"Just hope it's enough. What's the ETA on the next wave?" He asked, taking a sip.

"They're half an hour out," Crawford answered, lighting a cigarette. He held the pack out to Pointere but he waved them away. He enjoyed cigars but couldn't stand cigarettes. "Then an hour or so to load and refuel once they're on the ground."

"That will be the fourth wave, right? We still needing six?" Pointere asked.

"We can get the last of the people out with five. The loadmasters are cramming them in like sardines. A sixth would be nice, but it would just be for equipment and supplies. Nothing we can't do without or make a raid to somewhere on the east coast once we're settled." Crawford said, turning as Captain Blanchard ran up.

"Sirs," he said, then turned to Pointere. "Fence line defense is starting to crumble. We're going to have to pull back sooner than we hoped."

"Shit! Can we hold longer with some more men?" Pointere asked.

"No sir. Not with the numbers we have. The fence is just too long and the volume outside is growing by the minute. I can buy us some time if I can put the Ospreys up and use their miniguns."

"Do it." Pointere said immediately.

"Yes, sir." Blanchard spun and ran off, shouting into a radio as he headed for the flight line.

"Damn fine soldier," Pointere commented as they watched him weave through the workers.

"Yes, he is." Crawford said.

"How did he talk you into letting him stay?" Pointere asked, watching Crawford out of the corner of his eye.

"Let's just say it was a spirited conversation." The Colonel chuckled.

Both officers turned to look as six Ospreys lifted off in sequence from the end of the flight line. Spreading out, they all kept their engine nacelles rotated for vertical flight, hovering like a helicopter. Moving over the perimeter, they all began firing belly-mounted miniguns, raking the hordes of infected that were piled up against the fence.

The show was impressive, the tracers in the ammo creating the illusion that a solid stream of red, molten lead was connecting each aircraft to the ground. Thousands of infected were killed in only a few seconds. They were packed in so tight it wouldn't have been possible to fire a single round without hitting at least two of them.

The exhausted ranks of the Air Force personnel holding the fence cheered as the Marines continued to chew up their attackers. Body parts flew through the air and a fog of bodily fluids started forming. But the infected in the rear just flowed in when the bodies in front of them were destroyed. No fear or reason existed, only the desire to reach the flesh they could see and smell on the other side of the barrier.

50

Rachel was nearly deaf from the sound of the Bradley's chain gun and machine gun. They were holding the infected back, but barely, and not for much longer. They were burning through their ammunition at an alarming rate, but didn't have a choice. If the infected reached the runway, the plane wouldn't be able to land and all of this would have been for nothing.

"Viper flight, Ram two seven. What's your ETA?" Scott shouted into the radio.

"Three mikes," the response was almost instantaneous. "What's the situation on the ground?"

"Large force of infected to our east. We're holding, but our gun's going to run dry pretty soon."

"Copy that, Ram two seven. Pop smoke and we'll see if we can give you a little assist."

"Copy. Popping smoke," Scott answered, hitting a switch that ejected a smoke grenade to clearly mark their position. "Smoke is blue."

"What's going on?" Rachel shouted.

"Navy's here. They're going to give us some help with the infected." He answered.

Igor and Scott kept up a steady rate of fire, but the front ranks of the infected were spreading and not allowing them to stay concentrated. This reduced their effectiveness and allowed the leading edge of females to press closer to them and the runway.

"Viper flight on station. Copy blue smoke. We've got you Ram two seven." The pilot called on the radio, acknowledging he wouldn't fire on the location marked by blue smoke.

A moment later they could all hear the roar of jet engines through the hull of the Bradley, then a ripping sound that passed over them from right to left at high speed. A couple of seconds later it was repeated. Scott whooped when he saw hundreds of infected pulverized by 20 mm cannon fire.

Igor popped the turret hatch open and stuck his head outside to watch. The sound rattled Rachel's teeth as the jets returned, making another strafing run, then a third. Igor had stopped firing the chain gun, now using short bursts from the machine gun to clean up the few infected that had somehow not been killed by the aerial assault.

The pitch of the jets changed as they turned and lined up on the runway, touching down and quickly rolling to a stop not far from where the Bradley sat.

"Irina, tell Igor to keep his eyes open. I'm going out to get them loaded." Scott said, jumping out of his seat and hitting the ramp release button with the side of his fist.

The ramp dropped quickly, smoke and the stench of a battlefield swirling into the vehicle's interior. Scott grabbed a rifle and led the way out, Joe and Rachel close behind him. The machine gun kept firing occasional bursts as Igor kept the remaining infected at bay.

Running down the ramp they turned to their right, rounding the back corner of the Bradley and Rachel and Joe both almost came to a stop. Expecting some sort of passenger transport plane they were both surprised to see two F-16 Falcons sitting idling on the tarmac. Both pilots had already raised their canopies and extended a boarding ladder, which was nothing more than an aluminum pole with small pegs sticking out on each side.

They exchanged glances then picked up their speed as the two pilots climbed down to meet them. Each of them had a bundle under their arm. Scott ran up, meeting them and turning to see where Joe and Rachel were.

"...expecting a transport." Rachel heard him saying to one of the pilots when she got close enough.

"Nah, they wanted this done right," the pilot said, grinning. "That's why they sent us."

He turned and looked at Joe and Rachel, stepped forward and faced Joe. "Sir, please step over there with Lieutenant Henry. He'll get you ready and we'll get out of here."

"Ma'am," he said, holding what looked like a padded flight suit out to Rachel. Joe had walked over to the other pilot and he was offering the same thing. "Please put this on, and forgive the familiarity but you're going to need my help and we don't have a lot of time."

"What is it?" Rachel asked as the man shook it out and started lowering zippers. It looked more like a space suit with what had to be pressurized air connections in several places.

"It's a G-suit, ma'am." He said. All the zippers were open and he held it out for Rachel to step into. "If I have to make any hard maneuvers while we're in flight, it will keep you from blacking out."

Rachel worked her feet through the legs, the man stepping behind her and helping pull the tight suit over her hips.

"Why would there be hard maneuvers?" She asked as he grabbed her arm to help force it back into a sleeve.

"The Russians are still putting up patrols, ma'am. You're other arm, please, and bend to the side." He helped her contort her upper body, then she was in and he was back in front of her, yanking the rubberized zipper up to her neck. She spared a glance at Joe who was already dressed and climbing the ladder on the other jet.

The pilot escorted her to his plane. Before he could start her up the ladder she turned and faced Scott who was checking on the proximity of the infected. Igor was still firing the machine gun and once again an occasional burst from the chain gun.

"Find John," she said, pulling a surprised Scott into a hug. "Tell him where I am. Tell him…" She stopped herself. She was going to say, "I love him", but at the last moment held her tongue.

"Good luck," Scott said, stepping back from her embrace.

"Ma'am, up the ladder and in the back seat. Don't touch anything. I'll help you with the harness, helmet and mask once your seated." The pilot placed a firm hand on Rachel's back.

Turning, she climbed the ladder and carefully stepped into the cramped cockpit before sliding down into a seated position. The pilot appeared a second later, reaching on either side of her, then between her legs to grab straps. He got everything buckled, pulled them hard enough to pin her tightly to the seat, then connected several air lines to her suit.

He made a quick check to make sure he hadn't missed anything, then put a helmet on her head and fastened the integrated mask across her lower face. An oxygen line and a couple of wires in a bundle led from the mask to the console at her side. Tapping her on the helmet the pilot gave her a thumbs up, his eyebrows raised questioningly. She returned the gesture, unsure if everything was good to go or not.

He got situated in the front seat with an ease that came from lots of practice. A moment later the canopy descended, sealing tight against the body of the jet. The engines had been idling; creating a steady vibration that was transmitted through the seat into her body. Strangely it was almost comforting.

“Can you hear me, ma’am?” Rachel was startled when the pilot’s voice sounded in her ear.

“Yes, and my name’s Rachel, not ma’am.” She replied, unsure if he’d be able to hear her or not.

“Yes, ma’am. If you feel sick, there’s a bag between your feet. You don’t want to throw up in your mask if you can help it. Here we go.”

As he spoke the words, the vibration increased and the jet turned. Through the clear canopy Rachel could see the second jet, two helmeted heads tuned in their direction. She raised a hand, moments later the rear seat passenger returning the wave.

The pilot maneuvered the aircraft for a minute, getting it lined up with the center of the runway, the nose dipping slightly when he put on the brakes. She saw his head turn left, then right before going back to center. It bobbed slightly and suddenly the whole plane shuddered as the engines throttled up to a scream. Rachel didn't understand why they weren't moving, then she was pressed deep into the seat as he released the brakes.

The Falcon flashed down the tarmac, bellowing as it accelerated. Rachel could feel the bounce of every seam in the concrete in her ass as they rolled over them, then the tires left the ground behind. Her stomach dropped to her feet as the pilot lifted the nose almost vertically and they rocketed skyward. She could hear him communicating with the other pilot over the intercom in her helmet, not having a clue what they were talking about.

They continued climbing for a short time then he tipped the nose of the jet over and brought it horizontal. Rachel breathed deep, nearly panicking when she heard a hissing sound and looked down to see the legs of her suit slowly deflating.

"What the hell's going on with this suit?" She asked.

"Sorry, ma'am. I didn't have time to brief you. The suit will automatically inflate and deflate to counter the G forces generated in flight. Without it, all your blood would drain into your legs and you'd pass out and potentially die. By inflating, it squeezes your limbs and keeps blood in your core so your heart can still pump it to your brain."

"OK. Good to know." Rachel said. "How long will it take us to get to Seattle? And what's it like there? Infected everywhere?"

"I don't know what Seattle's like, ma'am. We're actually going to Whidbey. Whidbey Island Naval Air Station. It's about fifty miles from Seattle out in Puget Sound. That's all I know. I was just told to get you to Whidbey, nothing about what you're doing after that." He answered, turning his head to the left. "As far as flight time, I was told to get you there fast, so as soon as we top off the tanks we're going to boogie. It will be less than two hours."

Rachel looked in the same direction and saw the other plane, seemingly hanging in mid-air a short distance off and behind their wingtip.

"Top off? We've got to land?" She was surprised, but not as much as when the man chuckled and pointed at a speck in the sky above and in front of them.

"What's that?" She asked.

"Flying gas station, ma'am. Now, if you'll excuse me I need to step out and pump some gas." Rachel shook her head. What was it with these military guys? Everything they did was so amazing, yet they talked about it like it was just an everyday errand.

The refueling plane was the KC-135 out of Tinker Air Force Base that had launched with the first evacuation wave. It had stayed in the air to refuel any evac flights that were running low, the F-15 that was ferrying Dr. Kanger to Seattle, and service the two F-16s that were inbound. Flying nice and level and slow, it reeled out a fueling line with a drogue and two small winglets at the end when the pilot called on his radio.

Rachel watched in fascination as he brought the plane into stable flight, below and behind the tanker. A few moments later the basket of the refueling probe was "flown" into contact with the F-16s fuel probe by a crewman staring out of a small window in the back of the larger plane. Several minutes later they were full, disconnecting and moving well away to make room for the second Falcon to hook up and take a drink.

Fueling complete, the two jets banked sharply to the left and gained altitude. Rachel could see a compass on the panel in front of her and watched the little airplane icon settle on a direction of northwest. She looked out the canopy to her left, surprised to not see the other jet.

"Where did they go?" She asked.

"Half a mile to our port. Our left," the pilot said. "Keep looking in that direction. It's pretty humid. You should see them in a moment."

Rachel didn't understand what was going on, but did as she was told, keeping her eyes glued on the blue sky directly off the left wing. A few seconds later there was a large burst of white vapor, seemingly out of nowhere.

"What the hell was that?" She asked, concerned for Joe.

"That was the shockwave of a jet breaking the sound barrier. We just made one too."

"What?! You mean that was a sonic boom? Why didn't I hear it?" Rachel was excited, staring out, hoping to catch a glimpse of the other plane.

"You can't hear sound if it's moving slower than you are, ma'am." The pilot said. Rachel was sure she heard a smirk in his voice. "Fifteen hundred miles to Whidbey. We should be there in ninety minutes."

"If you call me ma'am one more time I'm going to punch you when we land." She said, amazed at the view of the Earth spread out beneath her.

"Yes, ma'am." He answered.

51

The holding effort with the Ospreys bought them some time. While the aerial miniguns were chewing up the infected, the ground defenders were able to take a short break, drink some water and regroup. But miniguns blow through ammo at an astonishing rate. And the supply was hardly infinite. They'd brought all they could scavenge, but there wasn't enough for a prolonged assault.

The Ospreys ran dry, one by one. As each exhausted their supply of ammo the pilot peeled away and returned to the flight line. The remaining rounds had already been divided up and ground crews quickly set about rearming the aircraft, but Pointere kept them on the ground. They would be the absolute last line of defense to keep the infected clear of the runway until the last evac flight could take off.

After that, well... He reached behind him with both hands, checking on the two large fighting knives sheathed at the small of his back. They were nearly as long as a Kukri, but where its blade was broad and curved for slicing, these were straight and narrow for stabbing. Satisfied they would draw smoothly when needed, Pointere turned to check on the loading of the fourth evacuation wave.

All of the C-130s were already loaded, the last one that was still on the ground roaring down the runway as he watched. The Globemasters, C5s and B-52s all had people queued up, loadmasters running up and down the lines screaming instructions. Though he couldn't see inside he had no doubt there were NCOs yelling and pushing, jamming bodies in as tight as they could.

Nine hours. That's how long it would take for the wave to reach Nassau, unload, return to Tinker, refuel, load the last of the evacuees and get back in the air. Nine hours. A short workday for a Marine, but forever when he and a handful of men had to hold off an enemy that didn't stop charging regardless of their losses. They didn't have to fall back to regroup. They would just keep coming in a relentless surge.

"Sir, it's time to pull back," Captain Blanchard said as he trotted up. "We've got infected making it over the top of the fence and we're starting to lose people."

"Fifteen minutes, Captain." Pointere said, looking over his shoulder at the flight line.

"Sir, if we wait, the defenders won't be able to make it across the bridges without being overrun." Blanchard said.

"Fuck!" Pointere thought, grimacing. "Very well. Issue the order to fall back and pass the word to expect infected inside the wire."

"Yes, sir." Blanchard turned away and started issuing orders over the radio.

"Nine fucking hours," Pointere muttered to himself.

"Sir?"

"Never mind." He said, not believing they could hold out for nine hours.

All around the base the sound of gunfire ceased as his order to fall back was relayed. The report of small arms had become a constant for the past several hours, and now it was shockingly noticeable by its absence.

"Get those fuel trucks pumping into the moat as soon as the defenders are clear of the bridges." Pointere ordered.

"Already issued the order, sir." Blanchard said, standing at Pointere's shoulder. They didn't want the highly flammable fuel in the open until the Air Force personnel that had been holding the perimeter were safely across the moat. One spark, or the discharge of a weapon could ignite it and cut off hundreds or thousands of men and women who would then fall to the infected.

"Why the Army, Captain?" Pointere asked as they waited. "You would have made a hell of a Marine."

"Thank you, sir, but there's several generations of Blanchards that would have risen from the grave and haunted me."

"Army brat?"

"My great, great grandfather was in the 1st Volunteer Cavalry in 1898." Blanchard said.

"Teddy Roosevelt's Rough Riders?" Pointere asked in surprise.

"Yes, sir. He came back from Cuba with Malaria and died a year later, before my great grandfather was born.

"He fought in World War I. In the trenches. Married an English girl and brought her home. They had my grandfather just in time for him to grow up and fight in World War II.

"He was in the 5th Ranger Battalion at Normandy. Toughest son of a bitch I've ever met. Sir. Anyways, he brought home a French girl and they had my father. My grandfather fought in Korea while my dad was growing up. Then my dad enlisted just in time for Vietnam. Four tours before he lost his legs to a VC trap.

"Then I came along. It was pre-ordained I'd join the Army by the time I was born. I'm the first officer in my family, and that was bad enough. If I'd picked the Marines, well they'd have strung me up. Trust me, sir. My grandfather may be 90, but I still don't want to mess with him." Blanchard grinned.

Pointere stood looking at the young man for a long moment.

"Captain, hasn't your family given enough? You shouldn't be here. Get on one of those planes. There's a lot more you can do for the survivors alive than you can by giving your life here."

"Sir, I appreciate you saying that, but my mind is made up." Blanchard said. "There's never been a Blanchard that ran from a fight at the expense of another, and it sure as fuck isn't going to start with me."

"Stubborn, isn't he?"

Both men turned, startled. Colonel Crawford stood behind them. He was dressed in full battle rattle, M4 rifle slung over his shoulder.

"Sir, I don't..." Blanchard stopped speaking when Crawford raised his hand.

"Captain, here's what's going to happen." Crawford said, stepping forward. "I'm staying and you're going."

"No, sir..." Blanchard started again, but went quiet when Crawford glared at him.

"The Colonel here is right. You've got a lot more to offer the handful of survivors of the human race. And throwing your life away, while noble and honorable as hell, is foolish. You're young. You've got a lot of years left to help these people rebuild.

"You're the smartest, most capable young officer I've ever had the privilege of knowing and serving with, and I have no doubt you're more than ready to lead these people. That's why these are for you."

Crawford extended his closed hand, opening it and dropping a pair of silver eagles in Blanchard's palm. Blanchard gaped at them before looking up to meet his commanding officer's eyes.

"I'm getting to be an old man, son." Crawford continued. "This new world, whatever becomes of it, isn't a place for old men. I've spoken with Admiral Packard and he supports my decision. It's done. And his orders are for you to get on the next plane out of here. Contact him when you get to Nassau. Is that clear, *Colonel*?"

Crawford stepped back, came to attention and raised a salute to Blanchard. Pointere immediately joined him, both of them waiting for the new Colonel. Blanchard looked up, his eyes damp, took a deep breath and nodded before coming to ramrod attention and snapping off a perfect salute.

52

The Air Force defenders ran, pounding across the bridges like the minions of hell were on their heels. And they weren't far behind. Without the constant fire from thousands of rifles, the infected were able to pile up and reach the top of the fence. The first females there became tangled in the coiled razor wire, their flesh slashed open to the bone.

But the ones behind them cared nothing about their fate, scrambling over them as if they were nothing more than another obstacle in the way. It started as a trickle, a few dozen females breaching the perimeter at half a dozen different locations. Then the first section collapsed under the weight of hundreds of bodies and the flood began in earnest.

Soon more sections broke open, and within a short time there were thousands of infected inside the wire. Females sprinted forward, drawn to the lights and activity at the flight line. Males shambled along in their wake in a single-minded pursuit of warm flesh.

The last bridge was pulled only a minute before a hundred screaming females arrived on the far side of the moat. The ones in the lead leapt, easily making it halfway across the ditch before they fell to the bottom. Several broke ankles or legs, but most landed and sprang back to their feet to charge the far side.

One of Colonel Blanchard's parting gifts had been an idea to slow the infected even further at the moat. There had been several thousand steel plates used for diverting jet blasts on a flight line in storage at the base. They had come from two other Air Force bases that had been decommissioned due to budget cuts. The DOD hadn't wanted to leave them to rust, so had paid a contractor handsomely to disassemble, load, transport and store them at Tinker.

The plates were ten feet tall, twenty feet long, curved and already had stout steel mounting rods attached to them. A veritable army of civilian workers had used heavy equipment all day to bring the plates out and drive their mounts into the ground along the inner edge of the moat. The concave side, the same side that would have taken a jet engine blast and diverted it safely upwards, was faced towards the moat.

Nearly doubling the height the infected had to climb to clear the defensive layer, the plates also presented a surface that couldn't be scaled. Because of this the infected couldn't get past them until they piled deeply enough to climb over those who went into the moat ahead of them. But long before hands would start grasping the top edge of the plates, Pointere had another surprise in store.

The infected continued pouring onto the base, the fence down in so many locations now that it hardly hindered their progress. At each point where a bridge had been across the moat, men held the tide back with machine guns as the curved plates were brought in and put in place. Once the gaps were sealed, it was a waiting game.

The fuel trucks began pumping jet fuel into the moat, the infected oblivious to the extremely flammable liquid that turned the ground under their feet to mud and soaked into the clothing they wore. Enough fuel had been set aside to top off the planes that would be returning for the final wave, the rest allocated for the defenses. When a truck ran dry, a driver would head for the closest access to the underground storage tanks.

More fuel was pumped in as the infected kept piling up. Watching from the roof of a large truck, both Pointere and Crawford stared in awe as every inch of land beyond the moat was quickly covered by the seething mass of bodies. The moat was already full to ground level and they were starting to pile up against the metal plates.

"How high do we let them get?" Crawford asked.

"Not much more," Pointere answered when sporadic rifle fire broke out as females began making heroic leaps and grabbing the top edge of the plates. "How long for the evac wave?"

"Seven and a half hours," Crawford answered, checking his watch.

Pointere shook his head and both men turned to look behind them at several large hangars. Five thousand men and women, including the Air Force personnel that had defended the fence all day were nervously milling around. If the Marines and Rangers didn't hold out, every single one of them would be dead before the sun came up.

"Pretty fucking stupid of you to stay behind," Pointere commented, fishing out his last two cigars and handing one to Crawford. "And what was that bullshit you were shoveling? Old man my sweet ass. What are you? Fifty?"

"Fifty two. On my next birthday," Crawford said, trimming the tip of the cigar with a small pocketknife. "It was the only way to get him to go, short of having a couple of MPs cuff him and drag him onto a plane. I wasn't going to do that to him. What about you? Why were you so quick to stay?"

Pointere ignored the question, taking his time getting the cigar lit, drawing deeply as he watched the surging infected. More and more rifles were speaking, knocking females off the top of the barricade. Generator powered floodlights had been set up to provide illumination for the workers as well as the Rangers and Marines. In the ghostly, white light he could see nothing beyond the moat other than a raging sea of death.

"Spark it up," he said into the radio Blanchard had left with him.

Moments later there were shouts up and down the defensive perimeter as the word was spread. He caught sight of a white phosphorous grenade that was lobbed into the moat, then there was a ground shaking whoomp as thousands of gallons of JP8 fuel ignited.

Flames shot fifty feet into the night sky, racing through the tens of thousands of tightly packed bodies in the moat until the entire defensive layer was burning. Thick, black smoke boiled into the sky, and the two Colonels could feel the intense heat wash across them. Defenders fell back, but the steel plates that were designed to deflect jet engine blasts did a good job of protecting those at ground level from the scorching temperatures.

Soon the smell of burning human flesh reached Crawford and he wrinkled his nose, pushing down memories of a lifetime of war. He and Pointere stood in awe as the fire consumed the infected, those behind pushing into the flaming cauldron of the moat without any regard for their own lives. Raising a pair of binoculars he surveyed the line, pausing in his scan when he realized what he was seeing.

“The females are holding back, clear of the fire.” He said. “The same behavior Major Chase reported. They’re getting smarter.”

Pointere raised his binoculars, grunting as he watched. "They're going to wait for it to die down, then charge the line."

"Pretty much," Crawford agreed.

JP8 burns at 6,000 degrees Fahrenheit and it consumed flesh and bone. The breeze was light and shifting, frequently blowing clouds of choking, black smoke across the waiting defenders. The Rangers and Marines began donning the respirators from their MOPP gear to filter the vile air they were breathing.

On the far side of the moat the females had stopped when the fuel was ignited, pulling back a hundred yards. Males continued to push forward, flowing through the static females and stumbling towards their death. The heat was so intense their skin began to blister when they were within fifty yards of the trench. At forty yards the hair was singed off their bodies. Inside thirty yards clothing burst into flame, yet they were undeterred.

Eyes boiled and exploded out of their heads. Skin melted away exposing the underlying muscle and bone. Before they even reached the edge of the moat, they fell to the ground, dead, as the water inside their skulls flashed to steam and boiled their brains. The females remained at a safe distance, impassively watching their brethren perish.

The carpet of charred remains stretched out from the defensive layer for close to thirty yards. The males from the rear continued to push forward, grinding the dead into ash under their feet, adding to the depth of the burned bodies when they fell.

"Hell is empty and all the devils are here." Pointere said, binoculars still pressed to his eyes.

"Shakespeare. The Tempest. Act 1, Scene 3, if I remember correctly," Crawford said.

Pointere lowered the binoculars and looked at him. "Scene 2, actually."

"Don't look so surprised," Crawford said. "I'm the one that should be impressed when a Marine quotes The Bard."

The radio clipped to Pointere's vest crackled and he moved it close to his ear to listen. After a moment he acknowledged the report and turned back to Crawford.

"They're pumping the last of the available JP8 into the moat. Time to make the rounds." He said.

The two men climbed down from their vantage point, heading in opposite directions. Soon, the fires would burn down and the females would charge. Modern weapons would only hold them off for so long, then all that would be left to the defenders would be personal, hand to hand combat. Until they were overrun.

53

The residential area at the bottom of the slope was quiet. Dark and quiet. Other than the sound of trash and leaves skittering down the streets, being tossed by a night breeze, nothing was moving. The houses were small and not particularly well kept. Most were in need of repair and paint, and the few front yards that showed any green were only growing weeds.

Not a good neighborhood. The kind where you expect to see Pitbulls chained to trees while sullen men work on rusting cars in the shade. But we didn't see any of that, though I would have been happy if we had. The complete absence of life meant that there had either been a house-to-house evacuation, or the population had turned.

I led the way through the empty streets, rifle in front and ready to go if needed. I hoped it wasn't needed, as I didn't have much ammo left. One encounter with even a small group of females, or any size group of armed survivors with bad intentions and I'd be dry.

Dog walked at my side, alert as ever as we pushed deeper into the abandoned city. Katie and

Martinez walked a few feet behind us. Katie carried my pistol, which was also low on ammo and wasn't sound suppressed. I'd reminded her not to fire if there was any possible way to avoid it. Martinez walked with my Ka-Bar knife held loosely in her right hand.

We weren't well armed, but we could still fight if we had to. I hoped that wouldn't be necessary. I was counting on finding a vehicle we could commandeer to get us across the city and to the airport where the National Guard air unit was housed. But so far there wasn't a single car or truck to be seen. At least none of the houses had garages, only a few of them even boasting a single space carport. That saved us the time of having to check every garage we passed.

It wasn't long before we reached a commercial area. Keeping to the darkest shadows I brought us to the rear of a squat, cinderblock building that had been painted white sometime last century. A dark neon sign advertised liquor and videos. There was a small door that opened into the rear lot that once upon a time had been protected by a heavy iron security gate.

The gate now rested in the gravel parking lot, twenty feet from the building. Large chunks of the exterior wall had been torn out when it was ripped away and the door it had protected was gently swinging back and forth in the breeze. The opening was black, the inside of the store even darker than the night, and I suspected there were similar security measures on the front that blocked any moonlight from making it to the interior.

I would have bypassed the building, but there was a ten year old Jeep Cherokee sitting in the back lot, front bumper pulled up close to the dirty wall. It didn't take Sherlock Holmes to realize it most likely belonged to an employee, or possibly the owner, of the liquor store. If we could find the keys, we had our ride to the airport.

"Check it," I hissed to Martinez as I kept the rifle trained on the open door.

"Locked up tight," she said a minute later.

Shit. I'd hoped we'd get incredibly lucky and the keys would be dangling from the ignition, the gas tank full and the doors unlocked. I might as well have been hoping for Santa Claus to swoop in and give us a ride. Either scenario had about the same likelihood.

"You two stay here and keep watch. Dog and I are going in," I said, not waiting for an acknowledgement.

Pausing to the side of the entrance, I checked on Dog. He stood directly in front of the opening, head stretched forward as he sampled the air. After a few moments of watching him and not hearing a growl, I stepped through into the pitch-black interior. It probably wasn't as dark as some areas of the caverns, but it was too dark for me to be able to see a threat before it was on top of me. I was very happy to have Dog at my side.

Moving deeper into the store I shuffled my feet as I walked. I had no idea what objects might be on the floor and I'd rather kick something than step on it and turn an ankle. The smell of alcohol was overpowering. Whiskey, rum, tequila, and the sickly sweet aroma of beer told me that there had been a lot of bottles broken and their contents spilled.

"Stay!" I mumbled to Dog.

There had to be a lot of broken glass on the floor and I didn't want him to slice his feet open. He hadn't alerted on the presence of any danger, infected or survivor, so I was fairly confident in proceeding without his nose, eyes and ears at my side.

I had only taken a couple more steps when the toe of my boot came into contact with a bottle, sending it spinning across the hard floor. There was a crunch under my foot, and I was glad I'd stopped Dog when I did. Moving on, every step I took was on shards of shattered glass, the crunching and cracking sounds seemingly as loud as gunshots in the silence of the dark building.

The store was small. No larger than the average convenience store. It didn't take long for me to reach the front, bumping into a waist high counter. Reaching out I could feel a chipped laminate covering, then something smooth that ran from the counter up as high as I could stretch my hand. A bullet proof sheet of glass, I realized after a moment. No. Not a good neighborhood.

And not good news. The presence of the protection against armed robbers meant the entire register and office area was most likely secured. I had hoped to either find a body with keys in the pocket, or keys left behind the counter, but my optimism was fading.

Covering all my bases I followed the counter, bumping along in the dark. Reaching a corner I turned and ran into a door that gave when my body touched it. Access to the register, and it was standing open. Stepping around it I stopped when my foot hit something that felt soft. Squatting, my suspicion was confirmed when I touched a body.

It was male, I could tell that much as I ran my hands over the corpse searching for pockets. I found a wallet, a pack of gum and a disposable butane lighter, but no keys. Flicking the lighter, I blinked in the light of the flame and looked at the dead man. He was middle aged with a swarthy complexion and closely cropped beard.

A conservatively colored Kufi, a traditional cotton cap worn by many Muslim men, covered his close cropped dark hair. His throat had been torn out, almost certainly by an infected female. Blood soaked the front of the knee length Kurta, a Muslim shirt, which he wore over jeans. His body had fallen across the threshold to the small, secured area, preventing the armored door from swinging closed.

Stepping over the dead man, I held the lighter higher and searched the area with my eyes. A cash register occupied most of the available counter space, a small calculator sitting next to it. On the next shelf down I recognized a rolled prayer rug, next to it the butt of a pistol. Grabbing the weapon I shoved it in my waistband and kept looking, finally spotting a large ring of keys.

The lighter's flame was shrinking, and I looked for another. A display stacked high with all different sizes was to the side and I was reaching for one when I spotted another display targeted at the impulse buyer. Small, LED flashlights. Grabbing one I clicked the rubber covered button on the end and it came on. Not a lot of light, but plenty in the small, dark store.

Shoving two more in my pocket for Katie and Martinez, I picked up the key ring and examined it. At least two dozen keys, more like what a janitor would carry than a small business owner, but there was a key with the Jeep name and logo stamped on it. Dropping the ring in my pocket, I was turning to head back to where I'd left Dog when something caught my eye.

Aiming the light I frowned when I realized what it was. A stack of Passports on one of the lower shelves. Picking them up I shuffled through, noting issuing countries of Syria, Saudi Arabia, Yemen and Kuwait. I began opening them, looking at the photos and names. There were twenty-four in all, each of them with a different photo of a young, Middle Eastern looking male, and each also contained a US Student Visa.

None of them were the man on the floor who was easily twice the age of any of the Passport holders. I started to get upset, then came to my senses and tossed the stack on the floor. This guy was most likely involved with terrorists. There was really no other reason for him to have all of these documents. But it didn't really matter. All of these guys were probably already dead, or had turned. And if they hadn't, they would soon.

Moving through the store was much easier with the little flashlight and I quickly found Dog sitting, waiting patiently for me. Grabbing several bottles of water off a shelf, I scratched his head and headed for the exit, clicking the light off and stepping to the side when I heard voices coming from the parking lot.

54

Peeking my head around the doorframe I got a good view of the lot. Katie and Martinez were standing behind the Jeep. Katie held the pistol up, aimed at a man carrying an AK-47. Two more stood behind him, equally armed. Martinez held my knife straight down behind her right leg.

The moonlight wasn't bright, but it provided enough illumination for me to recognize the three men. I'd just been looking at their photos in Yemeni Passports. Dog growled softly and I placed a hand on the back of his neck to calm him.

"This is our Uncle's store," the one closest said.

"Then back away and we'll be leaving," Katie said. She spoke in a loud voice and I knew she was buying time and trying to alert me.

"I do not think so," the young man said. "My cousins like American women. You should stay with us."

OK, enough. I was almost certain these guys were the remainder of a terrorist cell that had been plotting something before the attacks. I've known a few foreign nationals that were in the country for a variety of legitimate reasons, and not a single one of them would have been caught dead without his or her Passport and Visa.

Plus, I was watching the way these guys held their weapons and how the two in back kept up a constant scan of the area while the leader kept Katie and Martinez talking. They were trained. Maybe not by a real military, but by someone who knew what he was doing.

"And you do not want to fire that pistol," the leader said, stepping farther away from his comrades. "There are what you call infected not far away. The sound of gun fire will bring them here."

"Can't argue with that," I said to myself as I pulled the trigger on my suppressed rifle and put a round in his head.

Shifting aim to the next closest man I fired, but he was already in motion and the round punched into his shoulder. I adjusted and fired a second time as something flew towards the third guy. My guy's finger was on the trigger and when my follow up shot tore through his neck he pulled it reflexively and held it. His rifle was full automatic, and it ran through a full magazine as he fell to the gravel and began spasming.

The gunfire was loud and seemed to last forever. I shifted aim to the third man, but held my fire when I saw the hilt of my Ka-Bar sticking up from his throat. I'd forgotten how deadly Martinez was with a blade. She'd thrown the knife fifteen yards, at a small target, in the dark, and had hit the bullseye.

"Coming out," I called, just in case Katie was a little jumpy with the pistol.

Running across the lot, I checked each of the men to make sure they were dead. Retrieving the knife, I wiped it clean and handed to Martinez as she ran up. Dog had followed me, but backed away when she arrived. Fishing out the key ring I tossed it to Katie and while Martinez and I grabbed the rifles off the bodies and snatched up spare magazines, she got the Jeep open and running.

I was going to drive, Martinez climbing in the back seat and Katie scooting over, but Dog wouldn't get in the Jeep. With a sigh of exasperation I put the two women in front, Katie behind the wheel and got in back. Dog got in, then jumped over the seat back into the cargo area to be as far away from them as he could get.

"Which way?" Katie asked, reversing across the lot.

"East is the best I can tell you," Martinez answered. "Airport's on the eastern edge of town. Shouldn't be that hard to find. Tulsa isn't that large."

Gravel spun as Katie accelerated out of the lot and turned onto a four-lane street. Infected were already converging on the area, drawn by the very long burst of automatic weapon fire. They appeared out of alleys and from behind buildings, but Katie pushed our speed up and we quickly left the area behind.

"What the hell was that about?" She asked after a few minutes of driving. I was occupied with checking over our new arsenal.

"Those three were Yemeni terrorists," I said without looking up.

"What? How could you possibly know that?" Katie asked.

"Inside that store there was a stack of passports, each of them with a student visa. I had just looked at their pictures." I said.

"Sorry," she said. "You're right. They get in the country, then ditch their real passports and visas and carry forged ID with different names. Makes it a bitch to track them. That was one reason Homeland started recording the fingerprints of all foreign nationals entering the country."

"Well, doesn't matter any more." I said.

After a moment she nodded and focused on her driving.

"How did we make out?" Martinez asked, turning in her seat to look at the AKs.

"Three rifles. Well used, but in good condition. Three hundred rounds. Here," I said, handing one of them to Martinez along with a couple of magazines. She placed it on the seat next to Katie and reached back for another. Handing a second one over I passed a couple of bottles of water to her as well.

"By the way, that was a hell of a throw with the Ka-Bar." I said, leaning back in the seat, drinking deeply and looking at the dark, empty city passing outside the windows.

"Thanks," Martinez said.

"That wasn't exactly a compliment," I said and she turned around to look at me. "It's a heavy knife. For fighting. Stabbing. Slashing. The balance is all wrong for throwing, but you put enough force behind it to be accurate at forty-five feet and still bury an eight inch blade to the hilt. Seem normal to you?"

"When you say it that way... no, it doesn't." She conceded. "I just threw it the way I always do."

"And what you would normally throw weighs about a third of my Ka-Bar and is perfectly balanced, or so close as to not matter. Right?" I asked.

It was quiet in the Jeep as Martinez thought about what I had just said. She looked behind me at Dog, then back at me.

"Has he always been a party pooper like this?" She turned to Katie.

"If you only knew," she said, laughing. "He's the guy at the party that leans on the wall and watches everyone else. Even the drunks leave him alone."

"It's not being anti-social if you don't like the people at the party," I said.

"Whatever you say, sweetie." Katie said, grinning.

I rolled my eyes and sat back in the seat. If they weren't going to take this seriously there wasn't a damn thing I could do about it. Maybe I could have handled Martinez' sarcasm, or Katie's quick wit and smart-ass answer to everything, but together I didn't stand a chance in hell so I just shut up.

We drove on through the night, seeing the occasional roving band of infected. If there were any other survivors in Tulsa they weren't showing themselves. They were probably barricaded in something like a school or church and weren't about to step outside if they didn't have to.

"There," Martinez pointed to a sign that had an arrow underneath large letters that said "AIRPORT". Katie took the turn and accelerated onto a three lane freeway.

"Why are there infected here?" Katie asked once we were back up to speed.

"What do you mean?" I asked, trying not to sound like I thought she was an idiot for asking such a question.

"Fuck you, babe." She said in a gentle tone, which caused Martinez to snort a laugh. "What I mean is, why aren't all of them in Oklahoma City? Or at least on their way? Rachel told me about how the Russians are controlling them, causing them to form into herds. So, why are there any of them still here?"

"I have no idea," I finally said after trying to think of any reason. "Could they be people that were deaf and they can't hear the harmonic?"

"No way," Martinez answered. "Far too many infected still hanging around. My niece was born deaf and I remember my sister talking about the odds and the percentage of the population that's deaf. It's only something like one out of every thousand. That would mean there should only be two to three hundred deaf people in Tulsa. We've seen way more infected than that already."

"Then I've got no fucking clue, but if we get a chance to talk to someone who can actually do something with the information we should mention it." I said.

"See. Not such a stupid question was it?" Katie couldn't resist rubbing it in. "You forget, darling. I'm the brains and you're just the brawn."

It was quiet for a beat then both women burst out laughing. Great. The two biggest smart ass, sarcastic women I'd ever known were bonding.

55

The mortar crews had been firing for close to two hours. Between them and the rifles still protecting the tops of the jet blast plates, the infected were being slowed. Not held. That wasn't possible on open terrain, but they had been slowed to a crawl. The females' newly acquired desire for self-preservation was working in favor of the defenders.

Recognizing the danger posed by the mortars as they landed amongst the leading ranks, the females continued to hold back and let males shamble forward into the kill zone. Between the JP8 fueled fire, and now the mortars, there were multiple mounds of bodies outside the moat. Some of the mounds were fifty yards across at the base and over twenty tall.

But as many crates of mortar bombs as had been loaded on cargo planes and brought to Tinker, the supply wasn't infinite. Pointere grimaced when a runner found him and reported that they had consumed sixty percent of the stockpile. Sixty percent in two hours. They hadn't even gone through munitions that fast in Fallujah.

"I make four hours left. Any update from your end?" He shouted to Crawford over the roar of the battlefield.

"Maybe a little less. I heard from Blanchard and they got the planes off-loaded and back in the air in less than thirty minutes. They should be on the ground here in about two and a half hours." He shouted back.

"We've got at most ninety minutes of mortars left, then we're down to Claymores and machine guns." Pointere said.

"We need to arm the civilians," Crawford said. "They want to survive, they're going to have to fight."

Pointere nodded and made a call on his radio. A couple of minutes later a breathless Army Sergeant ran up, listened as the Marine Colonel yelled instructions in his ear, turned and dashed off.

"Let's put them on the line," Crawford said. "Pull them out when the planes are on the ground and ready."

Pointere nodded and looked around. Looked at the fighter and ground attack aircraft that were sitting silent on the tarmac. He'd made the decision to use all the available fuel for the moat, leaving enough for the evac flights only. Not one to second guess himself, he wasn't regretting the decision, just trying to figure out how to find some JP8 and get those planes in the air to aid in the defense.

"What are you thinking?" Crawford asked, also looking at the silent aircraft.

"Wishing I had more fuel," was the answer.

"You made the right call. That moat and the fire is the only reason we're still standing. It did a hell of a lot more than all those planes could have done."

Pointere nodded, finally shelving his musings and turning back to face the battle. Ninety minutes and the infected would start flooding over the moat.

56

"It's a fucking antique, sir." Martinez protested. "It should be in a museum somewhere."

We stood on the tarmac in the National Guard section of the Tulsa airport, looking at an aging Bell UH-1 or Huey. It may have been a museum piece to Martinez, but it brought memories from my youth flooding back and I couldn't help but smile.

"It's slow as my grandmother and handles worse than her walker," Martinez continued bitching. "It's loud as hell and... hell, there's got to be a Black Hawk somewhere around here!"

There wasn't. We'd already looked, and Martinez had looked a second time.

"It's also one tough son of a bitch, Captain." I said. "What's the matter? Afraid you can't fly something without all those fancy computers actually doing the work for you?"

"Fuck you, sir." She said. "There's not a rotor wing I can't fly."

"Then quit your bitching and let's get out of here while we can," I said.

"Yes, sir." Martinez mumbled, walking over to release the tie-downs that secured the rotor blades to the ground. Katie had stood back, watching the two of us.

"What?" I asked when I noticed her looking at me.

"She's like the little sister you never had," she smiled.

"Kind of," I acknowledged, shooting a look to make sure Martinez hadn't overheard. All I needed was for her to realize just how much of a soft spot I really had for her.

"You know, it's OK to let people know you care," Katie said, understanding exactly why I'd looked over.

"And ruin my reputation of being a gold plated asshole? I don't think so." I grinned. Katie just shook her head and followed me to the aging helicopter.

"Told you!" Martinez shouted. She was doing her walk around, checking whatever it is pilots check before taking off. “Right here. The airframe was built in 1961. 1961! Even you weren’t alive when this thing was built, sir!”

I just smiled and slid the right side door open, locking it in place on its track. The smells of aviation fuel, grease and sweat took me right back. Black Hawks, no matter how hard they’ve been used don’t have the character of a Huey. Or maybe I’m just getting old.

“Hey! I think I just found some patched over bullet holes. This baby probably flew in Vietnam!” Martinez shouted from somewhere under the front of the helicopter.

“Doubt it,” I said when she popped up at the side door. “We didn’t bring very many back. It was cheaper to just dump them in the ocean or leave them on the ground. Ever see the videos of Hueys being shoved off the decks of aircraft carriers after the evacuation when Saigon fell?”

“Before my time, sir.” She said, finishing outside and climbing into the cockpit.

After my experience with the Jeep I was prepared for Dog’s refusal to come near Katie. Getting her settled in the co-pilot’s seat, I sat down in the back and called him. He jumped in and started sniffing around while Martinez powered up the primitive avionics and started the engine.

She let the engine idle, warming up, and slipped on a set of headphones with a huge microphone that hung in front of her face. I watched her run her hands across the panel, familiarizing herself with the aircraft. After a moment she stopped what she was doing and rotated a dial on the radio.

"Sir, you need to hear this," she said after listening for a few minutes.

She flipped a couple of switches and a speaker mounted to the ceiling above my head began playing. I was listening to the comms of a unit engaged in a battle. The sounds of rifle fire and mortar bombs exploding were clear in the background every time someone transmitted.

"Can you tell where they are?" I shouted over the near constant chatter.

"No, sir. But they can't be far."

We sat there listening for a few more minutes, then someone referenced evac flights. This had to be at Tinker!

"Tinker, I think," Martinez said and turned around, concern creasing her face. I nodded, thinking and listening.

"Shut down, Captain." I said. "We need to find some goodies before we take off."

I jumped out the side door, Dog right behind me as the engine spooled down. Running to the hangar with the Oklahoma Air National Guard sign on it I tried every door I could find as Katie and Martinez ran up behind me. They were all locked up tight.

Jogging to the far corner, I forgot to exercise caution and ran directly into a male infected that had probably been drawn in by the sound of the Huey's engine. He wrapped his arms around me before I even knew I was in trouble and we fell to the ground. Dog grabbed his arm in his jaws and pulled, breaking the embrace and I was able to get an arm free and fend off the snapping teeth.

Several more males stumbled out of the darkness, excited by the sounds of the fight. One of them fell over us, landing on Dog and knocking him back. I kept rolling around, struggling against my attacker, hearing several quick shots.

Bumping up against the wall of the hangar I used my free arm to slam the infected's head against the corrugated steel. I kept at it, each blow making a hollow booming sound, but it was having an effect. His grip loosened and I yanked my other arm free. With one hand wrapped in his greasy hair and the other cupped on the point of his chin, I twisted hard to the side and up, feeling his whole body go limp when his neck snapped.

Pushing him off, I grabbed for the Kukri, pausing when I saw Dog and Martinez working together to finish off the last remaining male. He had it by the leg, keeping it off balance as she rammed the Ka-Bar into the back of its head. The body fell and they both turned, looking for another threat, but Katie had already put the rest down with her new rifle.

Seeing that all was clear, Martinez looked down at Dog and held her hand out. After a moment he lowered his ears and with his head below his shoulders, slowly moved closer and sniffed her hand. Finally he licked it and let his head come up slightly as she gently began scratching his ears.

Getting to my feet I ignored them and went around the corner, after checking for more infected, but there weren't any doors on the back. Running to the side closest to the Huey I picked a door and fired a short, full auto burst from the AK into the lock and deadbolt. The heavy slugs blew them out of the door and it started to swing open.

Yanking it out of my way I ran inside, clicking on the small flashlight. "Martinez, get those doors open!" I shouted as I moved deeper into the hangar. I was talking about the huge rolling doors, and I wanted them open to get what moonlight there was inside to help me find what I was looking for.

At the back of the hangar a large area had been fenced off with chain link that extended all the way to the ceiling. The weak light from the flashlight reflected off of rows of cabinets, stacks of wooden crates at the far end. A heavy chain and padlock secured a wide gate and I raised the rifle but didn't fire. The padlock was too heavy to be broken by a bullet.

Martinez had gotten the doors open with Katie's help and run over to stand next to me as I surveyed the supplies.

"What are you looking for?" She asked.

"I need in there," I said, dashing to a workbench in search of something I could use to cut through the fencing.

Martinez ran the other way and a moment later I heard a loud motor start up. Looking, I blinked when headlights came on and she rolled over behind the wheel of a tractor that was used to move aircraft in and out of the hangar.

"Grab that chain and wrap it around the padlock," she shouted, pointing at the far end of the workbench. "Then secure it to the hitch."

While I worked, she spun the tractor around and backed up to the fence. Chain looped through the one holding the gate, I hooked it onto the tractor and stepped back, making sure Dog and Katie were clear.

"Go!" I shouted.

Martinez hit the throttle, the fat tires spinning on the smooth concrete for a moment before gaining traction. The tractor shot forward, the chain jingling noisily as it paid out, then it went tight and the whole gate was ripped out of the fence. Martinez drove another thirty feet, dragging the big section of fence across the hangar, then came to a stop. Hopping off she unhooked, then climbed back on and spun the vehicle around to shine its lights into the caged area.

"Now, what do you need?" She asked, running over to join me. Katie was right behind her and I was glad to see Dog was next to her.

57

The mortars had run dry, the crews firing them grabbing their personal weapons and running to join the defenders that were behind the double ring of Claymores. Several thousand civilians were now armed with M4 rifles, sprinkled in amongst the Rangers and Marines. There were a handful of World War II and Korean War vets, many unable to walk without a cane or walker but still able to hold a rifle, that had declared their intention to fight to the last.

There were also women and children as young as ten holding rifles in their small hands. Everyone was frightened; several of the civilians expressing surprise when they realized the fighting men around them were scared too.

"Only fools and psychopaths aren't scared before a battle," Crawford heard a Marine Sergeant saying to a woman so terrified she was almost hyperventilating. "It's how you handle the fear that matters."

He would have liked to hear more of the conversation, but kept moving as he walked the lines. Pointere was doing the same thing, working the opposite side of the flight line. They were encouraging where needed, adjusting and directing people to plug gaps in the final layer of defense between the infected and the flight line.

The return flight of planes was half an hour away. They had to hold long enough for them to get on the ground, refuel, load and escape. Ninety minutes minimum. He didn't think it could be done, but kept his doubts to himself, constantly praising the defenders and telling them they would succeed.

Infected were flowing over the moat. Not in large numbers, yet, but the trickle that would become a torrent had begun. Everyone had been pulled back and the crew manning the firing panel for the Claymore mines was ready. All they needed was the order from Pointere.

Taking up position behind a machine gun emplacement, Crawford climbed to the top of a tall pile of sandbags to have a better view. Overhead, Osprey's hovered, keeping a constant eye on the entire perimeter and providing Pointere and Crawford with a steady stream of reports. Crawford had chosen the spot where he'd stopped because it was reported as the heaviest concentration of infected.

As the females continued to climb over the top of the blast wall, drop to the ground and sprint forward, specified Rangers and Marines began picking them off with single shots. They weren't going for head or heart shots, but targeting hips and legs. This gave them bigger targets and even though the females weren't being killed, they were going down and could only drag themselves forward.

Once they were on the ground and moving slowly, they were easier targets and were finished off by the civilians. This was working, but the front was steadily pressing closer to the defenders. As the volume of infected continued to grow there weren't enough rifles to target all of them quickly enough to prevent their advance.

Females that had held back when the moat was burning were now sacrificing themselves. Crawford didn't try to figure out the reasoning behind it, just noted it and filed it away. He remained stoic, standing on his elevated vantage point, watching through binoculars as the infected surged. The trickle had become a torrent in only a few minutes.

"Target only the front runners!" He shouted into the radio.

"Claymores, stand by," Pointere transmitted a moment later.

A solid mass of females was now running towards the defenders. The volume of rifle fire had increased and he could see the fastest females, those who had pulled out in front, go down in a tumble of limbs as their hips or legs were shattered by a well placed bullet.

"One hundred yards. Claymores ready," Pointere called.

The infected kept charging. With surprise, Crawford realized there were so many of them that he could feel the ground shaking all the way up through the sandbags he was standing on. Glancing around at the defenders lying on the dirt he saw them look at each other in fear when they felt the same thing.

The screams of the charging females were deafening. Tens of thousands of throats, all crying for blood. Their blood.

"Claymore outer ring only, fire on my command. Repeat. Outer ring ONLY! On my command," Pointere called on the radio, sounding calm even though he was shouting to be heard.

The infected kept running. Kept screaming. Crawford could see the blood red eyes in his binoculars, as they focused on their prey.

"Claymores FIRE!" Pointere ordered.

A Claymore mine is a simple device, nothing more than a convex shaped plastic container holding a layer of C4 explosive set behind 700 steel ball bearings. The convex design creates a sixty-degree wide pattern into which the ball bearings are propelled at 4,000 feet per second. Within the first fifty yards, nothing made of flesh and bone will survive. Out to one hundred yards, there's maybe a ten percent chance of survival.

Every man and woman felt the concussion of thousands of mines. Teeth were rattled and bones were vibrated. Around the entire perimeter, the outer ring detonated in a ripple, the electrical charge reaching the detonators at different times depending on the length of the wire connected to the master panel.

Hundreds of thousands of steel balls screamed outwards from where they had been embedded in an epoxy resin, each of them instantly breaking the sound barrier, which added to the volume of noise. Tens of thousands of female infected were shredded. Flesh was stripped from bone. Bones were broken and skulls crushed. Limbs were severed from bodies.

After the ear shattering blast, everything fell silent. There's a silence that descends over battlefields after the deployment of massively destructive weapons by desperate troops. The fighters on the side that launched the attack are holding their breath, waiting to see if they're going to survive another minute. The side that was just attacked pauses, partly in shock and partly in fear, waiting to see how badly they were hurt.

It's an eerie silence. Surreal after a long siege where there's been the constant sounds of battle for what feels like a lifetime. Many of the entrenched defenders had experienced it before. Some on beaches in Normandy or valleys in France and Germany. Others on the Korean Peninsula, or in the jungles of Vietnam and Central America, or the deserts and mountains of the Middle East.

Crawford hadn't been sure what to expect when the mines were detonated. He wouldn't have been surprised if the infected had just kept coming as if nothing had happened. He'd had a conversation with the Major about the defense that had bought time for evacuees in Murfreesboro, and how nothing could deter the advance of the enemy. Having witnessed it himself on smaller scales, he hadn't held out hope that the Claymores would do anything more than buy a couple of extra minutes.

So when silence descended over the area, and dust thrown into the air by the blasts began to clear, he was shocked to see a solid wall of females standing and staring. Their advance had stopped at the point where the devastation of the mines had reached, nearly eighty yards from where the Claymores had been placed.

"What the hell?" He muttered to himself, shaking his head and raising the binoculars to scan the perimeter.

In every direction the females had halted. This wouldn't have surprised him if they had been a normal enemy who felt fear, but he was shocked. He'd seen the females holding back at the moat, waiting for the fires to burn out, but not for a moment had he thought they could be brought to a halt like this.

"Any movement on your side?" Pointere's voice in his earpiece startled him, making him jump.

"No. They're holding for the moment," he answered.

Crawford listened as Pointere made calls to different junior officers spread around the perimeter. The news was all the same. The females had stopped and were just staring at the defenders.

"Sir, the front ranks are static around the entire perimeter, but there's lots of movement in the rear." This report came in from one of the Ospreys hovering over the battle.

"What kind of movement?" Pointere asked.

"Can't tell for sure sir. Stand by." One of the Ospreys changed position and descended to hover a hundred feet over a section of the infected. It slowly began drifting along the front as the pilots tried to see what was happening.

"Males, sir." The answer finally came after several minutes. "They are pushing males forward through their ranks."

"Goddamn it!" Crawford raged when he realized what the females were doing.

"What?" Pointere asked as he ran up to where he stood.

"Meat for the grinder," Crawford growled. "Just like they did with the moat, they're going to let the males come forward and absorb the worst of the damage and deplete our defenses. Enough males and we'll have to use the second layer of mines, then the females can charge in."

"They're that fucking smart?" Pointere asked, surprise clear on his face.

"Apparently," Crawford said. "Smart enough to fuck us."

58

The old helicopter vibrated hard as Martinez pulled back on the stick and lifted us into the air. The long, heavy rotors made the thumping sound unique to Hueys. The sound that for some reason always made me feel good. Maybe, just like the old fire house dog that jumped up every time he heard the bell, that rotor noise was such a part of my younger days that I got a little surge of adrenaline just from hearing it.

We had spent several minutes raiding the secure lockers in the hangar, finding most of what I wanted. Setting it aside, I'd left the heavy lifting for Martinez and Katie while I tackled the aircraft's side doors. It took some effort and some language my mother wouldn't have approved of, but with the help of tools from the hangar I had gotten them off their tracks, letting them crash down onto the tarmac. Next, I spent a couple of minutes removing the frames for the web sling seats in the back to make as much room as possible inside.

"What are you doing?" Katie asked, trotting up. She was carrying one end of a long, heavy wooden crate, Martinez following with the other end.

"Getting us ready," I said, grabbing the crate from them and hoisting it into the aircraft.

Prying the lid off, I had quickly installed a pintle in the mounting point on the side of the Huey's deck. Next came the vintage M60 machine gun, which attached easily to the pintle. I kept working as they brought out more of the gear I'd selected. Full cans of ammo were strapped down to the deck and I strung up the safety harness that would keep the door gunner from being tossed out when the deck tilted or the helicopter made a sharp turn.

More gear was brought out and secured as I took a moment to fashion a harness for dog out of the web sling seating I had previously removed. The deck of a Huey is slick, and with the side doors gone there wasn't much of anything to keep man or beast from being tossed out in mid-air. Makeshift harness firmly wrapped around his body, I called Dog in and connected a short lead from his back to a swivel hook set into the ceiling.

Finally ready, I strapped myself in behind the M60 as Martinez and Katie climbed into the cockpit. The engine fired up and the rotor was gaining speed as I pulled the charging handle on the machine gun. Then I had nothing to do except be a passenger as Martinez lifted off.

"This thing's a pig," she said after we had gained a few hundred feet of altitude and were pounding our way to the southwest towards Tinker.

"How about a little respect, Captain." I said. "Older and slower doesn't mean there's not still some sharp teeth left."

"Are you talking about yourself or the helicopter, honey?" Katie quipped, Martinez bursting out laughing.

Sighing, I wrapped my arm around Dog's neck and pressed my face against the side of his head. Maybe he had the right idea when he was staying away from those two.

Martinez gained altitude as we flew until even with the moonlight the ground below was only dark and featureless. Getting used to how the old girl handled, she made some maneuvers, swaying us back and forth. She put us into a dive, pulling out and powering back to altitude as she turned sharply. She might have a smart mouth, but the woman's skills with the stick were second only to her capabilities with a knife.

"You about done?" I asked after ten long minutes of aerial acrobatics.

"Sorry, sir. Just getting a feel for the lady." She sounded anything but sorry. "Maybe I was a little too hasty. She's not so bad."

I didn't take the bait, knowing there was no way I could hold my own with the two of them. Looking around I checked on Dog, very glad I'd been able to securely tether him. He was standing in the middle of the deck, all four legs splayed out to help keep his balance. His head was down, ears flat against his skull and he looked miserable. I rubbed his neck, turning back when Martinez spoke on the intercom.

"Sir, I've got a Navy flight on the radio. They're inbound to Tinker. You want to talk to them?" She asked.

Navy? What the hell? "Yes. Can you put them over the intercom?"

"Can do. Stand by." She said. "Go ahead sir."

"Navy flight, US Army helo." I said.

"Panther flight copies. We've got you inbound to Tinker on radar. We're coming to join the party."

"Damn good to hear that, Navy." I said. "Hope you brought some party favors. This is a BYOB event."

"Copy that, Army." He chuckled. "We're a flight of twelve Hornets off the Big Ronnie. We've got the life of the party tagging along, low and slow. We stopped off at Hurlburt in Florida and picked up Spooky. We're monitoring the comms out of Tinker. Sounds like one hell of a fight going on, but we can't raise a controller to direct fire." The Big Ronnie would be the USS Ronald Reagan, a newer generation supercarrier. Most likely in the Gulf of Mexico or off the southeastern coast for them to be able to stop in Florida, then reach Oklahoma City.

God bless the US Navy! When I heard "Spooky" I wanted to cheer. Spooky is an AC-130U gunship. An Air Force C-130 converted specifically for ground troop support. Heavily armored, it flies a low and slow orbit over a battlefield. Outfitted with a 25 mm GAU-12 Equalizer, one Bofors 40 mm autocannon, and one 105 mm M102 cannon, it can and does unleash hell on earth.

"You Navy guys sure know how to party," I said. "What's your ETA to target?"

"Twenty mikes for Panther flight. Thirty, three-zero, for Spooky." He answered.

"What's our ETA, Martinez?" I asked over the intercom without transmitting on the radio.

"Fifteen minutes," she said.

"Panther flight, I'll be your controller. Designation..." I looked around, trying to think of a call sign. Seeing Dog looking miserable I smiled and turned back to face out the open side of the Huey. "Dog four."

"Copy Dog Four. Will contact on this frequency when we're on station."

"Dog Four copies," I transmitted, then switched to intercom. "Martinez, give her all she's got. And turn up the overhead. I can't hear what's going on at Tinker."

A moment later the vibration increased as she pushed the old Huey to its maximum speed.

Soon after that the speaker over my head blared as she increased the volume.

"Claymores FIRE!" I heard.

59

As Crawford and Pointere watched, males kept pushing through the front ranks of the females to make their stumbling way across the field of bodies that had been shattered by the Claymores. Many of them tripped in their blind shamble, but many more managed to stay on their feet. They weren't moving fast, but they were advancing, their numbers growing.

Faster than it seemed possible, the open space between the final layer of mines and the females filled. The males packed together, the ones in front slowed by the footing, but as more and more of them trudged along their feet smoothed the way for the ones following. Soon, a solid wall of flesh was only twenty yards from the ring, the snarls and hisses reaching the defenders.

"Claymores stand by." Pointere transmitted over the radio.

Crawford checked his rifle, knowing that as soon as the last of the mines detonated, there would be a rush forward by the females. He glanced over his shoulder as a Globemaster thumped onto the runway, the ground shaking from the roar as the pilot used thrust reversers to slow the massive plane. At least they'd get some more people out before the defenses completely collapsed.

At the far end of the runway, evacuees were already queued up to start loading. Fuel trucks sat on either side of the tarmac, prepared to rush forward and hook up the moment the aircraft came to a stop. The engines would not be shut off, a risky procedure known as "hot" refueling. Normally, passengers would never be loaded with the engines turning as fuel was being pumped into the wings, but nothing was normal any longer.

"Claymores ready, on my command." Pointere broadcast as the males moved to within ten yards of the ring.

Crawford turned a quick circle, binoculars to his eyes as he checked on the readiness of the defenders. Machine guns were manned, a civilian sitting next to each gunner, prepared to hand them ammo or do anything they needed once the fight started. Each of them had received a crash course in what to do, and how, by the Rangers and Marines manning the guns.

"We're as ready as we'll be," Crawford said to Pointere, who nodded and keyed the transmit button on his radio.

"Claymores FIRE!" He ordered.

Explosions rippled around the perimeter a moment later, thousands upon thousands of males being blown backwards and falling to add to the layer of bodies on the killing field. Dust obscured the defender's view, but this time there was no silence. Screams from a hundred thousand throats sounded as the females surged forward.

A few machine guns opened fire immediately, the gunners nervous, firing blind through the dust and smoke. Ripping sounds began around the perimeter as the hovering Ospreys fired their miniguns. Hundreds, then thousands of females were shredded by the withering aerial fire, but in the end it had about as much effect as trying to hold the ocean back with a plastic shovel. More and more machine guns jumped into the fight as sprinting figures emerged from the dust, rifle fire picking up moments later.

Pointere shouted a few orders over the radio, but quickly gave up. No one could hear him and no one had time to do anything other than keep shooting at the screaming horde bearing down on them. Crawford had already raised his rifle, picking off runners with rapid but well placed shots. Pointere joined him, the two of them shoulder to shoulder on top of a pile of sandbags.

60

I could see the lights at Tinker well before we arrived. The only electric illumination visible for as far as I could see in any direction, they weren't hard to spot. I could also see anti-collision lights on several aircraft that were landing. Had to be the evacuation flights I'd heard mentioned on the radio, returning to pick up more people.

Leaning forward out the side door to get a good look, I glanced into the cockpit to see a compass. Holding a piece of paper down on my leg against the buffeting wind I drew on it with a grease pencil Katie had found in the cockpit.

"Panther flight, Dog Four. Copy?" I transmitted.

"Go Dog Four."

"Friendlies are defending the north-south runway. Civilians being loaded onto transport at the south end of the runway. You have eyes on the aircraft in the air?"

"Affirmative," the Navy pilot responded. "We're tracking them. Where do you want our first run?"

"Unknown at this time," I answered. "I'm still two mikes out. Stand by."

"Panther copies."

"Claymores FIRE!" I heard over the speaker at the same time as I received the Navy's response.

Watching, I saw a neatly defined perimeter around the runway and a couple of hangars appear as quick flashes of bright light when the mines detonated. I was impressed. That had to have been over a thousand mines, and I'd already heard a previous order for use of the weapons.

As we continued to approach I could see the winks of muzzle flashes and the path of tracer rounds as machine guns opened up. Watching for a moment, I spotted an area at the north end of the runway that was receiving the brunt of the attack from the infected. I also noted half a dozen Ospreys hovering over the perimeter, and getting closer I could tell they were firing their miniguns.

"Martinez, bring us in over the north end, and tell those Marines in the Ospreys to get the fuck out of the way!"

She descended fast and I could hear her yelling into her radio. Turning, she swung us into a hover a hundred feet over the heads of half a dozen machine gunners. To their rear was a large truck with thick bundles of wires that headed out in all directions. Had to be the master control for the Claymores.

"Panther, Dog Four," I shouted to be heard over the pounding of the rotors and the sounds of the battle beneath me.

"Go for Panther."

"I want half your flight on each side of the runway. Tangos are danger close. Friendlies are marked by small arms fire."

"Panther copies. On target in two mikes." He answered, still sounding calm and cool.

While we waited for the Navy, I swiveled the M60 around and added to the fire being pumped into the females. The machine guns on the ground were being run hard, without pauses to let the barrels cool. Normally that's not a good idea, but when the enemy is in your face the last thing you're worried about is ruining a machine gun barrel. You just stay on the trigger as long as you have ammo and a target.

The fire was devastating. High velocity bullets ripped through the herd, severing limbs, smashing bones and destroying internal organs. Females fell by the thousands, but for every one that went down there were more behind them, ready to take their place.

"Why did they hold back from the mines but charge into the gun fire?" Crawford wondered to himself as he changed magazines in his rifle. He didn't have time to think about it so he dismissed the thought and followed Pointere when the Marine slapped him on the shoulder.

Together they ran, firing their rifles as they moved. The emplacement closest to them was in danger of being overrun, the gunner firing at targets no more than ten feet away. A young female Airman was standing behind the gunner, firing her rifle on full auto to take the legs out from under the raging infected.

Crawford and Pointere arrived, taking up positions on either side of her and together with the machine gunner, all of them were able to stop the advance. But they couldn't push the infected back, no matter how fast they fired. The best they could achieve was to not let the females get any closer.

They all looked up in surprise when a helicopter roared into a hover directly over their heads, the door gunner adding to the fight. He worked the stream of bullets back and forth across the leading edge, shredding bodies. Slowly, the gap in front of them widened.

"How much longer?" Crawford shouted to Pointere.

"First one rolling in ten minutes. Forty until they're all in the air!" He shouted back.

At first, Crawford didn't recognize the rushing roar he heard approaching. His instinct was to turn to his rear and look, but he didn't dare take focus off the infected right in front of him. Then he heard the sound of heavy canons and a jet flashed by on either side of him, leaving a wake of destruction among the infected.

He heard another roar coming, then a second pair of jets screamed by, ceasing fire as they banked and rocketed skyward. A third pair appeared a moment later, then a fourth, fifth and sixth. The destruction they left behind was awe-inspiring.

In seconds, they had carved a one hundred and fifty yard wide swath of death out of the females with their Vulcan 20 mm rotary canons. The gunners quickly dispatched the few infected that were between the strike zone and them, then the firing slowed as there were no more targets inside a hundred yards. Crawford and Pointere exchanged surprised glances, then grinned like little boys.

"Get those fucking planes loaded, Colonel! Someone just bought us some time." Crawford shouted, turning to replenish his supply of magazines.

"Good shooting, Navy!" I shouted into the radio. "Hold until they start pushing in again."

"Panther copies. We'll be here when you need us."

"Isn't that Colonel Crawford down there?" Martinez yelled over the intercom.

"Where?" I asked, leaning out to look.

"Behind the emplacement to the left of the truck."

"Yep, that's him," I said, spotting the familiar figure.

"And here they come again," Martinez said a moment later. I looked up to see females surging in all around the perimeter.

"Panther, Dog Four." I transmitted. "Let's rinse and repeat. Just like last time."

"Panther copies," I heard, wishing it was daylight so I could see the Hornets turning and lining up for their attack runs.

The females had covered most of the open ground, running up against the machine gun and rifle fire, which slowed their advance and caused them to bunch up. That made them perfect targets for the Navy pilots. Less than a minute later the buffer had been opened back up, thousands more females dead.

The bodies were piling up, getting deeper by the minute. This hampered the infected's forward progress, but not enough. Without the air support they were able to start pushing in again.

"Panther, let's hit the bitches again." I said, closely watching the progress of the front ranks of the females.

"Copy Dog Four." He answered. "Be advised this will be our last run. Ammo will be depleted and we're almost bingo fuel. Spooky is five mikes out with the throttle through the firewall."

"Understood Panther, and thank you." I replied, looking at the ocean of bodies below me.

As far as the lights could reach there was nothing visible other than tightly massed bodies. If I could see out into the city or onto the prairie I suspected all that would be there was more of the same. I hoped the defenders could hold out until Spooky arrived on target.

61

"I've finally got the Colonel," Martinez shouted as the last Navy jet banked away to head south. She had been trying to break in on the defender's comm channel for some time, but for some reason they couldn't hear us even though we could hear them.

"Should I thank you for the air support, Major?" Crawford asked a moment later.

"Negative sir. They just showed up. I suspect we're seeing Admiral Packard at work."

"Well, they saved our ass, but it's about to get interesting again." He said. He and I were looking at each other as we spoke, him on the ground, me in the side door of a Huey a hundred feet over his head. "By the way, where did you get that museum piece?"

I imagined Martinez was grinning from ear to ear right about now. "National Guard, sir. They have all the cool hand me downs. You need to hold out for five more minutes. Spooky's on the way."

"That is good news, Major. I'm glad Sergeant Scott found you." He said, turning when the machine gun next to him began firing again.

"Sir? Sergeant Scott?" I asked, but he had already raised his rifle and was back in the fight.

Looking down the runway I could see long lines of civilians being herded into waiting planes. A Globemaster was in motion, lining up for takeoff and Martinez took us well out of its way. I could hear the bellow of its engines, even over the rotors and noise from the battle. It seemed to accelerate too slowly, and looked like it was barely moving when it lifted off the runway. The optical illusion created by very large aircraft.

The infected pushed in, screams audible even as we hovered. Watching from my vantage point the mass of bodies reminded me of the old movie The Blob. They seemed to flow over everything, just like that extraterrestrial gelatinous monster. Machine gun fire raked the leading edge, bodies falling to be immediately stepped on by the thousands pushing in.

Runners began breaking away from the main body as it pushed to within thirty yards of the defensive line. Rifle and machine gun fire cut them down, but in doing so gave up a few feet of ground to the herd.

“Spooky, Dog Four. What’s your time to target?” I shouted into the radio.

“Two mikes, Dog Four. Got you in sight. We’re going to have to hold back for a minute more. There’s a big bird about ready to go.” I turned and looked south, seeing a C5 Galaxy beginning to trundle down the tarmac to line up for take off.

“Copy, Spooky,” I said. “When you’re on target, defend the runway. You’ll see the perimeter. Friendlies are in a world of shit.”

“Spooky copies,” I heard, turning back to check on the line below.

Runners had broken away from the front edge, which was now only twenty yards from the defenders. Crawford stood next to two figures, one of them enough smaller that I suspected it was a woman, all three of them firing at the sprinting females. The machine gunner in front of them was working his fire along the front ranks, then had to pause to slap in a new ammo belt being held out by the civilian next to him.

The pause in fire from the machine gun was all the females needed. Two of the runners leapt, slamming into the gunner and his assistant as dozens more sprinted forward. In seconds they were pouring through the breach in the line. Crawford and the other two fighters formed a tight circle, backs to each other and kept firing.

"Katie, get back here!" I screamed, firing the door gun to give them some support.

"What?" She shouted in my ear a moment later.

"Unstrap me, then take over," I shouted back, not wanting to stop firing even long enough to change gunners. I felt her begin releasing my body from the straps that held me in place.

"What are you doing?" She shouted as the last buckle came free.

"Going down there," I said, sending a long burst into a group of runners who were almost to the line.

"Are you crazy?" She said, grabbing my arm.

"No time," I shouted, moving out of the way. Grabbing her hands I pulled her close, kissed her quickly then pushed her at the door gun. She started firing as she slipped into place and I quickly secured her to the helicopter.

Snatching an equipment bag from where it was strapped to the floor, I opened it and yanked out a pair of heavy gloves and the end of a fast rope. Slapping the gated hook over a steel stanchion, I kicked the bag out the side door opposite the machine gun. The bag fell to the ground, uncoiling the rope as it dropped. Turning my back to the open doorway, I pulled the gloves on, grabbed the rope with both hands and jumped backwards into the air.

62

I came down fast. Yes, it's called fast roping, but there's fast and then there's the fast I just did. I might have hurt something if I'd landed on solid ground, but I took my feet off the rope just in time to slam onto an infected's back. She fell, face first, and I let go of the rope and landed on her body.

I could feel her back break when my knees hit, and I let her absorb the rest of my momentum before rolling to the side and onto my feet. Females were leaping over the sandbagged machine gun to my left, the Colonel and his two companions still fighting to my right. Enemy too close for me to use the AK47 I'd taken off the dead terrorist, I pulled the Kukri and went to work.

The blade whistled as I slashed through flesh and bone. I wasn't necessarily going for kills, just keeping the screaming bodies away from me. I needed to clear enough of a path for someone to get back on the goddamn machine gun. Blood flew as I battled to move forward, the Kukri inflicting horrible injuries as I continued to wield it.

Punching with my left hand, grabbing and pulling bodies out of my way, I hacked and slashed like a man possessed until I reached the dead gunner. There was no time for me to look to see if anyone was close, and I nearly decapitated Colonel Pointere when he pushed past me and leapt for the machine gun. It took him a second to charge the weapon and swing the muzzle up.

Pressing the trigger he cut down dozens of females directly in front of us with a long, sustained burst, then began working on the ones right behind them. With the machine gun back in action I was able to wade in and clear up most of the females who had gotten through the line, Colonel Crawford and the blonde Airman taking down the last ones with their rifles.

Crawford looked at me and said something I couldn't hear between the hammering of machine gun fire and the blood pounding in my ears. I looked up as a massive C5 roared overhead, appearing to be traveling way too slow to possibly be in flight. Once it passed I scanned for the Huey, but didn't see it, then realized Martinez would have gotten out of the area for Spooky.

I heard the bass drone of the four giant turboprop engines a moment before the AC-130 passed overhead and opened fire. The 25 mm Equalizer is a five-barrel rotary canon and spits out 1,800 rounds a minute. The shells are about the size of my fist and traveling faster than 3,000 feet per second when they leave the barrel. They are absolutely devastating, and as the plane orbited it fired continuously.

Nothing was left alive in its wake. Hell, nothing was left intact, or even recognizable. Bodies just seemed to cease to exist, disappearing in a puff of pink mist if a shell hit them squarely. The leading ranks of the infected weren't pushed back, they were erased off the face of the planet.

After Spooky's second orbit we had a nice, wide buffer zone between the infected and us. There was some clean up, and the machine gunners made quick work of the incredibly lucky females that had somehow avoided the devastation. Starting his third orbit, Spooky opened up with the 40 mm Bofors autocanon, firing into the main body of the surrounding herd as it began to push forward.

Huge gaps were blown in the legion of infected by shells so powerful they had been used for anti-aircraft purposes in World War II. On the next orbit he continued firing the Bofors and engaged the Equalizer again. Two more orbits and we had a four hundred yard buffer.

Nearly every infected inside the defensive ring defined by the moat had been killed or maimed badly enough that they were no longer a threat. The few hundred that were still on their feet fell to machine gun fire. We were by no means out of the woods, there were still hundreds of thousands if not millions of infected pushing into the base, but we had some breathing room.

A plane roared overhead, taking off, followed closely by two more. Colonel Pointere was on his feet, the female Airman taking his place on the machine gun.

"Pull back now!" He shouted. "All personnel, evac now!"

Bending over he slapped the Airman on top of her Kevlar helmet, telling her to get her ass in gear.

"Don't know what you did, Major, but I owe you a beer." He said. "Now we've gotta move.

One plane left on the ground and they're holding it for us."

"Let's go," Crawford said, starting to turn towards the flight line.

"Sir, what were you saying about Sergeant Scott?" I stopped him, sparing a glance at the infected who were already pushing back towards us.

"He went out to find you with the two Russians," he said. "He got Rachel and a virologists onto a flight. I thought he had you with him."

"No, sir." I said, glancing up as Spooky started another orbit to buy the defenders time to get on a plane. "Never saw him."

"He's still out there, then." Crawford said, sadness on his face. "Find your wife?"

"Yes, sir. I did. And I owe you." I said.

"Bullshit," he said. "Who's in that flying antique?"

"Captain Martinez and my wife."

"Got room for another?" He asked, casting a glance over his shoulder at the defenders running for the last flight out. "Don't feel much like sitting under a palm tree in the Bahamas while I've still got people out there."

63

Tech Sergeant Zach Scott monitored the flow of diesel fuel into the Bradley's tank as Igor fired an occasional burst from the machine gun. Infected in the area weren't exactly thick, but there were enough of them that it was necessary to keep them pushed back while Scott was outside the vehicle. Igor was happily doing so, and while he wouldn't admit it, he was itching for another target to take out with one of the TOW missiles.

They were at a small truck stop in Fairfax, Oklahoma. Rachel and Joe had departed the previous day and they had set out in search of the Major, stopping to replenish the thirsty vehicle's tank. The power was off in the small town, but the Bradley had a pump powered by its engine, specifically designed for the siphoning of fuel from underground tanks. A one inch hose ran from an access port that was normally protected by an armored plate into the truck stop's storage tank.

"Radio is flashing," Irina shouted.

Scott looked up at where she had popped open the hatch over the driver's seat and stuck her head out of the protection of the vehicle. He waved to let her know he'd heard her and shut down the pump. The tank was full and he'd been carefully topping it off with as much diesel as he could squeeze on board.

Siphon hose coiled and back in place, he buttoned up the outside of the vehicle and headed for the rear door set into the ramp. Once back inside he made sure the opening was tightly secured before heading for the commander's seat.

A red light was blinking, alerting him that someone wanted to communicate over the FSOC system. Engaging the unit, he waited for the laser to lock onto the orbiting satellite and the comm status indicator on his display to turn green. When it did he recognized Blanchard's voice.

"Copy, sir." He said.

"What's your status, Tech Sergeant?" Blanchard asked.

"We're re-fueling and preparing to continue our search for the Major. Hope you're calling with good news that he's been spotted."

"Negative," Blanchard said. "Just the opposite, in fact. I just got off the phone with Pearl

Harbor. A Russian patrol intercepted the flight carrying Mr. Revard and Rachel. His pilot successfully evaded, but Rachel's plane took damage and she and the pilot had to punch out over Idaho."

ALSO BY DIRK PATTON

Unleashed: V Plague Book One

Crucifixion: V Plague Book Two

Rolling Thunder: V Plague Book Three

Red Hammer: V Plague Book Four

Transmission: V Plague Book Five

Days Of Perdition: V Plague Book Six

Rules Of Engagement: A John Chase Short Story

Afterword

First, I would like to recognize Air Force SSgt Z for earning his way into a very elite brotherhood. For what it's worth, you have my respect and admiration. Congratulations!

My thanks to many, but I have to single out Matt "Gunny" Zemeck, even if he did break my rifle, and "Colonel" James Pointere for being a good sport and letting me make him an officer. Suck it up, Marine!

Also, a special thanks to SH for his valuable and insightful suggestions.

It should be noted that the 20th Marine Expeditionary Unit used in this book is fictitious, (not MEU, just the 20th which doesn't exist), though there is absolutely nothing imaginary about a real MEU. Don't believe me? Ask a few thousand bad guys around the world!

The 5th Ranger Battalion noted in this book is not a currently active Army unit. It was last active in World War II, participating in the D-Day invasion of Normandy.

The 5th Ranger Battalion was activated on 1 September 1943 at Camp Forrest, Tennessee. During the Battle of Normandy, the battalion landed on Omaha Beach along with companies A, B and C of the 2nd Ranger Battalion, where elements of the 116th Regiment of the 29th Infantry Division were pinned down by murderous machine gun fire and mortars from the heights above. The situation was so dire that General Omar Bradley (the namesake of the Bradley Fighting Vehicle used in this book) was seriously considering abandoning the beachhead instead of sending more men to die. It was then that General Norman Cota, Assistant Division Commander of the 29th Infantry Division, gave the now famous order that has become the motto of the 75th Ranger Regiment: "Rangers, Lead The Way!"

The 5th Battalion Rangers broke across the sea wall and barbed wire entanglements, and up the pillbox-rimmed heights under intense enemy machine gun and mortar fire, and with A and B Companies of the 2nd Battalion and some elements of the 116th Infantry Regiment, advanced four miles (6 km) to the key town of Vierville-sur-

Mer, thus opening the breach for supporting troops to follow-up and expand the beachhead. Meanwhile, C Company of the 2nd Ranger Battalion, due to rough seas, landed west of the Vierville draw and suffered 50 percent casualties during the landing, but still scaled a 90-foot (27 m) cliff, using ropes and bayonets, to knock out a formidable enemy position that was sweeping the beach with deadly fire.

The 5th Ranger Battalion was deactivated 22 October 1945 at Camp Myles Standish, Massachusetts.

In Chapter 44, in his speech to his Marines, Colonel Pointere mentions Fox Company and Khe Sanh. Both of these battles, the former in Korea and the latter in Vietnam, pitted Marines against staggering odds in conditions worse than I can manage to put in writing. If you're in the mood to learn about some of the toughest men the Marine Corps has ever fielded, Google these two battles and read up on them.

I try to balance my writing to not lean too far to the "Military and War" genre. I get a LOT of emails encouraging me to put more detail in, but I never intended for this series to be about the military and don't want to weigh it down more than I already have when it's necessary to describe a weapon or ammunition.

The series is about surviving everything that can be thrown at you. Overcoming seemingly insurmountable odds by never accepting defeat. Beginning with book one, I've approached each chapter with two thoughts. What could possibly go wrong, and what would I do? The heavy presence of the military has evolved as I've kept writing, but that's because without them this journey would have ended before it really got started.

You can always correspond with me via email at voodooplague@gmail.com Visit my website at www.voodooplague.com and if you're on Facebook, please like my page at www.facebook.com/FearThePlague

I enjoy interacting with my fans and I answer all of my email… eventually.

Thanks again for reading!

Dirk Patton

2015

Made in the USA
Lexington, KY
21 April 2016